£1.00

D0620515

SUSAN MOODY, a former Chairman of the Crime
Writers' Association, is the author of the Penny
Wanawake detective series, and the suspense novels
*Playing with Fire*, *Hush-a-Bye*, *House of Moons* and *The
Italian Garden*, as well as *Misselthwaite*, the sequel to
Frances Hodgson Burnett's classic children's novel *The
Secret Garden*.

*Also by Susan Moody*

# Sacrifice Bid

## Susan Moody

**HEADLINE**

First published in 1997
by HEADLINE BOOK PUBLISHING

First published in paperback in 1997
by HEADLINE BOOK PUBLISHING

10 9 8 7 6 5 4 3 2 1

ISBN 0 7472 5617 9

Typeset by
Letterpart Limited, Reigate, Surrey

Printed and bound in Great Britain by
Clays Ltd, St Ives plc

HEADLINE BOOK PUBLISHING
A division of Hodder Headline PLC
338 Euston Road
London NW1 3BH

For all librarians, everywhere,
with thanks for everything

## ♣ 1 ♣

'And the rest are mine, I think.' Lolly Haden White spread the last four cards in her hand on the table. 'Two top trumps, ten of hearts is good, so is the six of diamonds.' She began to gather up the pack.

There was a moment's stunned silence, then Marjorie Curtiss said curtly: 'Excuse *me*.'

'What?' Lolly looked up and took in the expressions on the faces round the table. She looked bewildered. 'What's wrong?'

'That's the six of diamonds,' Marjorie hissed, pointing at the card.

'So?'

'Didn't you just trump my diamond king?' Marjorie looked triumphantly round. 'Didn't she? You saw it, Cassie, didn't you?'

'Well, yes, I have to admit that—'

'In other words, you cheated!' trumpeted Marjorie. She was good at trumpeting, a skill she had honed and refined during the years she had spent abroad following her managerial-consultant husband from rich picking to rich picking. 'You revoked!'

Cassie was alarmed by Lolly's reaction. Having flushed a

1

dark red as she realised her error, her face suddenly grew waxy-pale as the blood drained from it. One hand pressed the skin of her throat, the other, lying on the table, trembled convulsively so that the diamond ring on her fourth finger winked and glittered.

Leaning across, Cassie put her hand over Lolly's and felt it flutter under her fingers like a trapped bird. 'Are you all right, Lolly?'

'Y-yes. I think so.' Lolly turned to Marjorie. 'I'm so sorry. I don't know how I came to make such a stupid mistake. I'm . . . I'm not feeling well, I'm sorry.' She stood up, pressing her knuckles against the card table for support, looked vaguely about the room as if she had never seen it before. 'I am so very sorry to break things up but I think perhaps it would be better if I went home.' Her vowels, which were normally impeccably Home Counties, took on the faintly clipped accents of Kenya, where she had grown up.

From experience and observation, Cassie knew this meant she was really stressed. 'Do you want me to drive you?' she asked.

'No. I'll be all right.'

The three women at the table watched with some consternation as Lolly walked across the room to the door, one foot dragging slightly across the oriental rugs. Then Marjorie, remembering her manners, got up too and hurried after her. Cassie and Anne Norrington raised their eyebrows at each other as the two voices died away down the panelled hall.

'Look, Lolly, there's really no need . . .'

'I am sorry . . . I . . .'

'These things happen. You don't have to go . . .'

'. . . a headache . . .'

'. . . really wish you wouldn't . . .'

2

'Her game's gone completely to pot in the past few weeks,' whispered Anne.

'I've noticed.'

'We were playing at the Jenkins' last week and she was making the most extraordinary bids.'

'I know,' Cassie said. 'I was there.'

They heard the front door close and Marjorie's heavy footsteps on the polished parquet flooring of the hall. Sitting down at the table again, she smoothed the sensible pleats of her Jaeger skirt. 'I don't know,' she said, shaking her head. 'I shouldn't have said anything, I suppose. I didn't mean to upset her, but honestly . . . revoking like that. And last week at the Jenkins' she was making the wildest bids I've ever . . . oh, of course, you were both there.'

'You don't think it's . . .' Anne looked at Cassie '. . . premature senility, do you? Alzheimer's?'

'I hope not,' said Cassie. 'Not Lolly.'

But now it had been brought to her attention, she began to wonder. The onset of some form of mental deterioration might explain the shaking hands, the failing memory, the otherwise inexplicable lapses at the bridge table, the fact that her appearance sometimes seemed less bandbox smart than usual. As a former fashion editor on *Vogue*, Lolly had never dropped her rigorous sartorial standards, even after years of living in the country. Her expensive wardrobe was always immaculately maintained; her beautiful white hair done twice a week by Samantha Cook, who had been trained in a London salon. But this afternoon she had looked worn and old. There was a small mark on one corner of her Hermès silk scarf and the heels of her shoes were scuffed. In anyone else, such minor lapses wouldn't even have been noticed; in Lolly they told of a mind not at ease. There'd been a short period last year when her bridge play had deteriorated, but she seemed to have recovered from that. Until a few weeks ago. Not to be able to continue playing would constitute a small tragedy for a woman like Lolly, for whom bridge provided companionship, entertainment and mental exercise.

'Someone should have a word with Serena,' Marjorie said in her brisk way. 'She'd know more about it than we do.'

'Not necessarily,' said Cassie. 'But I have to go in her direction on my way home. I'll drop in and see if she's noticed anything.'

Driving home, she felt disturbed. Change was always disorientating, and not always for the best. If Lolly was truly undergoing some form of mental deterioration, then the existence Cassandra Swann had built up for herself could not continue as it had done over the past five years. It was on her thirty-first birthday that she realised life was finite, that she wouldn't live forever, that ever so gently, the doors were closing one by one. This fresh reminder of mortality was one she really did not need. Not now. Not today.

'*Deck the halls with boys of harley,*' trilled the angelic choir over the supermarket's PA system. '. . . *'tis the season to be charlie . . .*'

Yeah, right, Cassie thought sourly. Never mind the fact that distinctly unjolly rain had been pissing down for weeks on end or that the temperature was currently arctic. Nor that there were still more than eight weeks until Christmas. Which meant two months of Jingle Bells and Rudolph's sodding nose. Two months of charity Christmas cards, the very hideousness of their designs a reproach. Two months of fading tinsel and bloody Christmas garlands. Not to mention two months of hell spent trying to figure out how many presents she could buy for £21.28, which was all she currently had in her bank account, with very little prospect of adding to it. Already she was wondering whether people would notice if she didn't get them anything this year. In fact, all things considered, far from being jolly, 'twas a darn sight more like the season to consider slitting one's wrists.

She threw a double pack of loo paper into her trolley and tried to steer it into the next aisle without seriously damaging the pensioner who stood hesitating between a box of man-sized Kleenex and the own-brand recycled ones. Recycled nasal tissues: what a truly captivating thought.

*'Don we now our gay apparel,'* sang the choir, oblivious to political correctness, *'tra la la la la.'* Cassie dropped a packet of tampons in beside the loo paper. What was gay apparel, anyway? Pink T-shirts? Leather and tattoos? An earring? What exactly did Boys of Harley wear?

At the meat cabinets, all the prime cuts of beef were covered in red and yellow stickers indicating savage price cuts. She picked up a packet of fillet steak, studied it, put it back. Better pass on that one. Not only was there the risk of ending up mad as a cow to worry about, despite the vehement reassurances of the Government that British Beef was safe (and who trusted the Government these days? Not Cassandra Swann, that was for sure). There was also the melancholy thought that, even with the prices slashed, she couldn't afford to eat beef. Couldn't afford to eat anything, if the truth be told. In fact, the only reason she was here at all, about to spend money she hadn't got, was because earlier that morning, she had opened the fridge and found herself involved in a major Mother Hubbard incident. All it contained was half a lemon covered in tasteful verdigris, a can of non-alcoholic beer left over from the summer, and a jug of suspiciously viscous milk. Plus half a jar of black olives. There wasn't a lot you could do with that, nutrition-wise.

Her first instinct had been to ring up Charlie Quartermain and suggest they met for lunch, knowing she could pig out and he would pick up the tab. The instinct was unworthy. She knew that perfectly well. Nonetheless, she toyed with it for some time before rejecting it. It would, after all, be grossly unfair to trespass on his good nature. Especially when she was not prepared to offer a *quid pro quo* in the shape of allowing him into her bed.

Which is not, she told herself, looking at the pork chops on special, to say that she had not enjoyed their close physical encounter some weeks earlier. Not to say that at all. It was simply that since there was no future, could *never* be a future, for her and Charlie – not a shared one, anyway – it was unfair to let him think that there might be. And sleeping with him again would definitely give him that impression.

Putting the pork chops back, she sighed. It'd have to be pasta again. Pasta was good. Pasta was fat-free. Above all, pasta was cheap. The amount of it she ate these days, she was going to end up looking like an Italian mother-of-twenty. She stuck a couple of bags of fettucine into her trolley. Lolly's mental state was one problem; the car was another, the reason why she couldn't afford anything but pasta and bog-rolls, let alone Christmas presents. Its pulmonary wheezes had grown worse and worse until, a week ago, she had been forced to take it into the garage and hand it over to the two oily troglodytes who had been keeping it on the road for the past three years. Their bill had made her eyes water but at least the car now moved between points A and B without threatening imminent breakdown. Paying for it had cleaned her out.

Cleaned out the fridge, too.

The choir broke into a sickly version of *The Little Drummer Boy*, a song which, in Cassie's opinion, needed no extra help when it came to producing a feeling of nausea. She moved on to contemplate the chicken carcasses. In imagination, she saw one of them emerging from her oven, crispy-skinned, surrounded by roast potatoes, maybe a sausage or two, a jug of thick chicken gravy to hand, a roast parsnip somewhere in there as well. It wasn't gourmet dishes she craved, just rib-sticking ones. Her stomach rumbled. She was not exactly starving. She could manage to put toast on the table at breakfast time, make do with tinned soup for lunch. And in the past six days, she had been out to dinner twice, once with her business partner, Natasha Sinclair and her husband Chris, once with crime writer Tim Gardiner. Now it was nitty-gritty time. To eat or not to eat? On the one hand, it was good for the figure to go without food. On the other, starvation could be seriously life-threatening.

'Don't know how people manage these days, do you?' The tissue-ditherer materialised at her side and scooped two of the chickens into his basket. 'I mean, the prices and everything and it's not as if they made any concessions to us old folk. Look at me, I'm sixty-eight, live on my own, what do I want with a bargain pack of twenty chicken thighs, nasty stringy things? In addition to which they're pumped full of embalming fluid.'

'Embalming fluid?'

'That's what I understood. Apparently in America, corpses don't decompose any more. Open up the coffins and they're lying there as fresh as the day they passed away, because they've been eating chicken for years and years over there. At least, so I read in the papers but you can't trust a thing you read these days, can you?'

'I suppose not.'

He reached into the cold cabinet again and added a tray of chicken breasts to his basket. 'It's not what I spent five years fighting Hitler for, I'll tell you straight.'

'Gosh, I knew things were pretty desperate in the dark days of 1940, but I hadn't realised they were reduced to conscripting twelve-year-olds,' said Cassie.

'In a manner of speaking.'

'What manner would that be?'

'It's the principle of the thing, isn't it?'

'Anyway,' Cassie said, 'do you really count as an old folk?'

'Sixty-bloody-eight? I'd say so.'

'You look in pretty good shape to me.'

'I am. Eat properly, play badminton once a week, martial arts classes at the Centre, keep in trim. Age shall not weary me nor the years condemn.'

'I don't think you're exactly what the poet had in mind.'

The man fell into step beside Cassie as she walked past the fish counter. Enviously she noticed that, among other luxury items, his basket contained two bunches of asparagus and an avocado.

'Funny old world, isn't it?' the man said. Darting towards the seafood shelves, he picked out a packet of oak-smoked salmon, and put it with his other purchases.

'In what sense?'

'Here we are,' he griped, 'choking to death on fumes, poisoned by E-numbers, menaced by hooligans, no longer safe in our own homes when people like me—' he caught Cassie's eye and added quickly '—of my generation, that is,

8

laid down their lives to make this a land fit for heroes.'

'And heroines.'

'What?' He added a couple of bottles of wine to his basket. 'Oh, see what you mean. Yes, of course. The fair sex certainly played its part in the last war.'

'If you mention the Land Army girls, I shall mug you in the car park and steal your smoked salmon,' said Cassie.

'Not that I'm grumbling,' said the man, being a lot more economical with the truth than he was with his purchases. 'Never had it so good, really. But I'm one of the lucky ones. Got most of my faculties left, bit of a pension, don't need a home help though a lot of help they'd be if I did, they're not even allowed to replace a light-bulb these days let alone shift pieces of furniture or cook a decent meal. I mean, what do they think us old people want a home help for in the first place, not that "want" is the right word, when what we really *want* is to be thirty-something again?'

'Take it from me, being thirty-something isn't all it's cracked up to be,' said Cassie.

'That's what my eldest says. Swans up every now and then in this big car and tries to tell me how hard things are for him. I tell him all he's got to worry about is the threat of redundancy, which is a damn sight easier to face than the threat of extinction from a German artillery bombardment.'

'Not that you have any first-hand experience of either.'

'Not that I have any first-hand experience of either,' agreed the man. 'Though many of my generation did. But at least we didn't have to worry about jobs, that's one thing to be thankful for, though by the time the exploitist capitalist bosses had taken their cut, you didn't have much to take home to the wife at the end of the week, believe you me.'

'Still, you were able to make do, I expect. Always food on

the table, nice roast on Sundays, made your own entertainment, no doubt, singsongs round the family piano, game of Monopoly together, cards, that kind of thing. None of this gawping at the idiot box, watching filth and violence and sniffing glue.'

He looked at her with interest. 'You're taking the piss, aren't you?'

'Yes.'

'You seem like a nice kind of girl, too.'

'Oh, dear.' Social death or *what*, to be called a nice kind of girl by a man who called women girls and lied about his war?

'So why don't you let me buy you a cup of coffee in the cafeteria?'

'Well, I—'

'Better still—' He glanced at a gold watch clasped loosely round his thin wrist. 'Let's step across the road to the pub. I always fancy a little something at about this time.' He put out his hand. 'Brian's the name. Brian Arthur Edgecombe.'

Is this what it's come to? Cassie asked herself, while her escort chatted up the elderly barmaid. Cadging drinks off old age pensioners: can you really have sunk so low?

Brian Arthur Edgecombe proved to be a man with the right instincts. When he came back to their table he brought, without any prompting, not just her half of draught lager and his pint of bitter, but a couple of bags of crisps as well. Sometimes she thought she would kill for a bag of crisps.

'And your name is . . .?' he prompted, sitting down next to her on the padded pew.

'Cassandra Swann.'

'I've heard that name before somewhere.' He frowned. 'Now where would that be?'

'There was an article about me in the local free press once,' said Cassie.

'Why?'

'Dunno really. They get desperate at times. I'm a freelance bridge teacher.'

'Bridge. That's it.' Edgecombe snapped his fingers. 'You're engaged to a friend of mine. Charlie Quartermain.'

'En*gaged*?' Cassie felt her face grow hot with rage. 'I most certainly am *not*.'

'Oh? He told me quite distinctly you and he were going to be married.'

'I'm not engaged to anyone. And if I was, Charlie Quartermain would be the last person on earth I'd be engaged to.'

'Funny, that. I wonder how I got hold of the wrong end of the stick.'

'Probably because he handed it to you.'

'But you are ... um ... aren't you?' He wiggled his eyebrows about meaningfully.

'What?'

'You know ...'

'No.'

'Nudge, nudge, say no more.'

'You've lost me,' Cassie said in a manner which rivalled Aunt Polly at her iciest.

'Going out together, I mean.'

'That is the absolute bloody limit,' said Cassie. 'How *dare* Charlie spread such rumours about me.'

'So they're entirely without substance, are they?'

'Absolutely,' Cassie seethed. Her teeth were clenched together so tightly she thought that blood might start seeping out of her ears. 'Completely. If he's a friend of yours, you'll

11

no doubt be aware that he's something of a fantasist. Unfortunately, his fantasies appear to include me.'

'It seems a touchy subject.'

'I should damn well think it is.' She made an effort to control her fury. 'Tell me about you, Mr Edgecombe.'

'Brian, please.' He sucked his beer. 'Nothing much of interest to say, really. Retired now, of course. Wife and three grown-up kids. Did my National Service, took a course in wood-working, ended up teaching it for twenty years or so until the paperwork got too much to cope with, then turned a hobby into a living. Became a furniture restorer.'

'That's what I did, too. Gave up teaching biology in a girls' school and became a freelance bridge teacher instead.'

'Regret it?'

'Not for a single moment. At least . . . not until the bills arrive and then I can't help remembering that regular monthly cheque.'

'I'm with you there.' Edgecombe stood up. 'Want another?'

'It's my turn.' Cassie made a half-hearted attempt to look like someone ready to buy her round.

He stopped her. 'Wouldn't dream of it, my dear. My generation didn't let women pay for things.'

'Just saw to it that they didn't have money of their own to pay for them with, eh?'

He raised his eyebrows. 'Wearing a bra, are you? Or did you burn it? I do hope you're not going to turn out to be one of those dungareed feminists.'

'Not in a million years.' Cassie looked down at herself. 'I look dreadful in dungarees.'

While he indulged in further playful banter with the barmaid, she watched the television hung high up in one corner of the ceiling. It was fringed with silver foil streamers and a piece of plastic holly hung rakishly over one corner. On the screen, a man was leaning over a bent figure in a wheelchair, a soft pink blanket covering its ancient knees. She recognised it. The oldest woman in the world. A French-woman who'd been in the papers recently for being two hundred and ninety years old or something. 'And what, Madame,' the interviewer was saying, according to subtitles which ran along the bottom of the screen, '. . . what, Mad-ame, is your view of the future?' He held the microphone closer.

The aged creature stirred. Opened her mouth. Stroked her pink blanket. 'Very short,' she murmured. She smiled.

So did Cassie. Laughed aloud, in fact. It was nice to see that even though the old dear could have doubled for Methu-saleh's great-grandmother, she still had a sense of humour. At that age, short was probably the *mot juste*. She tried not to think of the various forms of slow and painful death to which she would like to put Charlie Quartermain.

'Christ,' Brian Edgecombe said, putting glasses down on the table and staring up at the screen. 'I hope they'll take me out and shoot me if I hang on that long.' He drank carefully from his pint. 'Can you imagine it: all your friends dead, all your children, your grandchildren, probably half your great-grandchildren as well? Who'd you talk to? What would you have in common with anyone else in the world? A bloody freak, that's what that poor old girl is. A statistical freak.'

'Isn't there a village in Peru where everybody lives as long as she has.'

'Maybe. But at least there's several of them. At least they can totter down to the pub together and swap reminiscences over a pint of fermented llama's milk.' He jerked his chin at the TV set. 'Who's that old dear got left? Nobody. What a nightmare.'

'She doesn't seem to mind too much.'

'I've got to the age where almost every day I hear that someone I know has died. My dread is discovering that I'm the last one left.'

'Sixty-eight isn't old.'

'It's not young, either.'

'This is true.'

He stared contemplatively at his foam-laced glass. 'When you're young, all the doors stand open. At my age, they're most of them closed.'

'Like what?'

He paused for thought. 'The clarinet, for instance. I've always wanted to be a jazz clarinettist, up there with the greats.' He sketched neon lights in the air. 'Think of it: Johnny Dodds, Benny Goodman, Brian Edgecombe.'

'Magic.'

'It's too late now, though.'

'No it's not. Anyone can do anything.'

'Thank you, Cassandra.' He shook his head gloomily. 'No. My fingers are too stiff. Arthritis and so on. And the other thing I always wanted was a fiftieth wedding anniversary party. I'd really been looking forward to that. Won't happen now, of course.'

'Oh dear. Did your wife . . .' Cassie simply could not bring herself to say 'pass over' '. . . die?'

'Die? No, she damn well did not.'

'Oh?'

'Took off to Florida with Bert Comstock – that's the newsagent round the corner from our house – is what *she* did. You'd think she'd have better sense. I mean, who wants to

14

live in Florida, for Pete's sake? All those blue skies and sandy beaches, palm trees and martinis by the pool, endless sunshine. The woman must be mad.'

'I'm really sorry.'

'Not as sorry as I am, Cassandra. Wouldn't even come to Cornwall with *me*, but some jumped-up seller of porno mags only has to whisper the magic words "Miami Beach" and away she goes, sexy underwear, two-piece bathing suits, frocks with necklines down to her waist, the ruddy lot.'

'Cornwall's quite nice, isn't it? I've never been there.'

'Neither have I. But what I kept asking her was: why him? What's he got that I haven't?'

'And what did she say?'

'A condo in Florida, is what she said. Couldn't argue with that, could I?'

'Not really.' Cassie could picture the wife, a bottle-blonde some thirty years younger than her husband, tied to an old man, looking for a bit of excitement. And finding it in the newsagent, a go-getting type with sleeked-back hair and a pair of designer jeans. Easy to see how it might have happened.

'What annoys me most, Cassie – you don't mind if I call you Cassie, do you? – what really gets to me is that there she is out there in ruddy Florida, lolling on the beach, being pawed by some Flash Harry with only one thing on his mind, while I'm still doing my shopping in Tesco's. Irritates the hell out of me, that does.' He supped deeply from his beer.

'Was she . . . how long had you been married?'

'Only forty-two years, that's all.'

'Forty-two? Gosh.' Forty-*two*? How *old* was the wife, for God's sake?

'Don't think me bitter, Cassie, but you'd imagine after

15

such a long time she'd have accepted that the parrots and the palm-trees weren't going to happen.'

'Except that they did.'

Brian snorted. 'A condo in Miami Beach. Well, she needn't think I'll have her back, not after this. It'll end in tears, you mark my words, but I shan't take her back. No way. Not after she's been screwing the ears off Bert.'

'Excuse me,' Cassie said. 'She's how old?'

'Seventy next birthday.'

'How old's the newsagent?'

'Eighty-three. Why?'

'And you're sixty-eight?' Her mind boggling like mad, Cassie tried to repress the doubtless politically incorrect notion that there was something unseemly about old people having sex.

'Right.'

'Brian, I want you to know something.'

'What's that?'

'You give me hope for the future.'

'Talking of the future, my dear, how about letting me take you out to lunch, one of these days.'

'What a splendid idea.'

'Let me have your phone number and I'll give you a bell some time.'

'I'm all anticipation.'

A thin layer of frost had formed on the car windows. Shivering, she switched on the ignition and turned the heater to high before scraping at the windscreen. If it even worked, she knew from experience that hot air would only start blowing through the fans as she turned in at her own gate. Still, miracles had been known to happen.

'*Come, they told me, pa ra pa ra pa,*' she found herself singing, tapping her gloved fingers in time on the steering wheel as she drove. '*A new born King to see, ta ra* . . . stop it, Cassandra. At once.' That was the trouble with the damned Drummer Boy: like dandruff, once it was in place, it was almost impossible to get rid of it.

She'd managed temporarily to shelve the problem – if problem there was – of Lolly Haden White. Now it returned with new vigour. Could there be anything worse than finding yourself gradually losing control? Once you reached a certain age, it must be an ever-present dread that things which only a short time ago were easy to do would become difficult; that your powers would start to fail but not so fast that you wouldn't be aware of your own degeneration. The father of a woman in one of her evening bridge classes had committed suicide a couple of years ago because he feared he was becoming an Alzheimer's victim and did not wish to become a burden.

'Just because he forgot things, some woman's name,' his distraught daughter had said, weeping, clutching at Cassie's arm, as though to reassure herself that flesh and blood still existed in an uncertain world. '*I* forget things.'

'We all do,' said Cassie.

'And he was so energetic,' the daughter said. 'Loved his garden, was taking a cookery course at the Centre in Bellington, rode around on his bicycle. You can't imagine anyone less senile. Just because he forgot someone's stupid name . . . it's just not *fair*.'

What is, Cassie wondered? We live in uncertain times, after all. And this is probably the least good time ever to be old, with the nuclear family a rarity, with grown children increasingly mobile as they move away from the places to which their

17

parents are attached in the search for ever more elusive jobs. And above all, with society increasingly geared towards the young, tending to stick the old on the back-burner, to disregard either their contributions or their abilities.

At the signpost which indicated the side road that wound its single-lane way to Larton Easewood, she turned off. Reaching the village, she drove down the High Street towards the green. At first sight, Larton seemed to be stuck in a Merrie England time-warp: a mixture of corn-coloured stone and Queen Anne brick, ancient hostelries, a butter market, a high-steepled church with some memorable stained glass. As she drove past the green, Canon Grainger, plumply black-skirted, emerged from the pub and hurried towards his rectory. What looked like a genuine yokel in old corduroys pushed a wheelbarrow picturesquely from right to left. A flock of shiny starlings was pecking at the grass like a group of eagle-eyed park attendants intent on cleaning up the litter left by thoughtless picnickers. The cold was intense enough to keep even the wannabe Hell's Angels indoors, though a scattering of beer cans and cigarette packets round the vandalised phone booth was a reminder of their usual presence. The bulk of a mobile library van stood as unobtrusively as possible under the bare chestnut trees, shivering every now and then as though with cold. There was something extraordinarily comforting about knowing that if you couldn't get into town to the library, then someone was prepared to bring the library out to you. But then the whole wonderful library system was comforting: one of the happiest memories of her childhood was the day she got her first card and was allowed to dig into the treasure chest of books on the shelves of her local library in Islington.

Turning at the traffic lights, she followed Market Street

until the village began to give way to fields and farmland, then pulled in at the Sinclairs' house.

'You look frozen,' Natasha said, letting her into the welcoming warmth of a country kitchen. There was an encouraging smudge of flour under one of her high Slavonic cheekbones.

'I am.' Cassie scanned the big scrubbed table. As she had hoped, a plate of fresh-from-the-oven peanut butter cookies sat cooling on a wire tray. She tried to calculate the number of calories each one contained, told herself that her weight had remained static for the past fortnight, then added that there was nothing wrong with the fuller figure and that she was merely pandering to social prejudice by worrying about her own. 'The car heater doesn't work properly and I can't afford to have it fixed.'

'One day soon we shall both be rich,' Natasha said.

Cassie had long ago given up trying to decide whether her friend's accent leaned more towards her Sri Lankan father than her Russian mother or vice versa. 'I hope I'm still around to see it.'

Natasha lifted one of the shiny lids on the Aga and set the big aluminium kettle on the hot-plate. 'Once our business takes off . . .' Bridge The Gap, the bridge sundries business which she and Natasha had finally got up and running – or crawling, to be more precise – earlier in the year, was doing reasonably well, but not doing it very fast.

'I don't think I can wait that long.'

'Why not?'

'I'll have died of starvation or cold. Or both.'

'Are things really that bad?'

'They're not good.'

'I have money. Or Chris does. We'd be happy to—'

19

'You've already paid for most of the equipment,' Cassie said firmly. 'I don't mind scrounging dinner off you – or, as it might be, the odd cookie—'

'Please, Cassie, help yourself . . .'

'—but I draw the line at money. Mainly because I can't really envisage a time when I'd be able to pay it back. Do you know I was reduced to letting an old boy on a pension buy me a lager and a bag of crisps this morning?' Cassie tried to keep her gaze away from the cookies but they were exerting an almost hypnotic attraction.

'I thought you were doing all right with your lessons and articles and so on.'

'I was. I am. Usually. It's the darn car. Plus Christmas. And one or two other one-off expenses which I'd been putting off for ages and have finally caught up with me. I'm going to have to take a part-time job, just to tide me over. I'll be all right by the time spring comes.'

'But it's only November. You can't go without food until then.'

'I'll look on it as a crash diet.' Cassie gave in and took a second cookie. 'These are delicious, Tash. But I didn't come for tea. Not really. I wanted to know if you'd heard any gossip about Lolly Haden White.'

'What kind of gossip?'

'Anything.' Cassie looked away. This was worse than she had anticipated. 'Anything about her behaving oddly.'

'I haven't actually heard anything direct,' Natasha said slowly. 'I'm not in her social circle. But we were having drinks at some fundraising do a couple of weekends ago and I did hear Serena Smith – that's her daughter – saying she was worried about her mother.'

'In what sense?'

'You know how it is at these charity things. It was in aid of the church roof, actually, and the Canon came bustling up, wanted to know if I'd be prepared to organise a fashion show and so on, and we got stuck into that. I haven't thought any more about it until now.'

'Serena said she was worried? What about, exactly?'

' "A bit concerned" is what she actually said. But at our age we all start worrying about our parents. If we've got any, of course.' Natasha smiled gently at Cassie, knowing that Cassie's mother had died when Cassie was six, that her father, Harry Swann, had been murdered some years later, that on her grandmother's death, the orphaned Cassie, aged thirteen, had been uprooted from her home above a pub in north London and transplanted to the coldly unwelcoming environment of the Norfolk vicarage where her Uncle Sam and Aunt Polly lived with their three thin daughters.

'Just as they worried about us when we were growing up, so we worry about them when they start to get old.'

'Except, with any luck we usually get a few good years in there when the kids are gone and the parents are still completely independent.'

Absent-mindedly, Cassie picked up another cookie. 'That's why I came. Lolly's been playing bridge so badly recently that you begin to wonder whether she's cracking up.'

'Serena would be more help than I can be.'

'I wanted to ask you what the word in the village was before I go and see her.'

'The village has remained silent on the subject. Has it occurred to you that maybe she's simply realising that after a lifetime of playing bridge, she can't be bothered any more, that there are other things she would rather do?'

'Wash your mouth out. What could she possibly rather do than play bridge?'

'Perhaps she's just worried about something. The three main things that upset older people are money, health or their children. Perhaps it's one of those.'

'It'd be easier to believe that,' said Cassie. 'Because nowadays, a woman of Lolly's age isn't considered old. And as for premature senility . . . it's just impossible to believe it.'

'Nonetheless,' said Natasha, 'it does happen. I know people whose parents have been quite a bit younger than Lolly and been diagnosed with it.'

'Next stop Serena,' said Cassie.

# ♦ 2 ♦

A qualified pharmacist, Serena Smith worked in the dispensary in Bellington Hospital. But though it was nearly six o'clock, Lolly's daughter was not at home when Cassie drew up at the gate of her neat little house on the outskirts of Bellington. After hanging around until the curtains at the windows patched with yellow rectangles started twitching up and down Lampeter Close, Cassie drove on through the driving rain towards Honeysuckle Cottage. Neighbourhood Watch works! At least six people would be able to tell Serena about the old banger which had been lurking outside her house, and several would probably embellish the information with descriptions of the sinister woman driving it.

Passing the Dower House in Firth, she slowed down, trying to decide whether to stop or not. She was rewarded, if that was the right word, by the sight of Charlie Quartermain helping a large old man out of his car. It must be his father: although she had never met him, she knew that the old man was due to pay a visit around now. Charlie had forced her to invite him to lunch with her a few months earlier but, for various reasons, the meeting had never materialised and she had been pleased rather than not, suspecting that Charlie had made their relationship out to be warmer than it really was.

At the foot of the short flight of steps up to the front door, the old man irritably shook off Charlie's helping hand and made some obviously disparaging comment. Glancing exasperatedly heavenwards, Quartermain began a shrug which was cut off abruptly as he caught sight of Cassie's slow-passing car. Waving energetically, he ran straight out in front of her, forcing her to brake violently enough for the car to skid on the wet tarmac and end up stalled, with its nose buried in the bank of laurels which stood between the Dower House and the road. One of the wipers carried on wiping, the other stopped halfway across the windscreen. How much was that going to cost to fix?

Heart hammering with the rush of unexpected terror, she rolled down the side window as Charlie approached her car. ''Ullo, darlin','' he boomed. 'How're—'

'What the bloody *hell* do you think you're doing?' she screamed. Somewhere at the back of her head, she heard Uncle Sam's sententious tones: 'Remember the Bard's words, Cassandra: *Her voice was ever soft, gentle and low, an excellent thing in woman.*' Bully for bloody Cordelia, Cassie used to think. When danger threatened, she preferred the more contemporary advice to run in circles, scream and shout. Which she did now. 'Dammit, I could have been *killed*!'

'Thought you might like to come in and have a drink with me and Dad,' Charlie said, ignoring her rage. His huge face bobbed like a harvest moon in the space between the sill and the top of the window; he laid his large hand so heavily on the roof that she was afraid it would buckle.

'If I can't get this car started again, I'll have the repair bill sent to you,' she said. 'It's lucky I just had the brakes fixed, or I'd have run you over.' The conversation she'd had at lunchtime with Brian Arthur Edgecombe came back to her. 'And now I come to think of it, I damn well wish I had.'

'Do me a favour, girl.'

'Give me one good reason why I should.'

'Come in for a bit, will you? Dad's being a pain in the bum and having a third party round might ease the tension.'

'Not this third party. I've got a bone to pick—'

'Pain in the arse? Me?' Charlie's large father elbowed his son aside and took his place at the car window. 'Don't take any notice of him, Miss Swann – it *is* Miss Swann, isn't it? The lad's off his rocker.'

'Hello, Mr Quartermain.'

'Ted, please, m'dear.'

'Ted.'

'He could've caused a nasty accident, jumping out at you like that.' Ted said, rolling his eyes righteously at his son. 'Good thing there's nothing wrong with your heart.'

'My true love's got my heart and I got hers,' Charlie said, with a fatuous grin.

The fact that she had grown up with Uncle Sam made it difficult for Cassie to leave this misquotation uncorrected, but for once she managed to control herself. She looked at Mr Quartermain. 'Now I'm stopped I might as well come in, as long as it's understood that I'm coming in to talk to *you*. I've got nothing at all to say to your son.'

'That makes two of us,' said Mr Quartermain. 'Out the way, Charlie. Let the lady descend from her chariot.' He tugged at the door handle and got it open. 'Allow me, ma'am.'

'Thank you *so* much,' Cassie said graciously. The two of them marched inside, arm-in-arm, leaving Charlie to follow.

The wide hall of the Dower House was a mess of plaster

dust and trailing wires. Plastic sheeting lay bundled up in one corner and a pile of broken bricks and rubble had been cursorily swept up against the wall. A lavatory bowl in avocado green rested on its side, waiting to be removed. 'Improvements going right ahead, just like you planned,' Charlie wheezed from behind them.

'Correction,' said Cassie. 'Plans didn't come into it. My advice: that's all you asked for, and all I gave.'

'Advice. Right.'

'Charlie.' She took a step closer to him.

'Yer?'

'Could I have a word? In private?'

Over her head, Charlie addressed his father, raising his voice. 'Why don't you go into the kitchen, Dad? There's beer in the larder. Just want to show Cassie what's been done in the drawing room.'

'No need to shout,' his father said, proceeding down the long hallway towards the kitchen. 'I'm not deaf.'

'Except when it suits you.'

'I heard that, thank you very much.'

Cassie sighed and stepped into the drawing room. The builders had stripped the grubby cream paint from the extensive skirting boards and picture rails, then treated the bare wood with something which smelled of beeswax and lavender. Despite the pouring rain outside and the slow descent of night, the pine glowed warmly. Gleaming brass fire utensils stood beneath an ornately carved wooden mantel, decorated with ripe fruit and leaves in the style of Grinling Gibbons. 'Oh, it's beautiful,' she said.

'And I'm having them curtains made up. The ones you picked out. Should be quite nice in here when they're hung.'

A hideous suspicion seized Cassie. Could it be that he'd

been asking for her detailed suggestions on the refurbishment of his house with a view to claiming later that he'd done it all for her? 'Charlie.'

'Yuss, darlin'?'

'First of all, you know it makes me mad when you call me darling. Second of all, could you explain why you're going round telling people that we're engaged?'

'*Moi*? I never said any such thing.'

'Then why did a complete stranger come up to me this morning in the supermarket and say you'd told him we were going to get married? A chap called Brian Edgecombe.'

'I never told Brian we was engaged. 'Ere, you want to watch out for Brian Edgecombe, he's a randy old sod.'

'Don't be ridiculous. He's sixty-eight. Rather past that sort of thing, I'd have thought.' Though if neither his older wife nor the even older local newsagent was, why should he be?

'Don't you believe it, darlin'. Man like Brian's never too old for it. You tell him to keep his hands to himself when he's round you or Charlie Quartermain'll come round and smash his kneecaps for him.'

'I can look after myself, thank you very much. Also, I've told you a hundred times that we aren't going to get married.'

He said smugly: 'Yes, we are.'

'How often do I have to say that I don't love you, Charlie, and never shall?' she shouted.

'You do. You just don't realise it.'

'Charles, I'd sooner join the SAS than marry you.'

He merely smiled.

'And anyway . . .' She hesitated. 'Anyway, I'm involved with someone else.'

'Are you talking about that cop of yours? The one that keeps going back to his wife? I'd like to have a word or two with him, ask what the bloody hell he thinks he's doing, treating you like that.'

Cassie wouldn't have minded a word or two with Detective Sergeant Paul Walsh herself. She hadn't seen him for weeks but wasn't about to let Charlie know. 'Why won't you believe me when I tell you we're *never* going to get into any kind of permanent relationship?' she demanded.

'Because it's not true.'

His self-assurance enraged her. Nonetheless, with considerable effort, she adopted a more reasonable turn of phrase: 'I would rather have cancer, Charlie. I would rather *die*.'

She instantly wished the words unspoken. It was a toss-up which looked the more stricken: Charlie, or Bambi standing by the body of his dead mother. 'Charlie,' she said, softening her tone. 'This marriage business is a fantasy of your own. I've never subscribed to it, never given you the slightest encouragement.' She hoped he would have the sensitivity not to refer to the night they had spent together.

She hoped in vain. 'You were doing a fair old bit of encouraging that night we spent together,' he said.

'A gentleman wouldn't have mentioned that.'

'Who said I was a gentleman?'

'I was drunk at the time.'

'*In vino veritas.*'

She stepped away from him. Oh *God*. How could she have let this wretched man intrude so far into her life that she was actually choosing his damned curtains? 'That's it,' she said. 'That is absolutely it. I will never ever, whatever the circumstances, *ever* go out with—'

From the kitchen came the sound of glass smashing and muffled curses. 'Bloody hell,' Charlie said, 'what's the old eejit done now.' He made rapidly for the kitchen, followed by

Cassie. Ted Quartermain was staring down at the bottles he had evidently dropped on to the kitchen floor, splashing his trousers with beer and scattering glass across the flagstones.

'Couldn't help it, Charlie,' he said piteously. Although he was a big man, not yet shrunken by his years, he cowered as though he expected his son to start laying about him with a cat-o'-nine-tails. 'They just fell out me hand.'

'Where've I heard that one before?'

'Give me the broom, son,' quavered Ted, 'and I'll sweep it up.' He put one hand on the small of his back and winced.

'Knock it off, Dad,' Charlie said. 'I left my violin in my other trousers.'

'I'll do it,' said Cassie, instantly wishing she hadn't. She'd be offering to wash Charlie's shorts next.

'Never mind. There's more where that came from,' Charlie said. He opened the larder door, revealing a stone-shelved recess, and hoicked out some more bottles of beer.

When they were sitting round the kitchen table, Ted said to Cassie: 'Did you know Charlie's been trying to get me to come and live with him?'

'What? No. No, I didn't.' Cassie had been trying to decide what the delicious smell which hung richly over the kitchen was and had come to the conclusion that the oven contained a roasting duck.

'Just because I get a bit shaky sometimes, he wants me to get out of my nice little flat and move in here.'

'Nice little hell-hole would be nearer the mark,' snorted Charlie. 'Lift out of order most of the time. Dealers and addicts lying about in heaps. Joyriders. Break-ins.'

'I'm not afraid of them.'

'That's what worries me, Dad. And you've been having your turns more often than you used to.'

29

'My Gran used to have turns,' said Cassie.

'Come over all dizzy, did she?' said Ted, interested.

'That's right.'

'Legs give way sometimes, did they?'

'Like cooked macaroni.'

'It's nothing that a sit down and a nice drop of rum can't put right.'

'That's just what she used to say.'

'I don't know why you're so set against coming down here, Dad. You'd be a lot better off with me.'

'Bollocks.' Ted stretched his tortoise-wrinkled neck and spoke to Cassie. 'I tell you, girl, I wouldn't be seen dead living in a bleeding Dower House, and that's a fact. He's got ideas above his station, Charles has. Needn't bloody well expect me to have them too.' He winked. 'A residential home, now. I quite fancy moving into one of them. They have nurses in those homes, don't they? I wouldn't like to tell a nice young woman like you what I could get up to with a nurse.' His lascivious grin was so like Charlie's that Cassie laughed.

Charlie was not amused. 'I'm not having you in one of them places,' he said. 'No way. Sit about all day, that's all they do, waiting to die. And that's in the good ones. The bad ones, they tie the old dears to the bog seats, beat them up, sexually abuse them.'

'Wouldn't mind a bit of sexual abuse,' Ted said. He did something quite disgusting with his false teeth, shooting the lower set forward so that it stuck out over his lip, then dragging it back in again. 'Anyway, that's not what I heard. I heard they have outings, bingo, people coming in to talk to them, singsongs. Chess. I could play chess if I was in a home.'

'Chess? You've never played chess in your bloody life.'

'I could learn, couldn't I?'

'I'm not having it,' Charlie said. 'That's all there is to it.'

'Why not? If it's what I want?'

'Because I think you'd be better off with your loved ones, all right?'

'Loved ones, he says.'

'Put a sock in it, Dad, or I might just have to shove your dentures down your throat.'

'Oh, very nice,' said Ted. 'That's a really nice way for a son to talk to his old father, that is.'

'Belt up,' said Charlie. 'I mean it.'

Cassie stared. It was the first time she had seen Charlie look anything less than amiable. Except for the time he had rescued her from that loopy hotelier who was trying to kill her. Formidable was the word which had leaped into her mind then, and it did so now.

'Did Charlie tell you I was an ace backgammon player when I was young, Cassie?' said Ted.

'Uh . . . no.' What Charlie *had* told her about his father was that he'd been a merchant seaman who'd returned home one afternoon to find his wife in bed with the next-door neighbour, had divorced her when Charlie was six years old and emigrated to Australia for seven years, after which he had returned and been cautioned for beating up his wife's new husband when he discovered that the man had been physically abusing Charlie for years. 'Lucky not to go down for it, too,' Charlie had said, describing this to her one evening last summer. 'But after that, I moved in with the old boy and stayed there until I left school.'

'Do you play backgammon, Cassie?' Ted asked.

'I'm afraid not. Bridge takes up most of my spare time.'

She smiled at the older man. 'Have you heard about Charlie's Christmas entertainment?' She was fairly certain that whoever had put the duck in the oven had included both orange juice and rosemary.

'He never tells me anything,' said Ted.

'Don't talk daft,' Charlie said.

'It's in aid of Chadwell Court, the residential home in Steepleton.'

'Who resides there?'

'Feisty old buggers like you, Dad.'

'Then why can't I move in there too?'

'Because you're me dad.'

'Don't be too bloody sure of that.'

'And because I say so.'

'What's Charlie going to be in this entertainment?' asked Ted, nastily. 'The Fairy Godmother?'

'As a matter of fact . . .' Cassie began. Because that was more or less what Charlie had turned out to be. He had recently taken Chadwell Court under his generous wing, and had thrown himself into the organisation of a Christmas pageant in order to raise funds for a new wing to be added.

'Don't know why he's so keen on this bloody home,' whined Ted, 'when he doesn't think it's good enough for his old Dad to live in.'

'Did I tell you, Cass,' Charlie said, ignoring his father, 'that Robert Craufurd's agreed to come down?'

'That old shirt-lifter?' said Ted. 'Saw him once, in Sydney. A right ponce, he was, and no mistake. Mincing round in a velvet hat and tight trousers. Make-up an inch thick plastered over his face. And that was before he got anywhere near the stage.'

Cassie pretended she hadn't heard this remark. She widened her eyes. 'Heavens, Charlie: how did you manage to get *him*?'

'Apparently one of the old boys in Chadwell Court is Kenneth Langdon.'

'The actor?'

'Right.'

'I thought he was dead.'

'He probably is. Just hasn't started to pong yet,' Charlie said.

'Story of my life,' said Ted.

'You should bath more often then,' his son said coarsely. 'Anyway, Robert Craufurd used to be a friend of his and—'

'Nudge, nudge,' Ted said.

'—and so he said he'd come down for the sake of auld lang sin.'

'How droll,' said Cassie.

'Ought to be castrated,' Ted said.

'Shut it, Dad.'

Dad did. But not before winking at Cassie.

A call from Honeysuckle Cottage ascertained that Serena Smith had still not returned home. Putting down the receiver, Cassie tried to recall the woman's marital status: certainly there had been a Mr Smith at some point because she remembered an article about her in the local paper. Was there one still? Were there children? She'd taught a lad called Nicholas Smith once, when she was doing a stint of supply teaching at Bellington Comprehensive, but there was no reason to connect him with Lolly's daughter. She debated calling Lolly and decided against it, on the grounds that Lolly would certainly want to know the reason why Cassie needed her daughter's phone number, something Cassie was not prepared to tell her. After a drink, she recollected determinations she had made earlier in the year to be less reticent, less English, more friendly and proactive where others were concerned, and dialled Lolly's number after all. But here, too, there was no reply.

Though pressed by Charlie and his father to stay and have supper with them, she had declined. She told herself that she still had some pride left and to eat the food of a man she had just so comprehensively rejected, even if he was basting a crisply roasted duck at the time and there were roast potatoes all round it, would be boorish in the extreme. She had wavered when he got out a bottle of Cointreau and dashed it liberally over the bird, even more when she saw that there was onion nestling among the potatoes, but she had managed to hold firm. Outside the chippie in Frith she had wavered again, especially as Francesca Fratini, wife of the owner and one of Cassie's new bridge pupils, had told her that she was welcome to have fish and chips on the house, any time she cared to stop in and ask for them.

At home, she boiled up some pasta, drained it, added olive oil and grated cheese, set salad leaves in a bowl. Filling and healthy, she told herself. Also, dull. And nothing like roast duck. Or cod and chips.

She switched on the TV and found herself watching an arts show, featuring a smug Oxbridge know-all interviewing, one after another, a motley group of celebrities. A large man in butterfly-framed glasses pretended he was in fact a woman; a singer with a face so pared away by dieting and exercise that he looked as though he'd been made out of moulded plastic, like Action Man, sang a meaningless song with a lot of equally meaningless hand-gestures, and a pretty blonde bimbo in a white sharkskin trouser suit which showed her boobs bemoaned the fact that, because she was pretty and blonde, nobody would take her seriously.

'And now, our final guest,' said the know-all, adding some vaguely obscene comment which had the audience roaring. 'Actor Robert Craufurd.'

Cassie leaned forward. Until now, the number of times she had given the actor even a passing thought could be counted upon the thumbs of one hand. Yet twice today he had been thrust into her attention. She had never heard of him until a year or so ago when he took on the name part in *Harry Walkinshaw, OAP*, a TV series which had become an unexpected hit. The thick white hair, the lugubrious jowls and the absurd situations in which he found himself ravelled, as a new old age pensioner, seemed to have struck a chord with millions of the viewing public, even those who were nowhere near the age of sixty-five.

Prior to that, Craufurd had been famously 'outed' by one of the tabloids after having been discovered a couple of years ago more or less *in flagrante* with a local fisher-boy on a Greek island. Pictures had appeared; there had been a minor hoohah, accusations of invasion of privacy had been lodged with the Press Complaints Committee and upheld. Since Craufurd's speciality until the successful series had been the playing of fops in Restoration comedies and rather camp characters on TV, and since, until then, his name had never been linked with anyone at all, the general public had scarcely noticed, let alone cared. The incident had given his previously undistinguished career a much-needed boost, culminating in his own series and soon the leading role in a play specially written for him.

Cassie watched him stride forward across the set, one hand

outstretched towards the know-all. At the last minute, he dropped his hand and, instead, embraced the know-all rather more intimately than the know-all cared for, judging by the expression on his face as Craufurd released him.

'So,' he said, straightening his tie, waiting while Craufurd seated himself in the carefully suspicious manner made familiar over nearly a dozen episodes of the series. 'Tell us about your new play.'

Craufurd pouted. 'Is that all I'm here for?'

'What else did you have in mind?' The host, who recently had parted very publicly from his second wife for the sake of a fiery Argentinian authoress of magic realist novels, seemed a trifle nervous.

'Oh, come now, dear boy, you know perfectly well what I have in mind. If mind is the right word.' He leered at the audience, who roared.

'Dear God,' Cassie said.

The know-all straightened his tie again, although it didn't need it. 'Robert – may I call you Robert?'

'You can call me anything you like, duckie, as long as you don't call me after midnight.'

'. . . Robert, you're something of a man of mystery, aren't you?'

'How do you mean exactly, sweetie?' His eyes opened wide in parodic campness.

'I mean that, in a very public arena, you seem to have retained a considerable amount of privacy where your personal life is concerned.'

'Then you obviously don't read the papers, dear.' He turned to the audience. 'I bet all those lovely people out there do – of course they do: there's a man reading one now.' The audience obediently roared with laughter though Cassie

36

could not see what was funny about the remark.

'I'm not talking about your Greek holidays,' said the interviewer, attempting to wrest control back into his own hands, 'but your past life.'

'An open book, dear boy, an open book.'

'Particularly the early part of your career. Almost nothing is known about you, prior to your appearance in the Seventies in the Whitehall farce, *A Row of Tents*.'

'That might well be because there wasn't a great deal to know.'

'Are you going to tell us any of it?'

The actor raised one eyebrow in the manner made familiar by his TV character. It was calculated to get a laugh and duly did. 'Wait for the autobiography, dear boy.'

'But you will admit that since then you've spent more time out of the public eye than in it,' said the know-all, considerably less smug than he had been earlier. The lights showed the copious amounts of sweat which were gathering on his forehead and upper lip. This interview was clearly not going according to script. 'One might almost say in total obscurity.'

Craufurd tutted. 'Oooh, what a bitch she is,' he said. The audience laughed hysterically.

'How would you explain that?' persisted the know-all.

The actor leaned back in his chair. This was familiar territory. 'One of the inestimable advantages of being an actor is that, until your final exit line, you need never count yourself a has-been. You never know at what point in your career your face will start to fit. Look at the number of actors who only began to get top billing in their fifties or later, even though they might have been in the biz since their youth. In my case, it took me twenty-five years, as the man said, to become an overnight sensation.'

'What we're all dying to know is what you were doing before you burst on to the scene as Harry Walkinshaw.'

Cassie sat forward on the sofa. 'You're the only one with the slightest curiosity on the subject,' she shouted. 'And anyway, can't you see he's not going to tell you?' Why did the idiot keep flogging it? Any fool could see that, whatever he'd been up to, Craufurd intended to keep it to himself.

Craufurd ran a limp hand through his thick white hair in the defeated gesture beloved by those who watched his series. The audience tittered. 'If you ever find out, darling, do tell me,' he said. 'Frankly, I was under the impression that I was getting on with my life.' He composed his features into actorish gravity. 'I suppose that what I was doing, dear boy, was honing my craft.'

'And how did you do that?'

'How do any of us ac-taws do it? The obligatory stint in rep as the tea-boy, the spear-carrier, the anyone-for-tennis chap in white flannels. Then a transfer from the provinces to the West End. A season or two with the RSC, swishing about in plumed hats and skin-tight breeches.' He wiggled about and rolled his eyes suggestively. 'Lovely, it was. Mind you, I always played royalty if I could.'

'Really? Why was that?'

'Because if you're royal in Shakespeare, you don't have to carry spears *and* they give you a chair to sit on. Gives new meaning to the phrase "bums on seats", I can tell you. Especially at my age.'

'What came after Shakespeare, then?'

'Television. A short stint in Hollywood. Back to the West End. Believe me, an actor's journey from obscurity to fame is as classic as that of Odysseus returning to his homeland, or, indeed of those latter-day heroes, Stephen Dedalus and

Leopold Bloom, on their progression through Dublin that summer's day in June, 1904.' Turning to the audience, he began to recite, in a rich Irish brogue, the last line or two of James Joyce's *Ulysses*. '*And his heart was going like mad,*' he said orotundly. '*And yes, I said, yes, I will, yes.*' The audience burst into wild applause.

'Foiled again,' said Cassie, as the interviewer struggled to make himself heard above the noise. He leaned forward. It looked like they were back on track now. 'And you yourself, Robert, have *you* always said "yes"?'

'Always, laddie, always. One thing I learned early on in my career . . .' The actor stared into camera, holding it, giving it everything it needed which frankly was not much, '. . . is that, like Fanny Hill, I was never going to get very far if I said "no." ' Audience roar, camera pulling back, end of show.

All very interesting. Or not, depending on how much of a damn you gave about Robert Craufurd. Had it not been for his impending visit to Steepleton, Cassie would certainly have been lining up with those who gave none at all.

She tried Serena Smith's number again, wondering, as she did so, whether the subject of Lolly's possible mental deterioration was too delicate to be discussed over the phone. While she waited, she decided that it was.

This time, Serena was in and picking up. 'Serena Smith,' she said briskly, sounding very like her mother.

'My name's Cassandra Swann. We have met though you probably don't remember me but—'

'Bridge, right?'

'Yes. The thing is, I wondered if—'

'You play a lot with my mother, don't you?'

'That's right. I was hoping to have a word with you . . . could I drop by sometime?'

Serena did not ask what word Cassie wanted to have. 'Tomorrow morning?' she said. 'Coffee time?'

'Excellent.' Which gave Cassie time to find a tactful way of leading up to a conversation which she was certain to find both difficult and embarrassing.

There was no tactful way. In the end, seated at the breakfast bar of Serena's hi-tech kitchen with a cup of coffee in front of her, she said: 'I hope this doesn't sound as if I'm poking my nose into something which doesn't concern me, but I and a number of Lolly's friends are worried about her.'

'Worried? In what way?' Serena put her immaculately made-up face on one side and widened her budgie-blue eyes. Her expression was one of polite incomprehension but Cassie guessed that the question did not surprise her.

'She's always been such a brilliant bridge player, as you know,' Cassie said. 'She's been a county champion, for a start. But just lately, she's been playing like a complete novice. So I wanted to ask if there was anything in particular which might be bothering her at the moment.'

Serena lifted her coffee cup to her mouth and stared at Cassie through the steam which rose from its surface. Then she put it down firmly in its saucer. 'I've been dreading this,' she said. 'I know what you're talking about and I'm simply terrified that it's . . . well, that she's losing her marbles. Going ga-ga.'

There are no nice words for it, Cassie reflected. Senility, Alzheimer's, dementia; they all have such an ugly sound and such painful resonances. Drooling and damp patches left behind on chair seats, questions endlessly repeated, memory fading, family and friends consigned to the outer reaches of a brain no longer able to function. And worse, quite often: wild behaviour, aggression, hatreds surfacing, long-forgotten resentments seething, despairs and terrors, a state of anxiety which nothing can reassure.

'I suppose that's really why I'm here,' she said soothingly, hoping that this was true, that if she examined her motives, they would turn out to be something more admirable than the mere wish to keep a long-term reliable bridge partner. 'To ask if there's anything that her friends can do to help her.' She paused, then added: 'Or help you.' It was no secret that the lives of those caring for an elderly relative could be made an absolute hell.

'I don't know.' Serena rubbed a mark on the black-ash finish of the counter at which she sat. 'I just can't begin to think of the disruption it would cause if we have to move her in with us. Even if she agreed to come, which at the moment I know she wouldn't.'

'There are alternatives to having her living with you.'

'What, like a home, you mean?' Serena's blue gaze was very direct. 'That's absolutely out of the question. There's no way on earth I am putting my beautiful elegant mother into a home to sit in a high-backed chair and turn into a . . . into a v-vegetable.' She pressed her finger against her upper lip as though to hold back tears.

'Not all homes for the elderly are like that,' said Cassie. 'The one at Steepleton, for instance. They go to tremendous trouble to keep the residents happy and occupied. I run a bridge class there once a week and I'm always amazed at how much fun they seem to have.'

'I'm not letting my mother . . .'

'As a matter of fact, I took a bridge foursome there in the summer, one of them being your mother, and the Matron showed us all round the place. Lolly seemed rather impressed. Did she mention it to you?' Cassie remembered the occasion clearly, in part because Lolly, as well as being impressed, had also been upset, though she did not indicate why. She had been fine at first, but after they had been introduced to half a dozen of the inmates, she had adopted an extremely forbidding expression, all furled lips and knitted eyebrows, and though she had played without mishap, she had clearly been brooding on something.

'A place like that'd be far too expensive for us to pay for,' Serena said. 'Though, on the other hand, if she came to live with us, I'm afraid that . . .' She straightened her mouth into a thin line and then slipped off her high stool and walked over to the kitchen sink where she stood gazing between frilly net curtains at the garden outside. She turned and looked steadily at Cassie. 'The plain truth is, that my marriage is going through a rocky patch. And my husband has already said that if Mother . . . if she does go, you know, senile, he won't have her here. Says if I insist, then I'll have to choose between them, says we have to think of the children first, and they'll be the ones to suffer if we end up spending most of the time caring for her instead of them. I've told him that I'd do most of the looking after, especially since he's not even here most of the time. Not that it'll be very easy for me.' She reached out a hand and straightened a frill, picked a dead leaf off the plant standing in a ceramic pot. 'I know he's right, but I don't know what else I could do.'

'It's terribly difficult, I know.'

'I've got a colleague at work who's had to give up her job in order to stay home and care for her elderly father. She's completely tied, has no social life at all because he won't be left with anyone. He used to be such a nice old boy but he's turned into a tyrant who makes her life a misery, and on top of all that, she's reduced to trying to make ends meet on income support, after being used to a professional salary.'

'We don't know that anything's wrong with your mother. And even if there is, she's certainly not anywhere near needing constant care.'

'How do you know? I've seen her hand trembling as she tries to light the gas. I've watched her drop a pan of boiling water onto the floor. It might be down the front of herself next time. She often forgets to lock her front door. I worry all the time, Cassandra, in case she's driving the wrong way down the motorway, or pouring rat-poison over her corn-flakes or wandering round the village stark naked, or some-thing. All those silly things you read about in newspapers that confused old people do. And before you say that she's neither of those things, it wasn't until a few months ago that I even thought of her as old, let alone suffering from senility. It's as if one moment she was my mother and the next she was a doddering wreck.'

'I think you're exaggerating a little.'

'Yes, I know I am.' Serena turned and came back to the breakfast bar. 'It just seems better to face up to the full horror of it rather than ignore it and push it to the back of my mind.'

'You said this change took place a few months ago. Did anything in particular happen then?'

'I know she was horribly upset by the break-up of my sister's marriage, but I can't believe she would go on worry-ing about it to the extent of it causing her to start acting strangely. After all, she worked in London, she's always been dead keen on feminism and the right of a woman to be independent and all that. So Elizabeth's divorce can't have been too much of a surprise. And then there's . . .' Serena distorted her mouth in an expression of hesitant doubt.

'There's what?'

'Well, it seems a bit melodramatic, but I'd say she's actually . . . afraid.'

'What of?'

'That's the thing. When I asked her she just gives me her cold expression – I'm sure you've seen her do it – and tells me I don't know what I'm talking about. But I'm sure I'm right.'

'Do you mean afraid as in frightened by something particular . . . somebody threatening her or blackmailing her, something like that? Or more vaguely afraid, the way we are, that she might be losing her mind?'

'I don't know. I just don't know. But I'm sure it's specific, whatever it was. Last time I was there, for instance, the phone rang and she went absolutely white, as though she knew that if she picked it up, something really awful would happen. In fact, it was only Marjorie Curtiss checking up on a bridge date, but Mother obviously thought it might be someone else. But she wouldn't talk about it.'

'You said she'd been acting strangely.'

'Well, for instance, a few weeks ago, she came to have supper with us, as she often does, and watch a bit of television – though she'd deny it if you suggested that was the reason she came. She's always been a bit snooty about TV, makes a big thing of not having one herself, you know how people are, but actually quite likes to see it, although she pretends that she's only watching because we've got the set switched on anyway.'

'So what happened?'

'We were just finishing supper when her face went a horrible grey-white colour and she suddenly started talking in this very loud voice. Incomprehensible sort of stuff, most of it. We – that's me and the children, because my husband wasn't there, he's with his ship in the Middle East at the moment – we thought she'd had a stroke, at first, but she seemed fine after a bit. We called the doctor, of course, but he said it was just shock.'

'What could have shocked her?'

'When we asked her, she said she didn't know, couldn't remember. Something on the TV, I should imagine.'

'You were eating in front of the TV?'

'No, but it was on in the corner, very quietly.'

'Do you remember what was showing?'

'I didn't give it a second thought until later. What with the fainting and the doctor and everything. It wasn't as if we were watching it, but it was probably the usual rubbish.'

'The news?'

'I don't know.'

'*Coronation Street*? *EastEnders*? A sitcom?'

'I just can't remember. I have a feeling it was an old black and white film.'

'In that case, might it have been something which reminded her of her past? *Out of Africa* or something? Or could one of your children have said something to upset her?'

'I suppose it could have been that,' Serena said doubtfully. 'I have a feeling that they were showing that sitcom about the couple who're trying to get divorced because the husband's admitted having an affair – you know the one, I just can't remember its name – but they can't because they can't decide who gets what . . . well, that's not what it's about, exactly, but that's part of it. Maybe it reminded her of Liz. My sister. Come to think of it, the husband in that does look rather like Larry.'

'Larry's your brother-in-law?' Cassie was floundering a little here.

'Yes.'

'Have you asked your mother if that's what she was upset about?'

'No. She'd bite my head off if I did. And the thing is, we weren't actually watching the TV. She'd brought a bottle of wine, and we were enjoying that. But there were flaming rows about the divorce between her and Liz. Which is why she'd have to come and live with us if she can't cope on her own any more because I know she'd rather die than go and live with Liz and her new . . . um . . . partner.'

Serena obviously found the latest word for a live-in Significant Other as awkward as Cassie herself did.

'That's another thing,' Serena continued. 'Mother used to be so calm, so sweet. And now she loses her temper over the least little thing.'

'There was a bit of a fracas last year, wasn't there?' Cassie said.

'That's right. When she didn't get the Old School House which she's been trying to buy for years. That Indian doctor bought it, that poor man who was murdered, do you remember?'

'Yes, indeed.'

'It was so embarrassing. She went round there after they moved here and started yelling insults at them, the most appalling racist rubbish which I'd never have believed she could possibly say if I hadn't heard her with my own ears. But that was just an isolated incident. It's the more recent things which worry me.'

'She's from Kenya, isn't she?'

'Kenya?' The frown lines on Serena's forehead moved up

towards her smooth black hair. 'I don't think so.'

'Oh.' Cassie was surprised. 'I thought she was brought up there.'

'It was South Africa, as far as I know. She worked for one of the Johannesburg newspapers. But she was brought up in England. I'm absolutely certain of that.' Despite her words, Serena did not sound particularly sure of what she was saying.

'Someone told me that Lolly's mother used to teach at the Old School House when it was still the little local school, which is why she wanted the house in the first place.'

Serena looked embarrassed. 'I never heard that,' she said. 'I was under the impression that my maternal grandmother was rather upper-crust, certainly not the sort who'd be teaching in a village school. The truth is, my sister and I don't know anything at all about our mother's past. She always refused to talk about it. She always said that the past is dead and buried, and it's much more important to cope with the present and prepare for the future than to keep looking back.'

'So you never knew your grandmother?'

'None of our grandparents. They all died before we were born. In fact, we didn't know our father either, because he died too. Killed in a plane crash when we were too young to remember him – or I was, at least. Liz has a few memories but nothing very coherent.'

'It must have been hard for her to bring you up entirely on her own.'

'I think it was. There were no aunts and uncles, either, so no cousins. Not that we missed them particularly. We were a very close-knit little group, us three girls, as Mother used to call us. Looking back, I suppose we were rather an isolated kind of family, though there are lots like that, I imagine. It's bound to happen when an only child marries another only child.'

The lack of information nagged at Cassie. Although it had nothing whatsoever to do with the problem of Lolly's state of mind, she said: 'What did your father do?'

Serena shrugged. 'It sounds odd, but I really don't know. I think he was some kind of high-powered businessman – he certainly seems to have left us well-provided for. But mother simply wouldn't talk about him. Said it was too painful, that it took her years to come to terms with his death and she couldn't bear to revive old memories. And frankly, I don't know whether Liz and I simply lacked enquiring minds, but it never really seemed important. I mean, my father wasn't part of our lives, never had been, so what he did or where he came from was irrelevant.'

Cassie slid off her high-legged stool. 'We don't seem to have come to any conclusion, do we? I can't tell you how much I'd hate it if Lolly really was moving into some form of mental degeneration.'

'Especially since there's little we can do if she is.'

'Except prepare ourselves. But from what you say, with any luck it'll just be the business with your sister that's upsetting her.'

'Let's hope so,' said Serena. 'Because the alternative is too awful to contemplate.'

♥ 3 ♥

Natasha Sinclair's husband had gone to France, in order to attend a high-powered conference on information technology in a purpose-built centre called Sophia-Antipolis. When he informed her that he would be away for five days, Natasha had immediately drummed up as many of her women friends as she could for an impromptu evening of 'girlie bridge'. It was the expected way for a wife left on her own to fill at least one of the spouseless evenings at her disposal. No duplicate was played at these sessions, nor were they intended as a chance for a serious game; the cards were merely an excuse for getting mildly plastered and the letting down of hair. Cassie never missed one if she could help it. As a way of catching up on local news and the latest gossip, such occasions were invaluable. Tonight, particularly, she also wanted a chance to observe Lolly more closely.

When the first table had played two rubbers, Natasha called a break and passed wine-glasses round, while Cassie pulled the corks off bottles of Australian Chardonnay. As the conversation became general, one of the women said: 'What did you think of the sermon last week at St Bartholomew's, girls?'

Petra Lewis, an in-your-face feminist solicitor with an

all-women practice in Oxford, sighed melodramatically at this disempowering word. 'Girls!' she said. 'Honestly!'

Someone said coyly: 'I don't know about the sermon, but the preacher was rather dishy. Who was he, again?'

'The new Chaplain at St Frideswide's College,' another woman said. 'Apparently he was at Wycliffe Hall with the Vicar, before he went out to Africa.'

'Before who went to Africa?' asked Cassie.

'John Lightower. The Vicar. He was doing missionary work – you must have heard him talk about his time out there.'

'For talk, read bore to death,' said Petra.

'I don't think I've ever met him,' Cassie said, trying to get a mental fix on the incumbent of St Bartholomew's. In her mind, all vicars looked like Uncle Sam. The startling thing was how many of them also did in real life.

'You'd remember if you had. He's got masses of . . . what's the word I'm looking for?'

'Dandruff?' Petra said unkindly.

'Charisma . . . that's what I mean. He's very compelling.'

Another woman shuddered deliciously. 'When he looks at me with those eyes, I'd confess to *any*thing.'

'Well, his friend was pretty much the same.'

'Imagine being stuck in a life with *those* two!'

Someone with more courage than sense asked: 'Did you go to hear the Vicar's friend preach, Petra?'

'No, I bloody did not,' Petra said. 'I'm not in the least interested in the patriarchal attitudes of established religions, let alone in kow-towing to those who perpetuate them.'

'Oh, for heavens sake,' someone began. 'Surely that's rather un—'

Lolly cut in, her voice sharp and disapproving. 'Strictly

speaking, the man who preached is not the new Chaplain, since, as I understood it, the appointment has not yet been confirmed.'

'No, but it's pretty well cut and dried,' someone else said. 'My husband says it's only a question of dotting the "i's" and crossing "t's".' She looked round at the other women. 'And did you know that three of our last five new bishops have held exactly the same position?'

'Really?' said Lolly.

'Yes. It seems to be an established stepping stone up the church hierarchy.'

'Ever seen a woman bishop?' enquired Petra, as though she really wanted to know.

'Why did you go to hear this man preach, Lolly?' Natasha said. 'I thought you never went to church.'

'I don't normally. I am deeply disgusted by the Church and the men who serve it. But my daughter insisted I accompany her and out of curiosity, I agreed to go.' Lolly laughed grimly. 'Perhaps she feels that as I get older, I need to take out spiritual insurance of some kind.'

'And what did you think of it?'

'I was . . . extremely surprised.' Lolly said.

'What by?'

Lolly seemed perturbed by the way the women were waiting expectantly for her answer. 'Everything. It's been a very long time since I was last in a church.'

Marjorie said: 'Hugh Nightingale came and had lunch with us after the service. We knew him years ago, before he took Holy Orders. He trained with my husband, you see.'

'Isn't your husband an accountant?' said Natasha.

'That's right. So was Hugh.'

'Hey, that's a good one,' said Petra. 'An accountant turned

51

priest. Talk about money-changers in the temple.'

'I've met him before, too,' said Janice Frankum, who was dummy at the other table. She and her husband had moved into the area three or four months ago, though Cassie had not yet got to know her.

The others ignored her. 'I didn't see *you* in church, Cassie,' Marjorie said.

'That's because I wasn't there,' said Cassie.

'Ah.'

Everyone seemed to be waiting for some explanation and, like a wimp, Cassie found herself providing one. If she had been as confrontational as Petra, she would not have felt the need to come up with an excuse. But because most people knew that her uncle was a vicar in East Anglia, they somehow expected her to be tarred with the same brush as he was and she did not have enough self-confidence not to care if she disappointed them. She was not a willing liar, which said something, she liked to think, about her character. But once she got started, she produced falsehoods of astonishing quality. Sometimes she amazed herself with her fluency and invention. Sometimes her lies were so damn good that even she believed them. This was the main reason why she tried not to tell them.

And now, as the temporary focus of attention, she could feel a whopper coming on, unstoppable as a hiccup. 'I'd like to have gone, but a friend of mine came over from Ireland that day. Brendan . . . um . . . O'Rourke. He's a . . . a painter. And poet. You may have read about his last exhibition at the . . . the Cork Gallery.'

'Brendan O'Rourke?' One of the women turned to another. 'Didn't we go to see his show, dear?'

'No. You insisted on going to that frightful thing with a

cow cut in half in a tank. I'm sure his name wasn't O'Rourke.'

'I saw it,' volunteered a woman called Eileen Thatcher, a very small bespectacled teacher who had never before spoken in Cassie's hearing.

'The Brendan O'Rourke exhibition? Are you sure?' Cassie felt like some alchemist of the past, raising devils to do her bidding.

'Yes.' Ms Thatcher spoke firmly. 'There were a lot of paintings of streets in Belfast, and portraits of children against a background of war. There were some sculptures, too. What do they call it? Found art? Bicycle wheels with objects welded to them: empty baked bean tins and bullets and pieces of barbed wire. A statement about Northern Ireland which I found very moving. And each one had a poem set next to it.' She looked at Cassie, who was listening to this with horror. 'So you're a friend of his, are you?'

'I wouldn't go as far as to say I was a friend,' said Cassie hastily. 'More of a casual acquaintance, really. In fact, to tell the truth, I scarcely know him.'

'I'd simply love to meet him. Next time he comes to visit you, perhaps you'd bring him round for a drink.'

Cassie wanted to say that it was absolutely out of the question to do anything of the kind. Instead, she adopted an expression of regret. 'Well, as you probably know, he's extremely reclusive. In fact, this is the first time he's left Ireland for years. I'm sure you'll understand if I say I couldn't accept engagements on his behalf without consulting him.'

'Ah,' said Eileen. 'The artistic temperament. I understand absolutely. But next time he's over from Ireland . . .'

'Absolutely,' Cassie said, knowing he never would be. Poor Brendan, barely brought to life before he was scheduled to snuff it. On the ferry going back to Ireland, if she had anything to do with it. She started mulling over the details of his final moments. A massive heart attack? A fall overboard with too much of the Bushmill's taken? Or simply a fatal bout of fisticuffs with someone who disagreed with his views on Northern Ireland?

Marjorie Curtiss asked about the Christmas entertainment which was to take place at Chadwell Court. 'I thought I'd get tickets for my parents,' she said. 'It might cheer them up. They've been so gloomy recently.'

'Perhaps it's the time of year,' said Lucinda Powys-Jones in her smooth slow voice.

'How do you mean exactly?' said Marjorie, adopting the careful tone she might have used to a backward child. Though popular, Lucinda was not renowned for her IQ.

'Doesn't everyone get depressed when the leaves start to fall and the evenings get longer? I know I do. And my poor old parent-birds. It's called Mads, or something. I read about it in a magazine.'

'Mads?' Marjorie looked round at the table. The other women tried to hide their expressions of disbelief at learning that Lucinda could read. 'Aren't you mixing it up with beef, Lucinda?'

'Probably.'

'Sads,' Cassie said. 'I think that's what it is. Seasonal Affective Disorder Syndrome, something like that. Swedes get it a lot.'

'Swedes?' said Lucinda, opening her pretty mouth in wonder.

'Not the root vegetable,' said Cassie patiently. 'The people.'

'You can buy special light-bulbs for it now,' said Janice Frankum.

'I don't know about light-bulbs,' said Marjorie. 'But ever since Father broke his leg hunting, he and Mother seem to think it's only a matter of time before my brothers and I start looking for a convenient scrap-heap on which to throw them. Which is why I thought tickets to this entertainment thing would give them something to look forward to.'

'They'll probably think you're trying to hint that it's time they enrolled in the Home,' said Petra.

'Oh Lord. Do you really think so?'

'Isn't that friend of yours organising it?' Lolly asked Cassie. 'That big man whose clothes are too small for him?'

'He's not really a friend,' said Cassie, wondering why she could hear a cock crowing so late at night. 'And it's not so much that his clothes are too small, more that he can't find anything in his size which fits him.' *Damn*, she thought. Now they would all think she discussed Charlie's wardrobe with him when not only did she not do so, but having seen the size of his underpants, could think of almost nothing she wouldn't prefer to do.

'I took him to a shop which caters for larger sizes,' said Petra.

'Did you, indeed?' said Cassie.

'But they didn't have anything which fitted him except a T-shirt which must have come out of Omar the Tentmaker's workshop. It had Beavis and Butthead on the front: he wanted to buy it but I told him not to.'

Just how the hell did Petra come to be walking round Oxford with Charlie, buying bloody clothes? Cassie said to Lolly: 'Yes, Mr Quartermain *is* in charge of the theatricals. It's quite amazing how many people he's managed to bully into doing a turn for him.'

'Beavis and who?' Marjorie said.

'Don't worry about it, Marge,' said Petra. The three other women at the second table finished post-morteming their last rubber and joined in the conversation. 'Is it true Placido Domingo's going to come and sing?' one of them asked.

'I've got a loverly bunch of coconuts,' said Petra Lewis.

'I *beg* your pardon,' Marjorie said.

'Charlie's asked him to sing that,' said Petra. 'Or so he told me.'

'And what in the world did he answer?' Cassie attempted to stifle what she refused to accept was the jealousy churning in the pit of her stomach.

'He's going to try and fit it in, apparently.'

'Charlie: what a man,' sighed Natasha, glancing at Cassie. 'I know not everyone likes him, but he is so generous and so energetic.'

'So rich, too.' Another woman leaned forward. 'That gorgeous house.'

'You simply wouldn't believe what he spent on curtains for his drawing room,' said someone else. 'I have the same woman doing mine and she told me he insisted on having them made up in a particular way, even though it used up masses more material. Said they had to be exactly the way a friend of his had suggested.'

'Goodness,' trilled Natasha. 'I wonder which friend that could be.'

'I was told that he's persuaded Tim Holloway to recite 'Young Lochinvar' or something similar,' said Marjorie, a stalwart of the local Conservative Party. Holloway was the Member of Parliament for the district, and lived on the other side of Bellington in a choice country house. 'Apparently he jumped at the chance.'

'Tim'll be a hoot,' said Janice Frankum.

The others turned cold eyes on her. Cassie had had no difficulty in picking up the fact that in the short time she had been around, the woman had made herself fairly unpopular. 'Oh really?' someone said nastily.

'Yes. He was at school with my husband and was apparently frightfully good at that sort of thing, even then. Always had a major part in the school play and so forth.'

'According to the papers, he's tipped for a post in the next Cabinet,' someone said.

'God,' said Petra, in tones of deep disgust. 'How I hate those fat cats with their overstuffed faces and Savile Row suits and I'm-all-right-Jack mentalities. And all of them going to the right schools, speaking in the same dreadful voices, wearing the same stupid ties.' She stared belligerently at Marjorie. 'Don't any of them ever take a look around them and see what they've done to the country?'

'Pipe down, Petra. We aren't here to—'

Petra had no intention of piping down. 'Just to take one example, do any of them ever stop to consider that, in real terms, women are no better off today than they were twenty years ago? Does it ever occur to them that we—'

'Didn't I hear that one of the Royals has agreed to play the part of Mother Goose in this pantomime?' someone said hastily. Once Petra got started, it was hard to stop her, and since, whatever their own politics might be, most of the women present were married to dyed-in-the-wool Tory voters, tempers were apt to flare when she did.

'It's not a pantomime,' said someone else, raising her voice over Petra's. 'It's a Christmas revue.'

Cassie tried not to laugh as she asked: 'Which Royal do you think would agree to take part in a village panto?'

'Prince Edward would make a lovely Buttons,' someone said.

'What part could Princess Di play?'

Petra offered an offensive suggestion which Cassie quickly covered up by saying: 'I understand Charlie Quartermain's got a definite commitment from Robert Craufurd to come down and take part.'

Lolly made a sound somewhere between a snort and a gasp. 'Coming here? I hope not.'

'Who is he?' Marjorie asked.

'Oh Marge, you sound like a High Court judge,' said Petra. She was the same age as Cassie and consequently some ten years younger than most of the rest of the women there. She adopted a shaky old-fart voice: '. . . "Erm . . . exactly what sort of vegetable is a couch potato? Is Ice-T some kind of refreshing drink?" sort of thing.'

'Well, I'm sorry,' said Marjorie aggressively, not sounding in the least sorry. 'At my age, I really don't feel it's necessary to keep up with youth culture any more. I've done it once and that was enough.'

'Miniskirts, white lipstick, flares, was it?' said Petra.

'I'm fifty-two.' Marjorie was ruffled. 'You'll be asking why I'm not wearing a bustier and smoking crack next.'

'We *know* why,' Petra muttered.

'Herman and the Hermits,' Lucinda said. 'I liked them.'

Petra groaned rudely.

'I believe Robert Craufurd stars in that stupid sit-com about a chap learning to come to terms with being a golden oldie,' said Natasha, pouring more white wine into their glasses and passing round slices of layered cream sponge.

'But he's queer,' Lolly said.

'Gay, dear. Gay.'

'Whichever. He is, isn't he?'

'Very much so.'

'Does it matter?' Cassie said.

'What?' They looked at her in bemusement.

'What's sexual orientation got to do with anything?' said Cassie.

There were confused murmurings. 'It must be so ghastly for a mother to discover her son's gay, don't you think?' remarked Eileen Thatcher.

'Or her daughter,' said Lolly.

'Why?' asked Cassie.

'Yea,' Petra chimed in. 'Why?'

'Oh, come on,' Eileen said. 'I know we're all supposed to be so liberal these days, and in theory I don't mind other people's sons coming out, as they put it. But I certainly wouldn't want my Julian to come home one day and announce that he was homosexual. Quite apart from anything else, there'd be no grandchildren to look forward to.'

'A friend of mine's husband came home and announced exactly that,' said Petra. 'Said he was leaving her to set up with a man he'd met at a conference two years ago, and that they'd been having an affair ever since, and he couldn't go on living a lie a moment longer.'

'Heavens.'

'How vile.'

'What did she *say*?'

'She was pretty devastated. I mean, she'd got two kids and everything. But what else can you expect from bloody men?'

'That's utterly dis*gust*ing,' said Lolly. Her face was red and mottled; she was obviously made deeply uncomfortable by the conversation. Cassie wished they could change the subject.

'Somebody I know found that her husband was one of these cross-dressers,' said Anne Norrington before Cassie could think of something to change the subject to. 'She came home one day and found him in the bedroom, prancing around in a Janet Reger suspender belt.'

'Lucky him to be able to afford it,' said Cassie.

'But finding your husband likes women's underwear isn't as bad as discovering that he's gay, is it?' Marjorie said. 'If you're prepared to put up with it, cross-dressing doesn't really threaten your marriage, does it?'

'Or your view of yourself as a woman,' said Anne. 'Whereas if he was gay, it would make you wonder about yourself and whether he'd been making love with you simply out of duty, when all he really wanted was to be sleeping with a man.'

'Some people are perfectly happy to be bi-sexual,' said Cassie.

'That's even worse,' said Lolly. 'That's *horrible*. Degrading for both parties. I would find it so shaming, if it was me.'

'Why should *you* feel ashamed?' said Petra. 'It wouldn't be *your* fault. The bastards don't go round wearing signs announcing their orientation, do they? Especially if it might have a bad effect on their careers. Much better to con some poor woman into acting as an alibi while they further their ambitions.'

'Even so, I wouldn't be able to face myself in the mirror, if I knew my husband had been sleeping with men,' said Lolly. 'I would feel utterly . . . *contaminated*.'

'There's nothing wrong with being gay, you know,' said Cassie. 'It doesn't mean you've got horns and a tail.'

'You'll be telling us next that some of your best friends are gays,' Janice Frankum said with the kind of little laugh which went some way towards illustrating why nobody seemed to like her.

'As a matter of fact, they are. Some of my best godfathers, certainly.'

There was a faint but discernible wave of shock. 'That nice Robin Plunkett's gay?' someone said disbelievingly. A couple of women shifted their chairs, as though afraid of pollution.

'Ladies, *please*,' admonished Natasha, frowning at Cassie. 'Why do we always seem to get back to sex, whatever we start out discussing?'

'Because sex is the most interesting subject there is,' said Petra mischievously. 'Right, Cassie?'

♠ 4 ♠

Walking over Magdalen Bridge the next day, she looked up at the square golden mass of the tower and pondered the difference between ignorance and prejudice. At what point did one become the other? Or were they merely the two sides of a broken coin? The women last night spoke out of ignorance, rather than prejudice, yet the end result was the same. She leaned over the broad parapet of the bridge to look into the river, which was lined with leafless trees and bare black earth. Scuffed punts were chained together on the bank; a few mallards pecked busily here and there, their plumage shining again after the ravages of courtship, parenthood and moult.

Someone slapped her on the rump. Damn nerve. She turned, fists bunched. A voice said: 'Cassie Swann, as I live and breathe. I'd know that bottom anywhere.'

'Theo. Talk of the devil.'

'Oh?'

'I was just thinking about ignorance and prejudice.'

'And which am I?'

'Both, really.'

'Well, get you.'

Cassie took Theo's arm and walked on up the High. 'Let's

cut through and have a drink at the Turf.'

'I don't like the Turf.'

'The King's Arms, then.'

'I like that even less.'

'Then let's go back to your rooms and open a bottle of champagne.' Cassie pressed a hand against her head. 'I had rather more than I should have last night, and—'

'How much more?'

'At least half a bottle of Chardonnay more. And Robin always says that champagne is the best cure for a hangover that there is.'

'Who gets to provide the champagne?'

'You do, of course.'

'I wonder how I knew that.'

'You can afford it, you see, and I can't.'

In addition to being an English don attached to St Frideswide's, Theo Southgate was a writer of vigorously camp novels about contemporary life. He was also a good friend of her godfather, the novelist Robin Plunkett, who always referred to him as Tich for reasons which Cassie had no intention of exploring.

They walked up Longwall Street towards the more open ground at the end of St Cross Street where college playing fields sloped towards a branch of the river. Theo's college was a modern one, the work of a foreign architect who had achieved a remarkable homogeneity by designing every detail of the place, from library to lampshades, from chapel to chairs. Cassie had dined in hall there a couple of times, as the guest of Kathryn Laughton, née Kurtz, who had held a visiting fellowship there before falling in love with and marrying an old flame of Cassie's.

Theo's rooms, once you had closed the door behind you,

were a throwback to a different age and aesthetics. He had stripped out as many of the light wooden fittings as he was allowed to, given that the buildings were already listed, and installed his own eclectic mix of inherited furniture and artefacts: massive coffers of steel-hard oak, ornate breakfront bookcases, inlaid tables, strange chairs from Africa and India which colony-governing ancestors had brought back to their castles in Perthshire or their manor-houses in Devon. Horns and skulls and tusks stood about the place; brass trays and Victorian papier-mâché rubbed shoulders with Spode teacups and Staffordshire lambs.

'It's a good thing I'm always prepared,' Theo said, stooping to retrieve a bottle of Taittinger from a small fridge hidden beneath a flamboyant Indian shawl that must have been at least two hundred and fifty years old. He filled fragile crystal flutes and handed one to Cassie. 'Are we drinking to anything in particular?'

'Quiddities,' said Cassie. She sipped at the bubbles. As always, she thought that the appeal of champagne lay more in its connotations than in any oral satisfaction it bestowed upon the drinker.

'The whatness of things. Mmm. An unusual toast.'

'Sometimes I feel worn down by the gulfs which loom between people. The . . . well, what I was thinking about when you took liberties with my person – the prejudices and ignorance. No wonder nation is perpetually at war with nation.'

'I'd say that had more to do with territorial ambition than prejudice.' Theo surveyed her critically, head tilted. 'World peace aside, I'll tell you what. Since I last saw you, you've lost at least six, if not seven—'

'Pounds?'

'I was going to say ounces, but have it your own way.'

Cassie pouted. 'A pox on your ounces.'

'Cassandra, I know I'm not the first, nor will I be the last, to point out that you are an attractive and intelligent woman. Weight loss, whether it be measured in pounds or in ounces, will not render you any the more attractive, though it could possibly make you a tad more intelligent in that your brain might then cease to concentrate on inessentials like how much you weigh.'

'That's all very well. But look at this . . .' Cassie pulled up her sweater and with difficulty tugged her shirt from the tight waistband of her jeans. 'Look . . .'

'Must I?' said Theo, as Cassie pinched a chunk of stomach between thumb and forefinger.

'It's repulsive, isn't it?'

'No, actually. It's part of you and therefore charming. If I was even momentarily drawn to female creatures – in a sexual sense, that is – I would even now be surreptitiously loosening my clothing, preparatory to ravishing you among the silken cushions of my forebears. As it is, a boy can dream.' He sighed theatrically and filled their glasses again.

'Good stuff, this,' said Cassie.

'I should hope so. It cost a pretty penny.'

'Do you really think I've lost weight?'

'Not really, if you want the honest truth.'

'*You* have.'

'Really.'

'Almost too much, if you don't mind my saying so. And I speak not just from envy but also from concern.'

'At my age, you have to watch yourself,' said Theo. 'I'm edging towards forty-five and if I'm to continue to enjoy physical satisfaction with the person of my choice, I have to stay relatively thin.'

'There's a difference between thin and spectral. The skull beneath the skin is not a pretty sight.'

'True, Cassandra. Very true.'

'So what are you occupied with at the moment? Work or play?'

'Work. I've got a much heavier teaching load than usual this term since one of our tutors is away in Japan, and another's on maternity leave. Luckily we've got a most promising intake this year. They scarcely require guidance. In fact, I find myself taking notes from their essays to use in my lectures.'

'And your mamma, how is she?'

'Dear Mamma is as formidable as ever, though having some trouble with her corsetière as she does not hesitate to inform me at the top of her very loud voice whenever she visits the College. Particularly if we're standing in the Porter's Lodge amid a milling crowd of undergraduates, or passing the open windows of the Senior Common Room.'

'Oh please. Are there really such things as corsetières left? Or corsets, for that matter.'

'In my mamma's world, yes – that place near Harrods, for a start. But once she and her kind are gone, I fear that the last corsetière may immolate herself upon a pyre of ancient bust-bodices and crumbling whalebone stays.'

'There's a shop in Frith,' Cassie said, 'where they still sell those giant lock-knit bloomers and vests with sleeves and lisle stockings and invisible hairnets. It never occurred to me that anyone actually went in and bought them.'

'There are still a lot of old ladies about who need them. Not to mention actors. And even aged Prussian generals.'

'I used to help my Gran into her corsets,' Cassie said.

'Darling, didn't we all?'

'Every morning before I went to school.' Cassie was overcome by the memory of those unwieldy garments of shiny grey-pink material, festooned with hooks and eyes and buttons and pieces of tape which seemed to have no function. Sometimes the stiffeners would protrude, steel lengths made up of tiny overlapping circles which cut into Gran's soft bosoms. Sometimes Gran would groan with the discomfort of being encased in what was virtually a piece of armour-cladding and slap at her chest in the hope of making it easier to breathe. The corsets always had the same smell: Johnson's baby powder and 4711 Eau de Cologne and age.

'Thank God, my mamma has Mrs P to help her. Otherwise it would fall on me to lace her in each day, and heaven knows I've served my time with those bloody things. She tried girdles for a while, but they didn't produce quite the severely incapacitated look she was used to.'

'As though she'd been dipped in plaster of Paris and hung out to dry before she put her clothes on?'

'That's the one. Frankly, my dear . . .' Theo refilled their glasses and put the empty bottle into a military drum standing beside his desk. '. . . I attribute my sexual preferences to trauma brought on by blundering one night into a row of Mamma's corsets swaying on the washing line. Mrs P would have rather been gang-raped than hang them out during the day.'

'But you lived on a vast country estate in the middle of nowhere, didn't you?'

'Suppose the servants saw them, duckie. It might then have dawned on them that their mistress was a human being like themselves. And that would never have done.'

'Tell me about the new Chaplain-in-waiting or whatever it's called. Apparently he preached at one of the local parish churches a couple of weeks ago.'

'Nightingale? I wasn't on the appointments committee, but his credentials looked quite impressive. Rapid rise through the ranks, worked in the tropics for a while, aide to a bishop, roving troubleshooter, high-flier tipped for top office – that sort of thing. Never mind about the saving of souls: the College has to keep up its reputation for choosing the coming man since a lot of our chaplains have gone on to be bishops.'

'So I heard. What's he like as a person?'

'I only met him briefly. He seemed amiable enough. Ate a dinner or two in Hall, drank sherry with the SCR, did the usual sort of networking. I gather it's only a matter of form now: he should be joining us at the beginning of Trinity term.'

Cassie looked at her watch. 'I must go,' she said.

'Might one enquire where to?'

'I'm going to go and ask impertinent questions about the personal life of a complete stranger.'

'And what's making you act so entirely out of character?'

'Pity,' said Cassie. 'And terror.'

The house which Elizabeth Trowbridge, née Haden White, was currently occupying stood on the corner of a street in East Oxford full of identical Edwardian houses. All boasted green paint and stonework stained with dark dribblings from incompetent gutters. The front gardens of many had been landscaped with piles of bicycles customised by drippy white lettering or, in the more imaginative cases, by being painted pink with blue daisies or in rainbow stripes. For this was undergraduate territory, as testified by the thudding techno beat which pulsed from various poster-covered windows.

The front of No 37 contained only one bicycle, a mountain

bike in macho black, with thick-ridged tyres and a place for a can of water to clip into. Through the grubby ground-floor windows, Cassie could see a set of weights lying on the floorboards of what was otherwise an empty room. It looked as though the new man in Liz Trowbridge's life was a keep-fit enthusiast, unless they belonged to Liz herself.

Knocking at the door, she wondered how to broach the subject she had come to discuss. 'Hi, my name is Cassandra Swann and I wonder whether your mother is going senile,' didn't quite seem to cut it.

Wing it, she told herself, as the outline of a figure could be discerned approaching down the hall. The woman who opened the door did not resemble Serena Smith in any particular. In fact, she looked as though she could take on Mike Tyson and win without any trouble at all. One hand tied behind her back. One foot, too, probably. Cassie was tall: this woman was much taller. Cassie worried constantly about her weight: beneath the layers of denim it was obvious that this woman had taken the sensible course of action and given up worrying years ago. It was difficult to see much resemblance to Lolly here, but that didn't matter. Perhaps if Liz's new relationship broke up, Cassie should introduce her to Charlie Quartermain: talk about dinosaur calling to dinosaur. She reminded herself that this kind of sizeist attitude was exactly why her own life was such a mess.

'I'm Cassandra Swann,' she said helpfully, looking upwards and holding out her hand. 'I know your mother quite well.'

'Mam? Really?' The woman's face redistributed itself in what Cassie took to be a smile. 'Do you see a lot of her, just as a matter of interest?'

'I was with her yesterday evening, actually.'

'And did she seem all right?'

'As a matter of fact . . .' Good. It looked as though the subject of Lolly's problems was going to be raised without any effort on Cassie's part. '. . . She—'

'There's interesting. Didn't glow in the dark, did she?' The woman reached into the depths of her denim jacket and brought out a packet of Rizlas, a little metal gizmo and a pouch of tobacco. 'Didn't rattle a chain or two, or make wailing noises?' she went on, expertly rolling a home-made fag and sticking it into the corner of her mouth. Her Welsh accent held a silky menace reminiscent of a Hammer Horror vampire.

'Chains?' Was the woman mad? Cassie glanced nervously up and down the street, noting two small schoolboys in blazers one way, and a very bent old lady examining something in the gutter the other. Not much help there. Should this tall person attack her, it wouldn't be much of a contest. She laughed in jolly fashion. 'Not a lot of chain-rattling, as I recall.'

'Mmm,' said the woman. 'Only I wondered, see, because Mam's been gone now at least ten years and, just for the record, with every day that passes the keener my appreciation of her absence from the planet grows.'

'Gone? Oh, you mean—'

'Dead. Yes. Bloody old bat that she was.'

'Ah,' said Cassie slowly. 'So I take it that you aren't, in fact, Elizabeth Trowbridge.'

'As you so rightly say, I am not, in fact, Elizabeth Trowbridge.'

'And would you happen to know where Elizabeth Trowbridge is?'

'I would indeed. Why don't you come in and then you,

71

too, will know.' The big woman moved her face affably about some more then turned and headed down the passage towards the back of the house, leaving Cassie to close the door behind them.

The kitchen was inviting in an eccentric sort of way. A lot of second or even third hand pieces of junk furniture had been painted in a variety of brilliant colours and patterns, so that zebra-stripes jostled for attention with giant sunflowers, and galaxies of gold and silver stars glittered alongside a zoo of jungle animals. The walls were different colours: royal blue, dark red and eggyolk yellow; the kitchen table was decorated with varnished clouds, and all the chairs were splashed with spots, stripes, daffodils, exclamation marks: anything, really, which the artist's imagination could come up with.

'Well . . .' said Cassie, drawing a deep breath. In the midst of the riot of colour she could make out a plain green bottle and a wooden tray covered in découpé chintz roses which held a variety of poorly washed glasses.

'I teach art,' said the woman, as though that were sufficient explanation. 'And it hides the woodworm, see. If we won the lottery, we'd be out of here like a shot, before there's no furniture left and they start chewing us.' She picked up one of the glasses in a paw almost as large as one of Charlie Quartermain's. 'Wine?'

'I've just finishing drinking more than my share of a bottle of champagne.'

'You're in the right mood, then.' The woman slopped white wine into the glass and handed it to Cassie. 'I'm Jan Thomas, by the way.'

'From Wales.'

'How astute of you.'

'I'd been trying to work out why you reminded me of Anthony Hopkins,' said Cassie.

'My good looks, perhaps?'

Cassie laughed, attempting not to mind the imprint on her glass of a pair of lips which had not been efficiently dealt with during the most recent washing-up process. If not the one before. 'So,' she said. 'Liz Trowbridge.'

'What have you come to see her about, then?' Jan Thomas slumped down in a chair and stretched out her long long legs.

'It's a bit private, actually. Is she here?'

Jan looked down at her hands, clasped in front of her on the table. 'I'm afraid she's teaching. We both teach at the same school – I'm Art, see, and she's head of English and Dramatic Studies. But you can speak freely about whatever it is in front of me. Liz and I are very good friends, I promise you.'

'It's something of a personal matter. To do with her mother.'

'By . . . what's the old cow bitching about now?'

Cassie stared. To hear Lolly Haden White described in such terms had the same disorientating effect as sipping from a cup of tea and finding it was coffee. Or approaching a kitten and having your hand torn off at the wrist. 'What?' she said.

'Look, I only met the woman once, which was more than enough, and if she's a friend of yours, I apologise, but ever since Liz left Barry—'

'It's Larry.'

'Larry, sorry . . . her mam's been acting as though Liz has singlehandedly brought an end to civilisation as we know it. Won't talk to her, won't see her, sends letters back unopened. The whole Victorian from-this-moment-on-my-daughter-is-dead-to-me shtick. I'm surprised she hasn't hired a gang of thugs of walk up and down outside the house with banners saying Here Be Monsters. Or done it herself. Personally, I don't give a toss, but it really upsets Liz, see.'

'What does her new partner think about it?'

Jan looked at her oddly. 'Her new partner thinks it's a load of old horse manure, as you may have gathered.'

'Sorry?'

'*I'm* her new partner,' Jan said.

Oops. With a series of clicks, like a safe being opened, things fell into place. It explained everything, really, if Lolly's elder daughter had left her husband for a woman. Lolly's generation found it difficult enough to come to terms with male homosexuality; the female variety was untenable. And to have it brought so uncomfortably close might well have proved upsetting enough to produce in Lolly the symptoms which were alarming her bridge-playing circles, as well as the distress she had shown last night at the bridge evening.

'Ah,' Cassie said. She hesitated, then finished her glass of wine and stood up. 'I think really I've got the information I was looking for. We've been worried about Elizabeth's mother recently, but I think you've just made it clear why she should have been upset.'

'You sound as bad as she does.'

'In what way?'

'A homophobic, are you then, girl?'

'Not in the least. And I don't suppose Lolly is, either.'

'That's codswallop. Hear some of the things she said when Liz told her, you should.'

'Shock. Ignorance. I've never met Liz, but I bet she was rather truculent about it. In her place, I would have been. On the defensive.'

'I suppose she may have sprung it on her mother a bit,'

74

conceded Jan. 'But even so that doesn't excuse some of the crap she was hurling around.'

'You should remember which generation Mrs Haden White belongs to, and the kind of upbringing she was given.'

'*Why* should I?'

'Because a bit of patience on both sides will probably have better results in the long run than bridge burnings.'

'Maybe you should tell Mrs Haden White that.'

'Maybe I will.'

Cassie drove back the long way, via Larton Easewood, but Lolly wasn't at home. Just as well. She didn't imagine the older woman would be thrilled to learn that the details of her daughter's new liaison were common knowledge. Or, at least, known by Cassandra Swann. For that generation, respectability had always meant far more than it did to Cassie's contemporaries, and Lolly was particularly keen on keeping her private affairs private. Cassie had known her for some years now, played bridge with her regularly, met her on a number of social occasions, and yet she knew almost nothing more about her today than she had the first time they met. That keep-yourself-to-yourself, what-would-the-neighbours-say mentality had all but disappeared now. And much healthier it was too, though Tim Gardiner, her crime novelist friend, had sighed even more heavily than usual as he explained that the laid-back attitude of the nineteen-nineties, and contemporary views on divorce, had deprived detective-story writers, particularly those with amateur sleuths, of some of their best motives for murder.

'There's no social stigma attached to anything any more, you see,' he had said mournfully. 'So why run the risk of murdering someone when you could just as easily divorce them? And when people no longer care what other people think about them, there's no motive for murder as cover-up.' He gazed at her, his expression sad enough to wilt a palm tree.

'Mmm . . .' Cassie lived in fear of having to demonstrate her close familiarity with his works. She tried to remember the plot of his last book. There'd been a divorce of some kind in it, hadn't there? Or was it that his twee heroine, Pandora Quest – who reminded Cassie forcibly of her cousin Primula – was a divorcée?

Back at Honeysuckle Cottage, she worked for an hour in the garden, getting it ready for the colder days of winter. Clearing leaves, cutting back, lighting a bonfire. The pungent blue smoke drifted back towards the house, over the lily-pond and the roof of the converted stone barn which now housed the international headquarters of Bridge the Gap, to disappear among the ivy tendrils which covered the back wall of the cottage. It brought back childhood. Gran ferreting about in the yard behind the pub in the Holloway Road. Harry, her father, turning over the bitter London soil and snipping at the dead leaves of the lilac tree which grew in a corner against the back fence. Autumn standing on the edge of winter, the days closing down, shrinking: it was her favourite time of the year.

She sniffed deeply. After the smell of frying bacon, the scent of burning leaves must be one of the most richly evocative of all. By the side of the pond crouched the white cat which belonged to the farm whose fields abutted the hedge the end of the garden. A robin hopped nearby, head on one side, thin legs cheeky against its fluffed feathers. She had been here, courtesy of her godfather, for more than five years and while her natural habitat was the town, she had made accommodations, and knew she would miss this rural environment when she moved back to where she rightfully belonged. Were it not for the fact that Robin allowed her to live here without paying any rent, pretending that she was keeping the place warm for him while he sojourned at his house in France, she would long ago have returned to city life. She stamped on the edge of the spade and the robin hopped closer, knowing that when she turned the soil there was a chance of worms.

The thought of Lolly, alone in her house, afraid of some menace, unable to unbend enough to talk about it even to her own daughter, crept into her mind. Inside the house, she scrumpled up newspaper, added firelighters, kindling, small logs, and set a match to them. Once the fire was going she found a notebook and a pen and sat down on the comfortable sofa alongside the hearth with a glass of whisky in her hand. For no real reason except that of curiosity roused, she began to jot down what she knew about Lolly. It proved to be almost nothing, beyond the fact that her husband was dead, that she had two daughters and had grown up in Kenya. And even the information about Kenya seemed to be suspect, if Serena Smith was correct. She had been a journalist in her younger days, then worked for one of the glossy fashion magazines. Her mother was supposed to have taught at the village school, but that fact too, Serena had disputed. That was it.

Was everyone as enigmatic as Lolly Haden White? Were there people even at that precise moment trying to jot down what they knew about Cassandra Swann and coming up with more or less nothing? She thought not. Not after four years of semi-friendship. So one had to presume that Lolly worked at maintaining her privacy. Which raised the question of why.

Something bossy inside Cassie's brain asked why the hell not. Why *should* Lolly spill details about herself and her past life to anyone who passed? Not everyone was a garrulous big-mouth like Cassie Swann. And even garrulous big-mouths kept some things quiet. Look at Cassie's marriage, for instance: it was something she never spoke of. Most of her friends had no idea that she had once been someone's wife, partly because she found it painful to talk about and partly because she was ashamed of what she still viewed as a personal badge of failure. Why shouldn't others be the same?

It was, nonetheless, strange to think that she knew more about Charlie's father, whom she had met only once, than, after all this time, she did about Lolly Haden White.

# ♣ 5 ♣

The following morning, she was thinking about driving over to Larton Easewood when Kathryn Laughton née Kurtz pushed open the kitchen door, letting in a cloud of air silvered with frost. The tip of her nose was red; she was heavily wrapped in a long woollen sweater which hung several inches below her down jacket.

'Jesus H. Christ,' she said, clapping her hands across her body in a melodramatic way. 'Good thing I'm not a brass monkey.' She pulled off her striped mittens and blew on her fingers.

'Is it cold outside?'

'Nothing gets past you, does it?'

'Coffee?' Cassie poured some from the pot and pushed it across the kitchen table.

Kathryn took a sip. 'You shouldn't have bothered,' she said.

'I hope that's not a comment on my coffee.'

'Listen.' Kathryn pulled some of her hair down from under the knitted hat she wore. 'My brand-new husband's dragged himself away from me – oh Cassie, how can I ever thank you enough for letting me have Giles? – to go look at udders or something though I must say that until I married a dairy

79

farmer, I thought it was nursing mothers who got sore nipples, not cows.'

'Same thing, sometimes,' said Cassie. 'And if you wish us to remain friends, never, ever, mention sore nipples to me again. My cousin Primula is nursing her first-born and seems to think I'm interested.'

'Whoa,' said Kathryn. 'Down, girl. All I came round for was to ask if you could come to dinner on Thursday evening. Also to tell you how fantastically happy I am and how wonderful Giles is.'

'Dinner on Thursday?'

'Imagine.' Despite the fact that with a little more fur on her face she could have passed as a chipmunk, Kathryn managed to look dreamy. She clasped her hands to her bosom. 'My very first dinner party as a bride.'

'If you're planning to continue this nauseating display of Little-Womanism, I shall have to recollect a subsequent engagement,' said Cassie.

'You can't. I need you. I had to go over to Oxford the other day and be formally introduced to my successor – the guy who takes over the scholarship I had last year. And, incidentally, moves in to Ivy Cottage when Giles and I move out. He seemed kind of cute so I invited him over for dinner. And since he was standing next to someone else – the new college chaplain, – I invited him too. He's called Woodpecker, I think.'

'Nightingale,' said Cassie.' Hugh Nightingale.'

'How did you know that?'

'I cannot reveal my sources.'

'Anyway, will you come?'

'Must I? You're such a lousy cook.'

'I know that. But if we have plenty of booze, nobody will notice.'

'I'm having a slight cash-flow problem at the moment. Instead of bringing a bottle of inferior Bulgarian, which is all I could afford, why don't I cook for you instead? That way, I can be sure of getting a decent meal.'

Kathryn's Disney-cute face brightened. 'Hey, brilliant idea! If you give me a shopping list, I'll go buy everything for you.'

'How nice are these two guys you invited?'

'Pretty good, I thought. The songbirdy one is quite a bit older than we are, but the Yank is just right. And amusing too.' She remembered something. 'Talking of which, how is dear Charlie?'

'Why should you think I'd know?'

'Because I saw your car outside his place the other day.'

'He's fine.'

'Good. I'm really looking forward to this revue he's putting on. We're taking Giles's mom.'

'Is it the sort of thing Mercy would enjoy?'

'Giles is hoping it'll put ideas into her head.'

'You know Charlie wants to have Madonna jumping naked out of a cake, don't you? I hope Mercy doesn't get any ideas from that.'

'He's thinking more along the lines of voluntary removal from her house. Not that he wants to put her into a home or anything, but he does worry about her. He's afraid she's going to torch the place one night, and herself along with it. The problem is, she drinks too much.'

'Who doesn't?'

'That's what I tell Giles. But you know what an old curmudgeon he is.'

It was nearly noon by the time Cassandra was parking her car in Larton Easewood. She didn't bother to lock it: no self-respecting thief would waste time trying to break into her old rustbucket, let alone risk being seen in it by his mates.

Lolly's pretty little house stood back from the road behind a thick hedge of variegated box which shielded her against the idle glances of passers-by. Between the hedge and the house was an area flagged in York stone and set about with oak tubs which, in summer, overflowed with petunias and geraniums but now had a sadly moribund air. The skeletal remains of a clematis gripped the porch with tiny dried claws.

Cassie banged the knocker, noting that it was tarnished, noting, too, the dead leaves piled up under the bench in the porch. Clear indications of Lolly's state of mind. She had not telephoned beforehand, preferring to make it seem as though her visit was entirely impromptu.

When Lolly opened the door, she was wearing a striped butcher's apron. 'Oh,' she said vaguely, fumbling with the strings behind her back. 'I thought you were the postman.'

'Only me,' breezed Cassie in a manner she knew to be horribly reminiscent of Aunt Polly inflicting herself upon the undeserving poor of Uncle Sam's parish. She loomed a bit so that Lolly had no choice but to step back. 'I was passing and suddenly thought I might be able to cadge a cup of coffee from you.'

'Coffee?' The word seemed to be one which Lolly had never heard before.

'It's just about that time, isn't it?' Cassie peered at her watch in a jolly way.

'Oh, *coffee*. Of course.' Holding the apron in one hand, Lolly motioned Cassie into the hall. 'Do come in.'

'Thank you.' Cassie followed her inadvertent hostess down

the sanded floor of the hall towards the kitchen. Through an open door, she could see into the pleasant sitting-room where she had so often played bridge. The African masks on the walls, the clumsily carved stools and Benin bronzes, a primitive long-horned statue on the low table in front of the fire, provided a piquant contrast to the Home Counties chintzes and antique porcelain. From Cassie's passing glimpse, it appeared that Lolly had been going through old papers. The drawers of her writing desk had all been pulled open and a wastepaper basket stood beside it, overflowing with crumpled paper.

'So. How are you?' Lolly said, when she had settled Cassie at the table in the kitchen. If she thought it odd that Cassie should drop in on her today when she had never done so in the past, she did not comment on the fact but set about producing bone-china cups and a matching sugar bowl from a cupboard, and heating milk in a saucepan while waiting for the coffee grounds to settle in their glass jug.

'Very well. And you?'

'I'm sorry I behaved so badly the other evening,' Lolly said, busying herself with the plunger of the cafetière. 'It was disgraceful of me to leave you in the middle of a rubber.'

'Don't worry about it. We were ready to pack up in any case,' lied Cassie. She wished Lolly did not look so pale and seem so listless. That her hair did not appear to be in need of a wash and her cashmere cardigan did not cover a blouse which had obviously been taken off the clothesline and put onto Lolly without pausing for the touch of an iron. She added, before she could brood too much about lead-in lines: 'You seem worried, Lolly. Is there anything I can do to help?'

Lolly shook her head. 'I don't think so, my dear. But thank you anyway.'

'So you *are* worried about something?'

Lolly hesitated. 'Yes. There are one or two . . . I do have rather a lot on my mind at the moment.'

'Is it your health?'

'No. Nothing like that.'

'Only you seem to have been a little preoccupied recently. And,' Cassie continued boldly, 'your friends are anxious about you. Not to mention your daughters.'

'My daughters?'

'Serena and Elizabeth.'

'I do know who my daughters are, Cassandra.'

Cassie was encouraged by the note of asperity in Lolly's voice. 'I'll be quite frank,' she said, knowing she would never dare to be. 'We've all noticed that you've not been your usual self in the past few weeks, so much so that Serena mentioned it to me. She wondered . . .' Cassie swallowed, '. . . if perhaps your other daughter's recent split with her husband might be the cause.'

'I never liked Barry,' said Lolly.

'Isn't it Larry?'

'What?'

'Isn't your former son-in-law called Larry, not Barry?'

'You seem to know an awful lot about my family all of a sudden.' There was nothing in the least vague about Lolly's suspicious glance. 'You wouldn't by any chance have been checking on me, would you?'

'Absolutely not.'

'Has one of the girls put you up to sounding me out?'

'On what?'

'On the way that I—' The sentence stopped short.

'You what, Lolly?'

'That dreadful, dreadful . . .' Lolly began in a muffled

voice. Her face reddened; her eyes watered. From the pocket of her cardigan she pulled out a lace-edged handkerchief and dabbed at her eyes. 'On top of everything else. I'm sorry, Cassie, but really . . .'

'Lolly.' Cassie spoke gently, not quite sure what revelation she was supposed to have been given. 'I don't really understand what you—'

Suddenly Lolly was weeping, shoulders bent, handkerchief screwed up against her eyes. 'God knows Larry wasn't much to write home about, but that . . . that frightful creature my daughter is living with . . .'

'Jan?'

Lolly snuffled some more.

'Why do you think she's frightful?'

Lolly shuddered. 'So big . . . the size of her . . . Liz, so lovely and bright . . . actually in *bed* . . . that freakish . . .'

This was unblushing prejudice. Not to mention sizeism. 'You're over-reacting,' Cassie said.

'I drove over to Oxford when they first . . . when they moved in together. So perverted . . . so *obvious* . . . And it's all my fault.'

'How can it possibly be?' Cassie said. She put her arm round the older woman and guided her to a chair. Was Lolly going to blurt out some terrible perversion of her own, some sexual encounter – possibly with Larry – which might have put Liz off men for life?

Lolly merely snuffled.

'Whatever you've done, there comes a point where you can't blame yourself for what your children do,' Cassie said in a reasonable voice. 'Once they become adults, they have to take responsibility for their own lives.'

'So . . . *tall* . . . sleeping with my . . . it's horrible . . .'

'I've only met her once, but Jan Thomas seemed a perfectly nice person to me,' said Cassie. Which was a complete lie since the word 'nice' and the word 'Jan' could not have been less compatible. Interesting, yes. Intelligent. Competent. Unusual. All of the aforementioned. But definitely not 'nice'.

Lolly obviously agreed. 'Nice? *Nice?*' she choked. 'You should hear the things she called me. To my face. Quite apart from anything else, I'm Liz's mother, after all; surely she should have shown some respect.'

'But why should she?' Cassie picked up the coffee-pot and poured more coffee into Lolly's cup. She attempted jocularity. 'I bet you swept in at your most regal, didn't you?'

Lolly said nothing.

'They don't need your permission to live together, you know. They don't even need your approval. But I don't suppose you listened to a word either of them had to say, did you?'

'I didn't *want* to hear. As soon as I *saw* her ...' Lolly broke into fresh sobs, confirming Cassie's suspicions. Through the sobs, she could dimly hear self-recriminatory phrases: '... failure ... should have realised what would ... just didn't know ...'

'Didn't know what?'

Again Lolly did not answer. Instead, she wept some more, resting her forehead on her hand, fingers covering her eyes. After a while, she stopped and pressed her bunched-up handkerchief to her cheeks, mopping up the tears while she sought control of herself. Then, eyes red-rimmed, nose-tip flushed, she looked at Cassie. 'I apologise for breaking down. How terribly ill-mannered of me.'

'Didn't know what?' persisted Cassie.

But Lolly wouldn't say. 'Family matters,' she said forbiddingly, daring Cassie to probe further.

'Look, Lolly. I'm not as old as you are, and have nothing like your experience, but one thing I'm sure of, and that is that it's pointless to estrange yourself from your family.' Cassie tried not to think of her diminutive twin cousins, from whom she had spent most of her adult life trying to estrange herself. 'From what you say, you weren't that thrilled about Larry, but that didn't mean you didn't speak to Liz when she was married to him, did it?'

'That was quite different.'

'Why? And don't say, because he was a man.'

'You don't understand,' Lolly said with heavy weariness.

'But Lolly, these days nobody cares about things like that.'

'Do I really seem regal?' Lolly said, firmly changing the subject.

'Queen Victoria could have taken lessons.'

'Oh dear.'

'Not that we aren't deeply fond just the same,' Cassie added hastily, though this was a sentiment she would not normally have dreamed of expressing to someone as reticent about herself as Lolly. It had taken three years of playing bridge together twice a week before Lolly had even suggested that she drop the formal address of Mrs Haden White and call her Lolly. And why not? Unlike Cassie's generation, Lolly's waited until they were very sure of a person before acknowledging a level of intimacy by permitting the use of first names.

'Most of the time, regal is the very last thing I feel,' Lolly said. 'Confused would be more accurate. Especially at the moment.' She made an indeterminate gesture to indicate a generalised bewilderment.

'Look . . .' Cassie took a deep breath. Crunch time. Lolly

was not a person with whom you took liberties but she could try. 'Is it just the business with Liz that's upsetting you? We can't help noticing how your bridge game's gone off—'

'My bridge game? Is that all you're worried about?'

'. . . We've – your friends, that is – been wondering if it was possibly the . . . uh . . . that you might be . . .' She stopped, took a deep breath. Her first instincts had been right: Lolly was not a person with whom you took liberties.

'If you're wondering whether I'm going senile,' Lolly said briskly. 'The answer's definitely no.'

Cassie wanted to say: 'How do you know?' but settled for: 'So it's just that you're worried about Liz, is it?'

'Yes.'

'Lolly.' Leaning forward, Cassie put a hand on the older woman's sleeve, ignoring Lolly's faint withdrawal at this liberty. 'Is something frightening you? Is someone trying to bully you into something you don't want to do? Are you being threatened by someone?'

'Why do you ask?'

'Because if you are, then let us help you.'

'Us?'

'Your family. Your friends. It's absolutely pointless sitting here being terrified about something which might easily be sorted out.'

'Terrified,' scoffed Lolly. 'What absolute—'

The telephone rang out in the hall. Lolly went rigid at the sound, the blood draining from her face. In her lap, her hands clutched at the material of her skirt.

'Shall I answer that?' Cassie asked.

'No. I – I think I know who it is. I can ring them back.'

'Lolly, for heaven's sake . . .' began Cassie as the imperious ring of the telephone stopped abruptly.

Lolly visibly relaxed. She held up a hand. 'Whatever you were going to say, please don't. I've already said that there are a couple of things worrying me but since I do not propose to discuss them with you or anyone else, there's no point wasting time on them.'

'Right.'

'So, Cassandra, now that you've completed your mission of mercy, tell me what else you're up to at the moment.'

First round to Lolly. And probably last. Cassie couldn't see herself gearing up a second time to debate possible brain softening, certainly not with the owner of the brain under discussion. And in any case, from what she could see, it was disquiet rather than dementia that was causing Lolly's aberrations at the bridge table. So that was that, then. Whatever the disquiet stemmed from, it was Lolly's business, not Cassandra Swann's.

# ♦ 6 ♦

She had stayed behind after the bridge game two nights ago in order to help Natasha clear up. Over a final coffee, Natasha had mentioned that she was supposed to go and visit Bettina Maggs, the old lady from whom she and Chris had purchased their house some years ago. 'She bought a little cottage over in Market Broughton and was perfectly happy there until recently. I used to pop over and visit her occasionally. Then her son phoned to tell me that about two months ago she fell over while she was out shopping and broke her hip. And when she came out of hospital, she'd lost it.' Natasha looked extremely distressed.

'Lost what, exactly?'

'The ability – or maybe just the will – to look after herself. Personally, I think she's just frightened she'll fall over again and there won't be anyone around to help, but anyway, the son had to put her into a Home.'

'Such awful terminology,' Cassie said. 'As though she was a piece of unwanted furniture.'

'The thing is, I said I'd go and see her the day after tomorrow, and I absolutely hate letting her down but I'd completely forgotten that it's Daisy's school's Bring & Buy Day, and I promised ages ago to man the cake stall. And then the day after I have to go up to London . . . I shan't be free to see poor Bettina until the middle of next week.'

'Why are you telling me all this?'

'Guess.'

'You wish to impose on my good nature by persuading me to go and visit someone called Mrs Maggs, whom I don't know and who doesn't know me, thus embarrassing us both and probably boring us both rigid into the bargain. Am I right?'

'That's about the size of it,' Natasha had said cheerfully. 'Why don't you have another slice of this sponge?'

'You won't be able to get round me with a bit of left-over cake,' said Cassie.

Nonetheless, here she was, parking behind the Home for the Elderly where Mrs Maggs now resided. She walked into a tiled lobby which looked through glass walls onto what she presumed was a residents' lounge. High-backed chairs uphol-stered in shiny uncomfortable-looking green leatherette were ranged all round the walls of the long room. A variety of elderly people sat or slumped or slept in these chairs, their faces vacant, their hands idle except in the case of a grey-haired lady who picked continuously at the sleeve of the overwashed pink cardigan she wore over a pea-green nylon blouse.

Cassie's heart sank. One of these poor people must be Mrs Maggs. The sense of lives outlived, of time overstayed, was powerful. Did they really not get any stimulation? Did they spend their entire time here, doing nothing, their former personalities, the richness of their past experiences, all bun-dled away for ever? She wondered what, for instance, the tall headmistressy lady in a red dress with an expression of extreme anguish on her face had been. Or the old man in a jacket three times too large for him, whose fingers played restlessly with an unlit pipe.

She pushed open the door and stepped into a temperature hot enough to cultivate jungle orchids. A waft of stale air, heavy with the odours of food and disinfectant, only just covered up another deeper smell of incontinence and decay.

A black care assistant called Shona – the woman wore a plastic badge asserting this pinned to the bosom of her pink-striped uniform – pointed her down a corridor and told her to turn left at the end. 'Betty's in Number 89,' she said. 'Just keep walking – you can't miss it.'

'I thought Mrs Maggs was called Bettina.'

'Is she? Oh well, Betty's near enough,' Shona said cheerfully.

'Maybe, but—' But Shona was gone, walking briskly down the carpet-tiled corridor to where an ancient man lurched out of a doorway with his trousers round his ankles. 'Now then, Sid,' Shona said. 'We've got visitors. They don't want to see your family jewels, do they?'

The old man was in tears. 'I can't do me flies up,' he said. 'Can't get me fingers round the buttons.'

'Buttons? Have you gone daft or summing? It's zips these days, Sid, not buttons.'

Deftly, she led the old man back into the room, leaving Cassie with her half-finished sentence, her unarticulated thought. Which was that if someone's name was Bettina, then calling them Betty simply didn't do.

The Home had been built round an inner courtyard with a small lily-pond in the centre and a lead pipe that in summer would presumably play water. There were benches set round the pond; on one of them a woman in a nurse's uniform covered by a thick top-coat sat fiercely smoking a cigarette, her arms wrapped round her body for warmth. At the door of Room 54, an elderly woman stood with a coat wrongly buttoned and a large handbag.

''Scuse me, dear,' she said to Cassie. 'Do you know what time the next bus goes?'

'I'm afraid I don't,' Cassie said.

'Only I've got to get to Reading,' the old lady said. 'My son's getting married and he'll be so upset if I'm not there on this special day.'

'I'm sure he will be.' Cassie looked round. Should she be assisting this wild-haired woman to the front door and out into the street to wait for the next bus for Reading? Were the residents allowed outside unsupervised?

'Do you know what time the next bus goes?' the woman asked again.

'To Reading? No, I don't. But I could go and ask,' said Cassie.

'Would you, dear? That would be very kind.'

As Cassie continued down the corridor, she heard the old lady calling: 'Excuse me, but do you know what time the next bus to Reading goes? Only my son's getting married, d'you see, and I must get there on time.'

Oh dear.

A smell of loss permeated these antiseptic corridors. Loss of status. Loss of choice. Loss of a future. With shame, she recognised a conspiracy at work, society colluding to homogenise the elderly into a single group whose members felt nothing, were worth nothing, whose minds were as feeble as their bodies. And there was little she could do about it.

Several of the rooms she passed had their doors wide open. Some were crammed with personal possessions: others were grim, containing no more than a bed, another of the tall green chairs, a washbasin, testimonies to the truth of the fact that you come into the world with nothing, and leave it in much the same state. In some rooms, old people lay supine on their beds, staring at the ceiling with their hands clasped across their bodies, as though preparing for the long sleep. The place was suffused with a thick flat silence, as if life had long ago left this place and gone somewhere else.

At the end of the corridor, Cassie had reached Room 82, which meant one more turn to the left, along the third side of the quadrangle. Glancing through the open door of a bathroom as she passed, she saw two nurses struggling with an old man dressed in a thick lock-knit long-sleeved vest and underpants which had unmistakably been soiled.

Their faces were grim. 'You've been a naughty boy, Reg,' one of them said threateningly. 'You know what that means, don't you?'

The old man swore and cussed. 'A couple of whoors, that's what yez are,' he said.

'A dirty, dirty boy,' said the second nurse.

'It's not my fault,' said the old man. He tried to pull away from the women who held him firmly by the arms. 'Can't help it, ye' bastards.'

'Language, Reg,' said the first nurse.

'Fock off, fock off.'

'And we both know you could help it if you really wanted to.'

'But you like causing us trouble, don't you, Reg?' said the second. 'And we haven't got time for troublemakers,' She looked up and saw Cassie. Still holding on to the old man arms so tightly that his thin flesh bulged over her fingers, she raised her voice. 'Can I help you, dear?'

'I'm looking for Mrs Maggs.'

'Just along the corridor, dear.'

'Whoor,' shouted the old man. He farted loudly and at length. One of the nurses shook him so violently that his teeth flew out of his mouth and landed on the floor.

Cassie was appalled. Should she intervene, ask them what they were doing, why they were bullying an old man who clearly wasn't quite sure which day of the week was Tuesday? Yet there were always two sides to any question and she was not sure she had the right to interfere. Cravenly, she decided that, even if she did, it was a right that for the moment, she was going to leave unexercised.

The door of Number 89 was closed. Drawing-pinned to it was a calling card with the name Mrs Humphrey Maggs engraved on it in copperplate script. Cassie knocked. A voice called for her to enter. Opening the door, she went in. The room was small, made smaller by the amount of antique furniture which had been crammed into it. Every surface was covered with pretty *objets*: bowls of pot-pourri, silver-framed photographs, vases of flowers, tasselled lampshades, silver bonbonnières, mother-of-pearl inlaid trays. Over by the window, a grey-haired woman in a cashmere sweater was seated at a pretty walnut writing desk decorated with painted swags of flowers.

'Mrs Maggs?' Cassie asked. The room seemed a haven of civilised order after the unpleasantness of the rest of the place.

'Yes.' The woman turned and looked up at Cassie. 'Do I know you?'

'Not at all. My name's Cassandra Swann. Natasha Sinclair asked me if I would come and see you and explain why she's not here herself.'

'Cassandra Swann. You must be Natasha's business partner.'

'That's right.'

'And you live just beyond Frith.'

'Yes. How clever of you to remember.'

'How gratifying for me to be *able* to remember,' said Mrs Maggs. 'To realise that I still *can* remember. I've been in this dreadful place for almost five months and every time I see that sorry collection of old people shuffling about, with their minds gone, and those cruel, cruel nurses, I pray with every fibre of my being that I die before that happens to me.'

'I'm sorry.'

'Don't be. I don't resent being in here. I realise that my poor son had no choice, that between us we haven't the resources to pay for somewhere better – and even if we had, I can't see why he should beggar himself and his family for my sake. I, after all, have had my life; theirs is still going on.'

'Are those your grandchildren?' asked Cassie, nodding at a photograph of three young adults which stood on the desk. She perched herself on the side of the bed, since the seat of the easy chair held a pile of freshly laundered towels.

'My dear, you don't have to pander to what you perceive to be my interests. My knees may have gone, but my faculties certainly have not.' For a moment she looked pensive. 'It might be better if they had, then I shouldn't be aware of the horrors which go on every day in this place.'

'Does your son know about them?'

'Certainly not. And I would be horrified if he were to learn. He has more than enough to worry about already. He would try to take me away from here and find somewhere else. But I'm afraid there isn't anywhere else. So I keep smiling.'

'I admire you.' There was no point in being jolly, in

pretending that things were all right. Mrs Maggs was far too bright for that.

'The worst place is that dreadful lounge, as they insist on calling it,' said Mrs Maggs. 'It's nothing more than a waiting room for death. That's why I prefer to stay in my room. Although it gets a little claustrophobic, it's infinitely better than sitting out there with my hands hanging down, doing absolutely nothing, watching other people die.' She smiled. 'A curious word, lounge. In its meaning of drawing room, I mean. My mother would have died rather than allow us girls to lounge in our drawing room at home. It was all 'Backs straight, girls, remember your deportment, hold your head up, Bettina, straighten your shoulders, Annabel'. She was very keen on good posture, was my dear mother. That and a daily dose of Syrup of Figs.'

'My grandmother was the same,' said Cassie.

They both looked up as a scream sounded down the corridor and was cut off. 'Those dreadful women,' said Mrs Maggs. She shook her head.

'Should I go and do something?'

'My dear, there's very little you can do. Poor Mr Tallis has lost control of his bodily functions and they get a bit rough with him.'

'Can't something be done? I don't mean a cure, but . . . there are things, aren't there? Um . . . incontinence pads and so on.'

'Reg refuses to wear them. Says he wore nappies when he was a baby and he's not going to wear them now. It's such a shame. The terrible thing is, you can't blame the nurses for getting irritated. When you're seriously understaffed and there are forty other people needing your constant attention, they're very quickly going to run out of patience with an obstinate old man like Reg.'

'But all the same . . .'

'And the sad thing is, this kind of rebellion is Reg's only means of demonstrating that he's still alive, still a man, still has some dignity.'

'Funny way to show it.'

'It's all he has left.' Mrs Maggs shook her head again. 'Anyway, let's not dwell on it. Tell me how dear Natasha is. And those beautiful children of hers. I can't think of a family I would rather see installed in my much-loved house than the Sinclairs.'

They talked quietly of local events and happenings. Mrs Maggs, it appeared, had not been in the thick of village life but was nonetheless aware of the daily goings-on. 'And Lolly Haden White,' she said, at one point. 'How is she, poor thing?'

'Why do you say that,' Cassie asked.

'Poor thing? Because I've never seen anybody more determined not to enjoy themselves. I don't mean that she was miserable or anything like that, but it's as if she feels she doesn't deserve to have any fun. Oh, I know she enjoys playing bridge, and meeting people and so on, but there's such a sense of . . .' Mrs Maggs gazed out of her window which gave onto the rear of a pub, '. . . held-backness. I know there's no such word, but do you know what I mean?'

'Yes, indeed.'

'Almost as if she doesn't dare to let go.'

This was hardly the time or the place to bring up the possibility of mental deterioration. Nor would it have been relevant if she had, for Mrs Maggs continued: 'It's not as if it's something which had happened as she got older. Right from the first, after she moved here, she had that same tension about her. Corseted, that's the word. As though she were laced into the most cruel pair of corsets imaginable.'

'I wonder why.'

'I can't imagine why I'm pursuing this thought,' said Mrs Maggs. 'I really don't gossip much, but since I've been here, I've had time to think a lot more about my life. And for some reason, Lolly in particular has been on my mind. There is such a strong sense about her of a life unlived: at least I can look back and see how much I enjoyed what I was given.' She moved her head from side to side. 'Lolly always seems so unhappy.'

'I know.'

'I can't help feeling that if I'd persevered a bit more, I might have found a way to loosen her up. We were very close, you know, for a number of years. But things change, what were once priorities get pushed aside and new ones take their place. When Humphrey, my husband, retired, he and I did a lot of travelling, for instance, something we'd never had time for before.'

'Where did you go?'

'Oh, all sorts of places. Africa. The United States. India. Now that was quite an extraordinary experience. Have you ever been there?'

'Not yet.'

'Such a timeless country. We were fascinated from the moment we stepped out of the plane. Of course, we had connections: both my husband and I had brothers who served during the Raj and lived out there for years.'

Listening as she described some of her experiences, Cassie wished she had a tape recorder. Here in this little room with its view of dustbins and galvanised iron barrels waiting to be collected by the brewery, India shone and gleamed for a while, polished as a maharajah's ruby, intricate as the creepers which covered hidden, monkey-haunted temples deep in the jungle.

Cassie heated water in a saucepan, dropped in six nests of *fettucine*, waiting while they cooked, then added grated cheese. Behind a rusty tin of Lapsang tea on one of the stone shelves in the larder, she found an out-of-date packet of sunflower seeds; as she lifted up the packet, a spider with at least twenty legs scuttled rapidly towards the back wall and for a moment she contemplated chucking them into the garbage. She shuddered. Spiders. Her own personal Room 101 was full of them. Thank God there was still a bottle of brandy in the sideboard. She poured a stiff one and put the sunflower seeds into a frying pan with a drop of olive oil, shaking the pan with her other hand while they turned brown. She thought about Charlie Quartermain and the duck he had been roasting the other day. What it all boiled down to was this: how far was she prepared to go for a square meal? Or even a semi-circular one.

Going down that road was unprofitable. She poured a second large dollop of brandy in the hope of dispelling the profound depression which her visit to Mrs Maggs had roused, and carried a tray into the sitting room. Such dignity in the face of sickening indignity; poor Reg, with his pathetic attempt to make someone – anyone – see that he was still alive; and Millie, the lady with the handbag, who had accosted Cassie once again as she left, to ask when the next bus to Reading went. What was the solution for people like that? In these days of fragmented families, small houses, where else could they go when they could no longer look after themselves, except into retirement homes?

Bettina Maggs had been quite blunt about it. 'Euthanasia, my dear. It's got to come. It's already available in a limited form in Holland. And I read recently that in the northern part of Australia it's just been made legal. There are just too many of us old people, and I would be willing to bet that a very large proportion of us would be extremely happy to die at a moment chosen by ourselves, with dignity and no discomfort. I most certainly would.'

Cassie switched on the TV. The News that evening was even more dispiriting than usual. Continental Europe was being beastly to Britain by refusing to buy its BSE-infected beef, and the Prime Minister, with one eye on the forthcoming elections, was kicking the furniture about it while various ministers from EC countries explained in faultless English why they naturally preferred not to see their entire populations keeling over with mad cow disease. A man had been fatally stabbed while trying to stop a gang of yobs from breaking into his car. There'd been an oil-spill off Greenland, putting thousands of birds at risk. The body of an old-age pensioner had been discovered in his high-rise flat four months after he had starved to death. Shocked neighbours spoke of his reclusive ways, his refusal to open the door to them. 'He were proud,' his granddaughter said to camera. 'Wouldn't let the social services in, didn't want to accept charity.' She held up the medals her grandfather had won in the War, and wiped her eyes. 'A proud old man, he were. Would've been ninety next birthday. It's a bloody disgrace.'

What the disgrace was, she didn't say. Which in itself was unusual in this age when people tended to blame everyone but themselves for the things which were wrong: their parents, their siblings, their education, their government. Nobody ever took responsibility for themselves any more:

perhaps the old man had done so by deliberately starving himself to death. After all, at ninety, there was little to which to look forward. At least he had been living in his own quarters, and not locked up like poor Mrs Maggs, in a home.

Cassie thought of randy Brian Edgecombe, still chockful of vim. Twenty years down the track, would he too be a lonely recluse, too proud to accept necessary help? Come to that, would she herself, forty years from now? Surely not. It was impossible to imagine. Which brought her to Gran. God, how she missed Gran, with her corsets and her fags and her smelly old fur coat which still hung upstairs in the wardrobe of the spare bedroom. How would Gran have coped with extreme old age: with the same indomitable spirit as she had always shown? If she had not succumbed to a heart attack twenty years ago, she would be over eighty now. When Cassie was a child, Gran had always seemed so full of energy, so immensely powerful. Invincible. Simply that. Cassie had never considered her age, simply seen her as Gran. Rock in the midst of stormy waters. Calm eye in the centre of the hurricane. Looking back, Cassie could see now that running the pub singlehanded, coping with her grief over the violent death of her only son, left with the responsibility of bringing up a young grandchild, must have been tremendously demanding at an age when reserves are supposed to start running low. But Gran had never flagged. Not once. It had never occurred to Cassie that she ever would.

The News ended and she found herself staring wet-eyed at an idiotic gameshow host in a dinner jacket who was talking animatedly to a woman with dyed blond hair about the woman's willingness to make a complete fool of herself for the benefit not only of the studio audience but also for the millions back home. Mindless crap. She switched to another channel where an effete man with a quiff of dyed black hair spoke in disparaging terms about Fra Lippo Lippi. Pretentious crap.

She missed Gran. Pouring just a drop more brandy into her glass, she remembered the hard years of growing up in the Vicarage, a cygnet among ducklings, a thorn among roses. Her three girl cousins were so damned tiny. No boobs worthy of the name, hips you could strike matches on, thighs the size of empty toilet rolls. Whereas Cassie Swann, cockney-voiced, cheaply clothed, was quite the opposite. When her adolescent hormones began their manic surge towards maturity, she had grown taller and wider and rounder than all three of her cousins put together. She had not fitted into any of her clothes. She had not fitted into Vicarage life. Worst of all, she had missed her Gran more than she could ever have expressed and yet no-one had ever seemed to notice. Her physical needs had been taken care of. She was fed, clothed, educated. But after her arrival at the Vicarage, no-one had ever kissed her, no-one had given her a hug. Gran had never been mentioned. To Aunt Polly, struggling to maintain her middle-class pretensions on a vicar's pay, it must have seemed that the sooner Cassie forgot her origins in the Holloway Road, the better for all concerned. She probably saw Gran as nothing more than a fat old woman with an unacceptable accent, a vulgar partiality for port and lemon and a forty-fags-a-day habit. But to Cassie, she had been mother and father, she had been all the love and strength the world contained. Losing her had been far worse than the death of either her mother or her father. Gran had always been there, in the rooms above the Bricklayers' Arms, until the day Cassie came home from school and found her dead in her bed, beneath the grubby pink eiderdown which Cassie was allowed to snuggle under when she had a cold.

Sensing imminent breakdown, part genuine, part brandy-induced, Cassie picked up Tim Gardiner's latest publication from the sofa cushion beside her. So far, she had only skimmed through it, noting that his serial heroine had taken on the Water Board and deciding that it wasn't for her. During her recent outing with Tim, she had managed to imply that it was, by talking rapidly about water pollution and laughing merrily when all else failed. Now, blinking tears away, she looked at the flattering photograph on the jacket, which showed the author moodily lit from the side. He wore an adventurous safari jacket with just the suspicion of a black fedora – or was it a pompadour? – above his writerly brow. There was text beneath the picture. *Gardiner's crime novels offer more than just an absorbing puzzle*, she read. *This latest in the Pandora Quest series offers both an engrossing story and a critical commentary on the politics of culture.*

The politics of culture? What in the hell did that mean? And if anyone was interested, for Cassie's money, Pandora Quest was the wettest heroine since the Little Mermaid.

The telephone rang. When she picked up, a voice said: 'Cassie?'

Good question. At this time of night, who else was likely to be answering Cassandra Swann's phone? 'Yes.'

'It's Eric here.'

'Who?'

'Eric. Hyacinth's husband.'

'Oh sorry . . . *that* Eric.' It was Primula's husband Derek who was the headmaster, which meant Eric must be the estate agent, married to the slightly less objectionable of the two matched homunculae who were her twin cousins. 'How nice to hear from you.'

'Isn't it, though?' Despite his profession, Eric retained a certain measure of what lonely hearts ads termed GSOH. In Cassie's book, anyone who had to point out that they had a GSOH must, by definition, be singularly lacking in that department. In fact, the whole vocabulary of dating magazines caused involuntary retching. *Wants to share cuddles, laughs and good wine*. Oh please. *Likes theatre, travel and open fires* – well, who doesn't? It occurred to her that she had never asked Hyacinth how she and Eric had met.

'The point is,' Eric was saying, 'that Hyacinth asked me to ring and tell you that your Aunt Polly has gone into hospital.'

'Oh, my God.' Cassie sobered instantly. 'What for?'

'Tests.'

'What kind of tests?'

'They think she may have something quite serious.'

'Not . . . you don't mean cancer, do you?'

'The Big C,' said Eric heartily. 'That's the one.'

'Are they sure?'

'Not yet, obviously.'

'But what are the chances?'

'They didn't say.'

'Which hospital is she in?'

By omission rather than commission, Aunt Polly had caused the adolescent Cassie too much unhappiness for her to be desperately concerned now about the answer. If that made her a bad person, then so be it. While she took down the address and the name of the ward, Cassie reflected that though she had never liked Uncle Sam's cold-hearted wife – an emotion which was entirely mutual – nonetheless, she would not have wished such an illness on anyone.

'I'll try and drive over at the weekend,' she said, hoping that her car was up to the journey. One of the advantages of Honeysuckle Cottage had always been its lack of proximity to East Anglia; suddenly this seemed a definite drawback. Because it was so unworthy a thought, she tried very hard not to calculate the cost of the petrol she would have to buy to get to the hospital and back.

As if he could read her mind, Eric said: 'I wouldn't go haring over to Norfolk just yet, if I were you. Hyacinth said to tell you to wait until we've heard something definite. And the tests are going to leave the old dear fairly knackered. So a card or something would be best at this juncture.'

'All right. If you're sure.'

'Best if we just follow orders, don't you think?'

'The Nuremberg Defence didn't help the Nazis much.'

'If they'd been married to one of the Vicarage Three, they might have been pardoned on compassionate grounds.'

Heavens: a halfway decent joke. Sometimes – not often – Cassie wondered whether beneath Eric's estate-agent persona, there was a kindred spirit trying to get out.

'So how are things?' Cassie asked. She had not seen Eric since Uncle Sam's birthday luncheon party, earlier in the year.

'Can't complain,' said Eric. 'I expect you knew that Hyacinth's pregnant again.'

'Primula told me.' That, plus a lot of disgusting specifics about her own baby's bodily functions – many and varicoloured – which had left Cassie feeling distinctly unwell. It was a toss-up which were worst: those, or Primula's copiously detailed descriptions of her difficulty in breast-feeding and the physical symptoms this provoked. Listening with rising gorge, Cassie had sworn that if she were ever fool enough to let herself become pregnant, she would not, under any circumstances, discuss the processes thus unleashed with anyone at all. Not even the father. 'Congratulations to you both. When's it due?'

'Next summer.'

'Something to look forward to.'

'Isn't it, though? Sleepless nights, the old homestead knee-deep in tiny garments, wife the size of a moving van and half as sexy: it's just what any man expects the day he signs on the dotted line.'

'Do I detect a note of bitterness there, Eric?'

'Absolutely not. After all, you know what I always say . . .'

'Probably.'

'. . . I already had my fun, making the baby. Know what I mean?'

Perhaps she was wrong about the kindred spirit.

During this conversation she had been vaguely aware of action taking place outside the cottage, a scuffling on the doorstep, a single rap of the knocker. With the handset replaced, she went to the front door and pressed her ear against it. No sound. Nothing. She didn't want to open it. For one thing it was freezing outside. For another, who knew what insane axe-murderer might not be lurking on the doorstep. Reason told her that even an insane axe-murderer wouldn't lurk on the off-chance that she was going to open the door, that he would knock or rap or utter some kind of mad and menacing sound designed to lure her into his clutches. After a while, she decided to risk it and pulled back the chains, undid the bolts. Sometimes she wished that the large Alsatian called George which she had invented to forestall the unwanted attentions of a psychopath she had been teaching bridge to in the prison at Bellington really did exist. The thought of the non-existent Brendan O'Rourke, conjured so blithely from her light imaginings, made her decide that on second thoughts, it was as well it did not. Cautiously opening the door, she found a carrier bag from the Chinese takeaway in Frith.

A mistake had obviously been made. She wondered why the delivery person hadn't waited for her to answer his knock. Nonetheless, ravenous, she pulled it inside, carried it to the kitchen and opened it. Inside there were a number of foil boxes, each neatly labelled. Despite her assurances to herself that the order belonged to somebody else, she could not stop herself from ripping off the cardboard lids. Oh Lord. Crispy fried duck with plum sauce. Duck in black bean sauce. Pork with crispy noodles. A double portion of prawn crackers. Rice, glutinous, aglimmer with egg and peas. She drooled. Her mouth was full of desire. Tentatively she pulled a piece of the duck from its sauce and put it into her mouth. Delicious. She felt as though she hadn't eaten properly for a month. She extracted another piece, just to make sure it was as good as the first. If anything, it was better. She wondered what would happen when some irate customer phoned in to complain that his order had never arrived. She could always deny that it had been deposited on her doorstep. She could postulate a passing tramp. Oh God, the duck was delicious. She tried the rice. Perfect. *A point* – or whatever the Chinese equivalent was. The prawn crackers were perfect too. So was the whole shebang, including the bag this unexpected manna from heaven had arrived in. She decided that since temptation had been put in her way, it was not her place to resist it, fetched chopsticks from the kitchen drawer and settled down to enjoy herself.

Half an hour later, as she sprawled contentedly on the sofa

with one hand on her food-swollen belly, the phone rang.

''Ello, darlin'' a voice trumpeted. 'Enjoy your nosh then?'

'Nosh?'

'The Chinese takeaway.'

'It was you, was it?' She might have known. Especially since the delivery boy hadn't waited to be paid.

'Ordered it from the Pekin Garden, didn't I? Thought you was looking a bit peaky, last time I saw you. Like you hadn't been eating properly.'

'I haven't, now you come to mention it.'

Charlie's bellow was full of concern. 'What's up, girl?'

'Nothing much. Just a temporary cash-flow problem.'

'It won't help anything if you starve yourself.'

'Except my figure.'

'Lose an ounce and I'll have something to say about it, I can tell you.'

'Will you, Charlie?' Stomach full, she felt kindly towards him. Not just him, but the rest of mankind as well. Even Primula.

'Face like an angel,' he murmured. 'Body of a Venus.'

Normally she would have slapped him down. Instead, 'Oh, Charlie,' she breathed. 'Do you really think so?' Any minute now she was going to fall asleep.

As though sensing this, he said: 'Want me to come round?'

'What for?'

'Why d'you think, darlin'? To give you a bit of a seeing-to. Bit of a cuddle.'

She sat up. Jeez: give the man a millimetre and he took a journey round the earth. If Charles Quartermain were to advertise in the columns of a singles magazines, she rather thought he wouldn't bother with the GSOH side of things. Just get right down to the nitty gritty. 'Look,' she said, as

110

frostily as she could manage. 'I'm extremely grateful to you for your thoughtfulness and I won't deny that I thoroughly enjoyed your unexpected gift. However, I should remind you that I did not ask for it, and I would hate to feel that your kindness had any strings attached.'

'Blimey,' he said. 'You do talk nice. Did you make that up out of your own head or have you got it written down on a bit of paper?'

'Oh, Charlie. Why do you always spoil things?'

'Do I?'

'Every single time.'

He lowered his voice. 'When we get married, I don't want—'

'We are not bloody well going to get married,' she howled.

'—you to be under any false illusions.'

'Trust me: I'm not.'

'Want you to see me plain, girl. The whole man. Take me for all in all, this was a man.'

Quartermain quoting Hamlet? And getting it more or less right? Whatever next? 'Thank you, Charlie,' she said. 'I'm more grateful than I can tell you. I'm going to bed now and I'll—'

'Can I come too?'

'*No.*'

'Only got to say the word, darlin', and I'll be round in two shakes.'

'Thanks. But not tonight,' she said, and hung up on him.

# ♥ 7 ♥

When Cassie stepped onto the bathroom scales two days later, the needle havered a bit before settling at a figure which showed that she had, for the first time in months, lost weight. Disbelievingly, she stepped off onto the cold floor and then back on: yes, even after that giant Chinese takeaway the other evening and an unfortunate tussle with a pair of Eccles cakes which she had lost, she was nearly two pounds lighter than she was last week.

In addition, there was a cheque in the mail for an article she had written for a bridge magazine weeks ago and forgotten about. It looked as though she would be able to eat over the weekend – but wisely, rather than too well. She'd be able to fill up the tank of her car, too, if she wanted to. Which she did, but not just yet. During the night, lying awake and worrying about bills, she had decided to start using her bike again. As well as being ecologically sound it would be good exercise, and cost nothing.

After a meagre breakfast, she put on a jacket and went outside. It was cold, with the sky pale and heavy with potential snow. The wind whipped at the thatched roof of the cottage and gnawed at the conifers which marked the top of the sloping field of the farm over the hedge. A pearly-breasted wood pigeon walked over the soil she had managed to dig earlier in the week; in the field, seagulls squawked, their red bills and legs startling against the straight lines of plough. She dragged open the door of her shed-cum-garage and wheeled out the bike which leaned against the cobwebbed wooden wall. It had once been the property of Robin Plunkett's nanny; like so many of her goods and chattels, it had ended up in Robin's possession and thus, by default, in Cassie's. It was black, oldmaidish, uncompromising. It had sit-up-and-beg handlebars. Withered string netting encased the rear wheel, designed to prevent long skirts catching in the spokes. It even had a clip attached to the frame into which a sporting person could insert a lacrosse stick. This was the sort of bike which intrepid women with umbrellas and jaunty boaters might have mounted for a spin down Brighton esplanade in the golden Edwardian summer.

She examined it doubtfully. Was this biking lark such a good idea after all? It was easy to picture Mary Poppins riding round Kensington Gardens on it, a lot more difficult to imagine Cassandra Swann perched on the saddle, freewheeling down the hill into Frith. Small boys might be tempted to throw stones; dogs would certainly bark. And it only had the one gear. Which made the hill down into Frith possible but the hill coming back out of Frith considerably less so. Behind the hedge which screened the front garden from the lane, a discreet purring noise indicated that some kind of expensive vehicle was in the process of pulling up. She heard a car door slam, footsteps, Quartermain's rusty breathing.

'Gawd,' he said.

'Good morning, Charles.'

'You a mind-reader or what?'

'How do you mean?'

'I just came round to ask you if you knew anyone with a bike like that.'

'Why?'

'Because me dad's come up with this great idea for the Christmas show at the Home. We could make a real production out of it. "Daisy, Daisy, Give Me Your Answer Do". What d'you think?'

'Sounds all right.'

'Picture it,' said Charlie, his huge hands sketching it in the freezing air. 'We can doll the local jailbait up in those kind of governessy blouses and nice sexy skirts, tarty lace-up boots, parasols, know what I mean?'

'I can't say I care for your sexist terminology,' Cassie said primly, 'but I do get the idea.'

'Perambulate them about a bit, get them to show their legs during the verses. And all the old dears can join in the chorus. We could move on to "Knees up Mother Brown" and "My Old Man Says Follow the Van", turn it into a singsong for them: they all like that sort of thing.'

'Where does the bike come in?'

'Someone can wheel it up and down in the background . . .' He opened his mouth, displaying dentistry of the sort a Cro-Magnon might have winced at, and rumbled something tuneless.

'What?'

'I said: You'll look sweet upon the seat of a bicycle built for two.' An unbecomingly lascivious grin crossed his broad face. 'Here, I wouldn't mind sniffing your—'

'Don't!' Cassie said sharply, glaring at him. 'Just don't say it, Charles.'

He realised she was serious. He took the bike out of her hand and stroked the rusted handlebars. 'They don't make

115

'em like this any more, do they? How much do you want for it, then?'

About to say that it wasn't hers to sell, Cassie hesitated. Nanny was long gone; Robin had never learned to ride a bike and certainly wasn't going to start now. 'How much are you offering?'

'Tell you what . . .' He avoided her gaze, staring thoughtfully into the interior of the shed. 'I'll do a swap.'

'What kind of swap?'

'New bikes for old. A mountain bike, ten-gear job with them fancy thick tyres and lights and I'll throw in a carrier, for this. What do you say?'

'I say that's very generous of you. I also say that I wonder whether that's really why you came by, or whether the idea only popped into your head when you saw me with the bike.'

He held her gaze. She had never noticed before just how clear his eyes were, and how sweet his mouth. 'How'd you mean, girl?'

'I think you've adopted me as your favourite charity, Charlie.'

'My favourite woman, yer. Dunno about favourite anything else.'

'The thing is, I really appreciate your kindness to me, but I can't keep accepting it. A takeaway meal is one thing. A new bike is quite another.'

'If I don't get the bike from you, I'll have to look somewhere else. The "Daisy, Daisy" number's a great idea, but it's not going to work without a bike.'

'I don't believe you. But because I'm a shallow, weak-willed unprincipled person, I'll go along with you. As long as there's no strings attached.'

'What sort of strings?'

'Like the two of us going to bed together.'

'The thought never crossed me mind,' said Charlie. 'Want to hop in the motor and we'll drive over to Bellington, choose a bike, maybe have a spot of lunch at the pub?'

'All right.' Cassie despised herself. But there might be some truth in Charlie's assertion. And the thought of the mountain bike was extraordinarily attractive. She just wished the offer had come from someone else. Like, say, lugubrious Tim Gardiner, or even Detective Sergeant Paul Walsh, her vacillating lover. Dream on. Not in a thousand years could she imagine either of them getting involved with a Christmas spectacular for the old people, nor buying Cassandra Swann a new bike.

The bike was beautiful. Even stripped of the ludicrous piece of plastic holly with which the company sought to persuade potential buyers into forking out a three-figure sum in time for the Yuletide overspend, it remained black, moody and very contemporary. She felt slim and elegant on it. Her hair rippled behind her in the breeze, her pert breasts thrust at her white angora sweater, her profile was sharp and eager as her long slim legs propelled her forward into the future. And that was before she even left the bike shop.

Seeing it, she thought: the hell with it. The worst Charlie could do was manoeuvre her into sleeping with him again and, despite what she'd said earlier, she was prepared to go along with that if she had to.

'It's gorgeous, Charlie,' she said, wishing she owned a white angora sweater, that she had pert breasts rather than two drooping balloons. Shame wormed its way towards wherever it was that her conscience lurked. She was prostituting herself. Using Quartermain. Taking advantage. Of his generous heart, of his professed adoration for herself. Aunt

Polly would have been down on that like a ton of bricks. Not so much on moral grounds as on social ones. This was not ladylike behaviour. And if you *were* going to take advantage of a man, please let it be a belted earl at the very least, or failing that, a public-school man, preferably in a secure profession. Charles Quartermain and Aunt Polly had never met: if there was a God, they never would.

Petra Lewis came to mind. She would have poured scorn on Cassie's hesitations, urging her onwards with manhating cries. Men have used women since the dawn of time, she would say. It's time for some table-turning. Trouble was, Cassie was not convinced by these arguments.

Nonetheless, the bike *was* beautiful. She felt like a child on Christmas morning. If it had not begun to snow in a tentative sort of way, she would have considered cycling the five miles back to Honeysuckle Cottage. As it was, she allowed Charlie to stow it in the capacious boot of his car before he drove her out into the countryside to have lunch at a riverside pub. A fire burned in the big hearth; there was roast lamb on the menu; the place was awash with inglenooks and ancient beams. Through the window, a subsidiary of the Thames undulated its way between leafless willows. The piped music was not Christmas-orientated. Substitute Paul Walsh for Charlie Quartermain and what more could the heart desire?

She stifled this unworthy and ungrateful thought. There had been a period when even being in the same room as Charlie had made her cringe. Time, and enforced proximity, had changed some of that but nonetheless, nothing could alter the fact that he was not her companion of choice and never would be.

Over lunch, Charlie talked enthusiastically about what he

was now referring to as a Christmas extravaganza, particularly the giant iced cake from which he was hoping to persuade Madonna to spring in an ermine-bordered red bikini, to peals of silver bells rung by the residents of the Home.

'You can't,' Cassie said. 'They'll have strokes. All that excitement'll be too much for them. And anyway, she'd charge far too much.'

'Actually,' he said, 'I was wondering if you'd understudy her, just in case she doesn't accept our invitation.'

'Me? I haven't worn a bikini since I was five. When my Gran took me on a day trip to Frinton-on-Sea.' She could still remember the cold sand between her toes, the grey sea, the dog turds and broken glass which made the beach an obstacle course. It had been wonderful. They had fish and chips for dinner, with fancy little wooden forks, and winkles for tea, with a strawberry ripple cornet for afters. She remembered Gran hoicking up her dress, rolling her lisle stockings right off her varicosed legs and wading in to the sea, saying how good it made her bunions feel. She remembered the deck-chair attendant patting her head, flirting with Gran, giving them an extra hour free because Gran's mum came from Preston, like his auntie Nell. Gran had bought her a stick of rock and she'd sucked it all the way home on the coach, her tongue turning bright pink, the purple letters – Frinton-on-Sea – standing proud of the rest of the rock.

'Me mum liked Clacton,' Charlie said. 'That's where we always went.'

Silence fell between them. Cassie didn't add that when she was ten, Gran had taken her to Clacton for a nice change. She did not feel comfortable with the notion of experiences which she and Charlie shared. She did not want him invading her memories.

After a while, she said: 'Got any more ideas for your Christmas extravaganza?'

'Lots.'

Cassie listened. Some of his plans seemed a little over the top. The massed choir of Santa Clauses, for instance. The team of trained reindeer prancing through the old folk's lounge bedecked in sleigh bells. Hot toddy tastings. But hey, that was Charlie. Go figure.

Clerical garb brought Cassie out in hives, a fact she attributed to her Vicarage years, when Uncle Sam had worn his dog-collar all the time and his cassock most of it. So it was a relief to see that the Reverend Hugh Nightingale was dressed in nothing more threatening than a dark suit and a silk tie patterned with nasturtiums. Observing the spill of tangerine and apricot, she reflected that this, thank heavens, was not the kind of cleric who had stepped from the pages of a Barbara Pym novel. Clergymen so often looked as though their under-wear was hand-knitted. Not this one. As Kathryn introduced him, he gave it the whole ball of wax: bright-blue eye contact, double-fisted hand-shake, presidential-candidate smile. Main-taining social contact at such intensity must be exhausting. He was tall, firmly built, in his early fifties. His hair was blow-dried and thickly silver; a scar ran from his left eyebrow down to the strong line of his jaw, giving him a rakish and macho air. Cassie had no difficulty in accepting that he was destined for the ecclesiastical glory which both Theo and Marjorie had predicted. His smoothness would have had even more charm if he hadn't so obviously believed it too.

Quinn Macfarlane, the new Visiting Scholar, was no also-ran in the macho stakes. He was big and blond, with the kind of craggy face that Robert Redford used to such good effect as the Sundance Kid. Meeting him, Cassie's susceptible heart raced as her hormones made a mad dash for the nearest exit from her body. Macfarlane shook her hand, holding it a fraction longer than was necessary. 'Hi, there, Cassandra,' he said. 'Good to meet you.'

She smiled, trying to make it look sultry rather than because her brains had leaked into her groin. 'Hello,' she said. As subtle rejoinders went, it could scarcely be faulted.

'I gather we're to be neighbours,' said Macfarlane. 'As soon as Kathryn and her husband move out of here.'

'You bet,' said Kathryn. 'It'll be just you and her and a bunch of cows.'

'Sounds good to me.'

'You'll have to look after each other.'

'I could handle that.' Macfarlane smiled, eyes crinkling up like a sea-captain's as he strains to see landfall on the horizon. 'Yes, ma'am.'

Through a haze of lust, Cassie could see Giles on the other side of the room, being irate with a tray of ice-cubes, while the Reverend Nightingale looked on, amused.

'I . . . uh . . .' she said. It came out as a sort of gulp. '. . . something on the stove.'

Kathryn followed her into the kitchen. 'Drop-dead gorgeous, or what?'

'Brandy,' Cassie said faintly. 'Before I go into meltdown.'

'I'll bet he's got a pair of rocks on him,' Kathryn said, slopping Hennessy Four Star into Cassie's glass.

'But does he know what they're for? With looks like that, he's liable to have the brains of a charcoal briquette.'

'Get real, girl. He's got this scholarship, for God's sake. He must at least be able to read joined-up writing. Maybe even tell the time already.'

Cassie laughed. 'Would it matter?'

'Actually,' Kathryn said, peering into a pan which held chestnuts and braised mushrooms in a reduced red wine sauce. 'He's an assistant prof from somewhere in Arizona, so he can't be just a sex-object. I can't remember what his discipline is, which gives you the perfect opportunity to bat those eyelashes of yours and ask. God: this smells absolutely fantastic, Cass. Ever thought of hiring out as a cook?'

'Not until now. But it's certainly an idea.' As Cassie put the finishing touches to things, she realised that it was, in fact, a darn good idea. An idea which might bear serious consideration. If she could be bothered. Christmas was approaching with all the subtlety of a nymphomaniac: if she put her mind to it, it might be possible to earn enough to tide herself over until her current cash-flow problem eased itself.

She was home just after midnight. Quinn Macfarlane had offered to walk her back but she decided she should play hard-to-get and refused. The night was full of cold starlight; a pale gash of moon hung low over black hedges. In the frozen fields, cows murmured and she could even hear the rustle of the river beyond the hill.

Falling into bed, she decided that it had been a good evening. Though she said so herself, the food had been delicious and the wine superb. Quinn Macfarlane was definitely a Good Thing. Even Giles had relaxed, his usual air of disappointed suspicion giving way to an unaccustomed mellowness. Hugh Nightingale had proved to possess a dry self-deprecating sense of humour which overrode a certain artificiality of manner. Cassie had recognised it at once as the defence mechanism adopted by those who have to deal too often with the general public. Uncle Sam was the same.

Around one o'clock, the telephone rang. She awoke, head thick, brain confused. Where . . . what? . . . She fumbled for the cordless receiver beside her bed, then remembered that she had taken it into the bathroom with her the night before and not put it back on the stand. Its battery would be completely run-down. Cursing, she heard her own voice on the answering machine downstairs, briskly demanding that a message be left, then, as she half-fell down the steep stairs into the sitting room, a confused noise which sounded like someone sobbing. 'Please . . .' the word emerged from the depths of stricken cries. 'Cass – oh, I'm sorry, but could you . . .'

The sound broke off abruptly. What had *that* been all about? She played the message through a couple more times but was unable to identify the voice. Irritating. She went back to bed.

It was early afternoon when she finally groaned out of bed, staggered downstairs and made a pot of Dynorod-strong coffee. It was years – weeks, anyway – since she'd last had a hangover. Not that she had one now. But if she dropped anything on the floor, she wasn't going to bend over and pick it up. Not today. Perhaps not until the end of the week. She put some clothes on and went out into the bright chill air. A brisk cycle ride would put her right.

Returning, she found a grateful message on the machine from Kathryn, another which sounded like a heavy breather with a head cold, which she took to be Charlie Quartermain though he didn't speak. Whoever had called her during the night had not rung back. Belatedly, she remembered 1471, the caller identity number, but it was too late now to try it. She was fingering the whisky bottle, thinking about hairs of dogs and wondering about the relative position of yardarms to sun when the telephone rang. A voice said: 'Cassie?'

123

'Paul!' She hadn't spoken to him for months but just one phoneme and she was hooked again.

'I'm on the mobile.'

'Where are you?'

'On my way. Don't go out.' The phone was put down, leaving her as breathless as a teenager. Damn. No time to have a bath, shave her legs, wash her hair. She dashed up the boxed-in stairs into the bathroom and brushed her teeth, slapped on some makeup, tore off her ratty old guernsey and put on a silk shirt instead, brushed her hair, squirted perfume.

She barely had time to be downstairs again, looking casual, looking cool, trying not to chew off the lip gloss, when the roof of his car slid past the front hedge and came to a stop. She told herself once again that their relationship was over. They were no longer an item. Face it.

Nonetheless, part of her refused to believe it. Her pulses fluttered like a schoolgirl's as, through the diamond-paned windows of the sitting room, she saw him walk up the path to the door and heard him bang the knocker against its plate. She told herself not to remember the time, not so long ago, when he would simply have walked round the side of the cottage and let himself in through the back door. Why had he come? Did he want to see her again, and if he did, what would her response be? He'd split up with and gone back to his wife, Barbara, so many times that Cassie had lost count. On top of that, last time they'd had an emotional (and very physical) reunion, she'd laughed at him as he made a hash of putting his underpants on again, and he had not seen the funny side. Which, unfortunately, had made it all the funnier. Paul was definitely not a GSOH sort of guy.

Would she be willing to resume their relationship, if that's what he wanted?

She had opened the front door to him before she could resolve the question. One look at his face told her it was probably not going to come up for consideration, either then or in the next hundred years.

He walked past her and she smelled his familiar scent, trying not to go weak at the knees. The one time that jealousy and heartache had impelled Cassie to seek out the Walsh residence and peer through the windows, she had seen that Barbara was an anorexic bleached-out blonde with a sharp face and a small mouth. Why a man like Walsh, with his university degree and his fast-track promotion prospects, should have married her was something Cassie had not dared to ask. Perhaps he didn't know himself.

'Drink, Paul?' she said, conscious of the whisky bottle and empty glass on the table in front of the fire. He'd think that she had taken up solitary drinking. He'd be right.

'No, thanks. I'm on duty,' he said brusquely. He excelled at brusque. She wished he didn't make her feel quite so much like a fifth-former queuing up outside the headmistress's study waiting for her turn to be torn to shreds by a lifted eyebrow and some withering contempt.

'Ah. So this isn't a social call?'

'No.' He stared at the swell of her bosom under her shirt. 'Why? Did you think it might be?'

'Of course not.'

He pulled out a pocket-sized recorder and after checking the batteries, sat down and set it on the low table in front of him. 'I'd just like to ask you a few questions,' he said. 'If you don't mind.'

'And if I do?'

'You can either come down to the station with me, or call a solicitor. Up to you.'

'Paul, what the hell is this?'

'If you'd stop interrupting and making objections, I'd tell you.'

'I haven't interrupted once.'

'It's about Mrs Haden White,' he said.

'*What* about her? What's wrong with Lolly?'

'Who says anything's wrong with her?'

'Oh God, Paul can't you stop acting like something out of *NYPD Blue*? Lolly is a friend of mine – at least, she's someone I've known for a long time – and you wouldn't be here asking questions about her if there wasn't something wrong.'

He got up and came and sat on the sofa beside her. He took her hand. 'I'm sorry, darl— . . .um, Cassie, but I've got bad news. Mrs Haden White was found dead this morning.'

'Where? What do you mean? What kind of dead?' Cassie couldn't take in what he was saying. Lolly, dead? 'How, for God's sake?'

'Her daughter couldn't get any answer when she rang this morning, and couldn't get into the house when she went round. So she called us. And when the local man showed up and searched the place he found . . .'

'Found *what*?'

'I'm afraid they found Mrs Haden White's body in the back garden.' He squeezed her fingers, which lay numb in his. 'I'm really sorry, Cassandra. I know you knew her. You mentioned her several times during the . . . the time we spent together.'

'Lolly's dead,' Cassie said. 'I can't believe it.'

'Not only dead, but it looks very much as if she was murdered.'

'You're saying that someone killed *Lolly*?'

'That's the way it looks, yes.'

'But who on earth would want to murder her? What possible reason could there be – an inoffensive old lady like her?'

'There's all sorts of possibilities. It could have been a break-in that went wrong. Or maybe she came home and found someone turning the place over. It might even have been sexually motivated.'

'Oh no.'

'You don't know what turns some of these low-lifes on. Don't forget, there're a lot of nutters roaming loose, and you never know what's going to start them off.'

'Sexually motivated,' Cassie choked. 'I just can't . . .'

'It's only one of a number of possibilities. We won't know anything for sure until we get the report back from the path lab.'

'I don't want to hear this.' Cassie tried to put her hands over her ears, but he pulled them away.

'Just because this is a nice bit of countryside, Cass, doesn't mean that the people who live here are nice. But like I say, at the moment we haven't the faintest idea why she was killed. It could be anything. Maybe it's as simple as someone taking offence at something she said or did. From what I've heard, she was pretty skilled at the old verbal GBH. On top of that, she had a family. Have you ever known a family where everything was sweetness and light? I don't suppose hers is any different. We're looking at everything.'

Cassie thought of Jan Thomas and Liz, two rational intelligent women. Could Lolly's hostility to their partnership have been the spark for murder?

Paul looked at the whisky bottle. 'On second thoughts, perhaps a small tot would keep out the cold. It's damn parky outside.'

Cassie poured him one and another for herself. 'I'm terribly upset by this news,' she said. 'I don't know if she was an admirable person but she was always so ... so brave, never letting her standards down, never giving an inch ...' Tears had come into her eyes as she spoke and now they began to fall.

Paul set his glass carefully down on the table and put his arm round her. 'Don't, Cassie,' he soothed. 'I know it's dreadful but—'

'The thing is, we all knew something terrible was happening to her, just from the way her bridge game went off, let alone the change in her appearance.'

Paul inched the recorder closer to her. 'How do you mean, exactly?'

Cassie explained it all, outlining the conversations she'd had with both Serena and Lolly herself. Continued: 'I went round to see if there was anything I could do. We were afraid it was Alzheimer's.' She thought back. 'And now I come to think of it, she did say that she was preoccupied about something. But she wouldn't say what it was. Lolly isn't— ...wasn't the sort of person who took kindly to people prying into her affairs.' She dabbed at her eyes and felt the pressure of Paul's fingers against the top of her arm.

'Cassie,' he said.

She turned her head and looked into his eyes. Those amazing eyes, the colour of water under overhanging trees, with the flecks of green and black in them. Despite the news he had brought her, desire flooded her. Her mouth felt swollen and lascivious; her breasts were heavy. God, how she longed for him to touch them the way he used to. The golden image of Quinn Macfarlane flashed across her mind like a hundred-yard sprinter and was gone. Charlie

Quartermain lumbered briefly through her thoughts. 'Paul,' she murmured.

'Cassie.' He reached towards the recorder on the table, felt for the switch without removing his gaze from hers, turned it off.

'You keep asking why anyone would want to kill Mrs Haden White,' Paul said. The two of them were in dressing gowns, sitting at the kitchen table. 'The first question you'd have to ask is: who stands to gain from her death?'

'Gain? I can't imagine that she's got a lot to leave,' said Cassie. 'There's the house, I suppose—'

'In this area, it's got to be worth well over a hundred thousand.'

'—and presumably she had an income.'

'From the look of the house, she didn't look as though she was short of a bob or two.'

'I don't think she was. She always dressed well, gave drinks parties and dinner parties, changed her car every two years, was always going up to London for concerts and the theatre, that sort of thing.'

'You don't do that on a state pension. Middle-class habits need a middle-class income. She probably had a lot more than you think.'

'It never occurred to me to think. But even so, Serena and Elizabeth – the daughters – are probably the only beneficiaries and I can't imagine either of them would kill their mother for the sake of a half-share in her house.'

Paul sighed. 'You'd be surprised what people will do, and how little they'll do it for.'

'But her *daughters*?'

'If not them, what about their husbands?'

129

'Serena's husband is with the merchant navy. And Elizabeth – she's left hers.'

'Divorced?'

'Not yet. Not as far as I know.'

'Ah. Perhaps he's decided to get in quick, before it's too late for him to dip his fingers in the honeypot.'

'That's horrible.'

'Murder *is* horrible, Cassie. You know that. And you know as well as I do that most murders are committed by the victim's nearest and dearest.'

Something was bothering Cassie. 'Why should Lolly have been outside in this kind of weather?'

'Obvious, isn't it? She was trying to get away. She certainly put up a fight before the bastard finally got her.'

'Oh *God* . . .' Cassie gagged on her mouthful of coffee. 'That's appalling.' Lolly, unsuspecting, letting someone in for a late cup of coffee, only to realise she had invited her killer into her house, running through the rooms, fumbling with bolts and chains, trying to get away, screaming perhaps for help and none coming. But who was after her? And why?

They had played back the message on her machine. 'I can't tell whether it's a man or a woman,' Paul said.

'Let alone whether it's Lolly.'

'I'm not even sure that word is "Cass" – it could just be a gasp, a deep breath so she could scream. If it's a she. Pity you didn't think to dial 1471 right then. If you don't mind, I'll take this tape with me. We can run it past our voice-identification team.'

Cassie could not stop thinking about that choked-off cry. Logic told her that it couldn't have been Lolly, calling for help. Lolly would have called Natasha, who lived nearby, or Serena, her daughter, or the people next door, before she called Cassie.

Nonetheless, she knew that the possibility would remain to haunt her. And added to it, the dim picture of a hand clamping down on the terrified old lady's fingers as they held the receiver to her ear, the receiver which might have brought help and protection. Not that Lolly was old: never for a moment had Cassie seen her as old, merely as not young. The papers would refer to her as elderly, since she was, after all, over seventy.

'Oh, Paul. Suppose it *was* her. If only I hadn't drunk too much last night, if only I'd remembered to replace the cordless phone by my bed.'

'What then? Even if you had, by the time you'd called the police or driven over to Larton Easewood yourself, it would have been too late.'

'Was it a man?'

'Could've been either. So far, we've no clues at all, except it was probably someone she knew, since she'd not only let them in, but was making them coffee. And it must have been someone strong: she was manually strangled and even given the fact that she wouldn't have been able to put up much of a struggle, that would still require a certain amount of force.'

Irresistibly, the image of Jan Thomas's hands crept into Cassie's head. They were big hands. Strong hands. And when motivated by anger and the desire to protect, how easy might they not find it to snap an elderly woman's neck?

'So there was no sign of a break-in?' Jan might have had access to the keys to Lolly's house, either from Liz or via Serena.

'Not according to preliminary findings.' Paul poured more coffee into his mug.

'You said you came here to ask me some questions. Have you asked them?'

'Nearly all of them. I'll probably have to come back to you

for more specific information about Mrs Haden White once we've been able to fill in what happened to her in the last couple of days: where she went, who she was with and so forth. And there may be some background detail you could be helpful with.'

'Surely her daughters would be more—'

'Close family sometimes know less than friends. Mrs Haden White might have confided things in you that she wouldn't dream of saying to them.'

'I can tell you now that she didn't. She wasn't very forthcoming about her private life – and even the little I thought I knew now seems open to question.'

'In what way?'

'For instance, she's given Serena one version of her life and me a rather different one. Maybe that's because one or other of us misunderstood what she meant, but I think she may just have been covering her tracks.'

'Why would she want to do that?'

'Interesting, isn't it?'

'It could be. For now, though, I think we'll concentrate on her present rather than her past.' He pushed back his chair and stood up.

Cassie did the same. 'So . . .' she said.

He stared over her head. 'Before I get dressed, there is one last question.'

'Yes?' Only the table prevented her from leaping across it and jumping on him.

'Can I come back?'

'Back?'

'To you.'

'What about Barbara?'

'It's over, Cassie.'

'You've said that before.'

'This time it's for real. She's got another chap and she's pregnant by him. She won't be coming back – and even if she wanted to, I wouldn't have her.'

'So Cassandra Swann will do until you find someone else, is that it?'

'Of course not. I just felt I had to give my marriage a second chance.' He caught her look and said quickly: 'All right: and a third. But it's finished between us. Finally done.'

'I don't want to go through it all again, Paul.'

'You won't. I promise.' He took a step towards her, and opened his arms. 'I swear it, Cassie.'

A bitter little voice at the back of her brain said: *There's one born every minute*, but she ignored it. 'Really?'

'Cross my heart.'

'Oh, Paul.'

He bent his head and kissed her. He put a hand inside her dressing gown and cupped it round her breast, easing her back across the kitchen table, pulling at the belt of his own robe. He moved to stand between her thighs. 'Cass,' he said hoarsely.

The kitchen door rattled open; she remembered that they'd forgotten to lock it last night in their eagerness to get to bed. A familiar voice began: ''Ello, darlin'. How're you—' then broke off.

'Jesus!' Cassie struggled to get up from her recumbent position on the table. Not easy unless you worked out at the gym a lot more regularly than she did. Paul simply stared at the visitor, his state of arousal rapidly vanishing.

Charlie had a package in his hands, which he put down on the kitchen counter. 'Just wanted you to have this.' He nodded at Paul then turned and went out, closing the back door quietly behind him.

'Damn,' Cassie said. 'Hell and damnation.'

'Was I dreaming, or did a gorilla in a red sweater just come in and then go out again?' Paul said. He pulled his dressing gown tightly round himself. 'Friend of yours, was he?'

'In a manner of speaking.'

'Feels free to walk in and out of your house, does he?'

'This *is* the country, Paul.'

'Even in the country, you'd think this early in the morning you'd be allowed some privacy. Anyway, he knows how to break up a party. I'll give him that.'

'He wasn't to know.'

Paul looked at his watch. 'I'd better go.'

Later, after he had driven away, Cassie stood at the window of the sitting room. She did not want to think about Lolly, violently dead. It was too painful to consider that terrified chase through the house, the knowledge that help, if it came, would be too late. Instead, she tried to give serious consideration to her relationship with Paul and the question of whether she should resurrect it. But all she could see was Charlie Quartermain barging into the kitchen and the look of hurt and bewilderment on his face when he saw her.

'Damn it,' she said aloud. 'It's my house, my place, I can do what I like when I like. With *whom* I like. I am not answerable to Charlie Quartermain. I owe him nothing. I will not feel guilty.'

Nonetheless, she did.

♠ 8 ♠

Lolly Haden White's death left surprisingly few ripples in her immediate circle. People expressed their horror at her violent end, mourned her, came to her funeral once her body had been released for burial, wrote letters of commiseration, and then resumed their lives with scarcely a break to mark where she had once made one. They were not to be blamed for this. Perhaps it was because she had so jealously guarded her privacy, but while recognising her significance in their small society, few felt that Lolly had been a close friend.

Cassie was unable to share this sanguine view. Along with a handful of others, Serena had asked her to come back to the house after the funeral: Jan Thomas hadn't been there but an unsmiling woman with curly auburn hair was introduced as Liz Trowbridge, Serena's sister. She had nodded at Cassie but otherwise displayed no interest at all in the people who had been her mother's friends. The fracture in relations between mother and daughter had probably been in existence long before Jan Thomas came on to the scene. Nonetheless, Cassie felt that, for propriety's sake, the woman should have been friendlier, even given the circumstances of her mother's death.

It was not simply that she herself had become involved with Lolly in a particularly personal way in the days before her death. It was also a compound of admiration for her indomitability, for refusing to succumb to the pressures of growing old, and of deep concern at the fears that perhaps at last she was being engulfed by forces too strong for her to overcome. Although Lolly's death could hardly be described as a life cut short, it was nevertheless one Cassie did not wish to dwell on. Knowing it was irrational, she could not rid herself of a feeling of responsibility. If poor Lolly had opened the door to her murderer, was it because she had grown too gaga to take even minimal security precautions? And if so, should Cassie have seen the signs and warned someone? No one could possibly blame her, since it was not her job to do so, and Lolly's own daughter lived close at hand, but in spite of that, the feeling of blame persisted.

Unusually, Paul Walsh was keeping her informed of the police enquiries and the directions in which they were heading. In the past, he had always refused to tell her anything about his cases, even when they concerned people with whom she was involved. Now, he seemed keen to share the progress of the investigation, which so far had been fairly slow. The only reasons for Lolly's death that they could come up with appeared to be either a bungled burglary or some as yet undiscovered financial motive, since nothing in her past had so far been unearthed which could have led to her murder at such a late stage in her life.

'She seems to have lived a blameless life for at least thirty years,' he said, sitting up in bed with Cassie one Sunday morning. For once, he had not been called away to some emergency. The bedroom windows were double-glazed with frost; the papers were strewn about the covers. 'If she'd got so seriously up anyone's nose that it led to murder, in a place as small as Larton Easewood everyone would know about it. But so far, we haven't found a thing.'

'What about the years before she came to live here?'

'We're looking into it,' Walsh said, in the stiff tone which meant he had not yet turned anything up. 'We haven't traced the husband yet.'

'You won't, either. He's dead.'

'Dead or alive, so far we can't find any record of him. I suppose Haden White was her real name, was it?'

'I've no idea.'

'Perhaps it *is* something to do with her past, rather than her present.'

'If you think about it, it's not very likely, is it? If we know she's done nothing in particular since she came to live in the village, whatever it was would have happened years and years ago. Besides, revenge is supposed to be a dish best eaten cold.'

'Cold, maybe. But not bloody deep-frozen. Why would anyone wait until the poor old thing is – what was it, seventy-one? – before taking their revenge?'

'She was seventy-two, actually. She threw a party to celebrate. I remember her saying something to the effect that like the Vicar of Wakefield, she only had one virtue to perfection, which was prudence, and that it was usually the only virtue left at her age.'

'Gawd.' Walsh reflected for a moment. 'Prudence: is that all we've got to look forward to? Doesn't sound like much fun, does it?' He turned to Cassie and stared into her eyes in a way which he knew perfectly well turned her to mush.

'Talking of fun . . .' Cassie lifted the covers and stared down at the body of her lover. '. . . I have this strange feeling that a spot of extreme imprudence is about to burst over me any moment now.'

'Not *over* you, darling. That would be a terrible waste.'

'It's much more likely to be something that's happened in the past few months,' Cassie murmured, her head tucked into the side of Walsh's neck, her leg sprawled across his body.

'What is?'

'The reason for Lolly's murder.'

'I'm off-duty.'

'Or are you going down the passing axeman route?'

'What?'

'The guy stopping in for a bit of mayhem on his way to a Psychos Anonymous meeting.'

'That's always a possibility.'

'But unlikely.'

'Unlikely.'

'I keep thinking of Hilda Murrell,' Cassie said. 'There was obviously some kind of secret service skulduggery going on there. And she too was an elderly lady living an apparently blameless life, only interested in her roses and her bridge, as far as anyone knew.'

'So far we haven't been warned off by the MI5 lot. Anyway, we've checked. Mrs Haden White was never employed by any of the security agencies.'

'But you *wouldn't* have been warned off, would you? Because then you'd know it was more than burglary or the desire to benefit from her will.'

'Talking of which, turns out Elizabeth Trowbridge's husband is having financial problems and since they're still legally married, if she inherits, he'd definitely stand to gain when it comes to drawing up a divorce settlement. We're checking him out quite hard.'

'Serena's husband is an officer in the merchant navy, isn't he?'

'Cruising the Indian Ocean, as far as we've been able to find out.'

'So at the moment, you haven't a clue why or how Lolly was killed?'

'I wouldn't say that.'

'You would if you were honest.'

'All right. Not a clue. Not the least smidgin of an idea. At least . . .' He held her chin in one hand and gave her the full benefit of his ardent hazel stare. '. . . not about that.'

'Don't,' Cassie said. 'When you look at me like that, I'm as putty in your hands.'

'That's why I do it.'

'Since none of my windows need replacing, what are you planning to do with me then?'

'I'll show you.'


Fresh out of the bath, Cassie sat in the kitchen with a cup of coffee, smiling in a fashion which she was fairly sure would have nauseated anyone whose opinion she respected. This phase in her on-again-off-again relationship with Paul Walsh probably wouldn't last any longer than any of the others but what the hell? Why not enjoy it? At the age of thirty-three or thereabouts – even to herself she preferred to be circumspect – a spot of rosebud-gathering was in order. Jesus had saved the world by the time he was this age; Alexander had conquered it. Whereas she hadn't even learned to control her computer.

Paul, she thought. Paul Walsh.

Mrs Paul Walsh.

Cassandra Walsh.

Mrs Cassandra Wa—

She sat up with a jerk. What was she playing at? Mrs Paul Walsh? Wash your mind out with soap. She caught sight of the package that Charlie had left on the counter after bursting in on her and Walsh. A flush heated her face. Embarrassing or *what*? She was about to get up and unwrap it when she heard a knock at the front door.

Serena Smith was standing on the doorstep. Her face was pale; out here in the daylight, Cassie noticed strands of grey in her thick black hair which she could not remember having seen before. 'Could I come in for a moment?' Her husky voice was slightly breathless.

'Of course.'

Serena hurried down the narrow passageway into the sitting room and seated herself heavily on one of the sofas on either side of the hearth. 'I didn't know who else to turn to,' she said. 'By rights it should be Liz, but the way things were between her and my mother before she ... she died, I'd rather not ask her.'

'Ask her what?' Cassie said gently. She sat down beside Serena. 'What's wrong? Of course I'll help in whatever way I can.'

'It's Mother's house.' Serena stopped. Bit her lip. Fiddled with the strap of her bag. Lolly's murder seemed to have aged her by twenty years.

'Yes?'

'It'll have to be ... to be cleared out. And I just can't face it on my own.'

Cassie wasn't sure she could either. How easily she could imagine Lolly's disapproval if she knew that a comparative stranger like Cassie was going through her things, invading her privacy, prying into matters which didn't concern her. *Prudence*: it was an old-fashioned virtue in this kiss-and-tell, I-want-it-now age. Lolly had been prudent for reasons which had seemed good to her; it didn't take much effort to appreciate how passionately she would have preferred her secrets to remain undiscovered.

She asked only: 'Are you sure I'm the right one to ask?'

'I don't know who else would be better. Mother was always a very private person, I know that, but she was fond of you, more than most, to tell the truth.'

'Well, I'm very—'

'But it's not just that. I'm afraid of breaking down if I'm on my own. All her things . . . her pictures, her book still by the side of her bed, the special coffee she used to buy in Soho, all the . . . the memories and things from . . . from when Liz and I were little . . .' Serena rooted in her bag for tissues as tears overflowed down her face and she began to sob.

Cassie put her arm round the older woman. 'There's nothing I can say. Nothing I can do to bring her back.'

'She brought us up entirely on her own,' sobbed Serena. 'She was so brave, so strong. I always recognised that, even when she . . . she . . .' She pressed the balled-up tissues against her eyes. 'Who'd want to murder her, Cassie? That's what I can't work out. Why not leave her alone, whatever it was? What's she got that an intruder needed to kill her for? She'd have gladly handed over anything, rather than risk her life.'

'Are you sure? From what I knew of her, she had a highly developed sense of fairness.' And given that, Cassie thought, would she not have preferred to see her killer brought to

justice than allowed to get away with something?' 'I can just
see her refusing to give some drunken punk her best silver.
Can't you?'

'I suppose so. Except that nothing was stolen, was it?'

'As far as you know.'

'Something like this certainly makes you realise how
meaningless possessions are, doesn't it?'

'And how important it is to live life to the full.'

'Yes.' Serena pulled back her bowed shoulders, wiped her
eyes again and put the tissues neatly into her bag. 'You know
what people are like. If you're there, I won't break down so
easily. Mother didn't approve of tears, she thought they were
a sign of weakness. She said we weren't given more to bear
than we could cope with and we just had to get on with it.
But Liz and I are so different, that if I did need to . . . to, you
know, have a quick weep, I'd rather it was in front of you
than her.'

'Oh, Serena.' What kind of legacy had Lolly left, that her
daughter should be apologising in advance in case she
displayed a perfectly natural emotion? 'You can cry as much
as you like. I'll probably cry alongside you.'

'Thanks, Cassie. Thank you for understanding.'

'So when do you want to start? The sooner the better, I'd
think.'

'I've still got some of my holiday allowance left. How
about tomorrow? Nine o'clock?'

'I'll be there.'

Lolly's house had the watchful air of a dog still waiting for
its master to return. There was something desperate about the
familiar sitting room, normally so meticulously kept, now
covered in fingerprint powder, the cushions scattered, an

upright chair lying on its back, the shards of broken glass still scattered on the carpet. Cassie didn't want to think about how it got broken or who knocked over the chair. The hideous aftermath of violent death. But more, too. The disintegration of something which, at its edges, had been Lolly: the atmosphere she maintained, the guarded persona she presented. Now it was spread-eagled to the incurious gaze of anyone who wished to pick it over, whether officially, as in the case of the police, or privately, as she was about to do.

'Where should we start?' Serena sounded nervous.

'In here?'

'I suppose so. The appraisers from the auction house in Bellington are coming over later: we're planning to sell some of the good stuff and then let the place for a while, so it's Mother's private things I need to deal with. Letters and diaries, if there are such things. Her clothes. Her jewellery. Stuff like that. Her ... her toilet things ...' Serena's voice wavered and her eyes filled. 'Oh dear ... I really hoped I wouldn't embarrass you like this.'

'Serena. It's not embarrassing, it's absolutely natural. Please just cry if you want to, I completely understand. My mother died when I was six and I don't remember much about it, but when my father, and then ...' Cassie, too, found speech difficult. 'When my Gran died, I wasn't allowed to cry, and it's taken me years to get over it. I'm not sure I have even now.'

'OK.' Serena grew brisk, dashing tears away with the back of her hand. 'Why don't we go through the things in here first. Anything you think I ought to see you can set on one side. Everything else can be torn up. All right?'

'Yes. As long as you trust me.'

'Of course.'

★ ★ ★

At lunchtime, they broke off briefly to eat the pastrami and Swiss cheese rolls which Serena had brought with her. They had been through the drawers and pigeon-holes of Lolly's bureau, the oak breakfront which stood in one of the alcoves, the coffer under the window. For the most part, these had proved to be empty: the papers which seemed worth keeping had filled no more than a quarter of one of the cardboard boxes which Cassie and Serena had picked up from the supermarket in Bellington.

'She'd already done some of this herself,' Cassie said, as they sat perched on kitchen chairs with mugs of coffee in their hands. She avoided looking out of the windows at the shed behind which Lolly's body had been discovered.

'Sorry?'

'Lolly. Your mother. She'd already thrown a lot of papers away. I dropped in to see her a couple of days before . . . and she was clearing her desk out. I saw the papers all screwed up and in the wastepaper basket.'

Serena stared at her. She raised one hand slowly to her mouth. 'You mean . . . as though she somehow expected that she was going to die?'

'More like someone tidying up her desk,' said Cassie, as matter-of-factly as she could.

'But why should she do that?'

'People do, you know. Especially older ones. Otherwise they'd all drown in a sea of paper.'

'Not my mother,' Serena said, shaking her head.

'The grandmother of a friend of mine gave away almost everything she owned to her children when she turned seventy-five, on the grounds she wouldn't need it any longer,' said Cassie, trying to ignore the head-shaking which was getting alarmingly emphatic, so much so that briefly she wondered whether the shock of Lolly's death had temporarily unhinged her daughter. 'Got rid of papers and everything, and then had to ask for them all back. She eventually died on her eighty-fifth birthday, from too much champagne.'

'But my mother wasn't like that. She didn't drink champagne, for one thing.' Serena said this without the slightest trace of irony.

'Ah,' said Cassie.

'It was one of her things, you see, to deal with her correspondence as soon as it arrived. She told me once that *her* mother always used to do that and it was a habit she'd adopted herself. So there was no need to get rid of things because if there were any papers in her desk, they were ones she'd want to keep.' She glanced over at the box, which had once held tins of condensed milk.

The matter had seemed a small one, otherwise Cassie would not have risked upsetting Serena by mentioning it. 'Everyone gets these let's-have-a-clear-out days,' she said as lightly as she could. 'Even I do.'

'My mother didn't,' Serena said stubbornly. 'She got rid of it there and then.'

Cassie could think of no response. Serena was right. There had been no scraps of paper lurking at the back of Lollie's drawers, no dustballs or bent paperclips, no old snapshots and fuzzy mint imperials, the way there would have been in Cassie's house. Was she simply a compulsive tidier or was she someone anxious to leave no secret clues, no vulnerable points which could be exploited? Whichever it was, it seemed clear that Lolly had been almost neurotically obsessed with privacy.

She changed the subject. 'You told me the other day that

145

you and your sister grew up very isolated. No grandparents, father dead, no aunts and uncles,' she said. 'Did that ever strike you as odd?'

'Why should it? Lots of families don't have any family – if you see what I mean. In China, for instance, there's a whole generation growing up without even cousins, let alone siblings.'

'Yes, well . . .' Making allowances for Serena's distress, Cassie didn't point out that Lolly was not and never had been Chinese. 'I can see that if Lolly was an only child, and so was your father, there wouldn't be aunts and things. But if you think about it, doesn't it seem odd that all four of your grandparents should have died? I mean, when you were children, your parents can't have been so old that it would be natural for their parents to be dead.'

'They might have been elderly parents. After all, my mother was over thirty-six when she had me: that was quite old for those days.'

'I mean,' Cassie said carefully, 'is it at all possible that for some very good reason, she was lying?'

'What about?'

'I don't know. Maybe about your father being dead. Or one or other set of grandparents. I mean, I heard that her mother taught at the village school here in Larton Easewood but you said that wasn't true at all. So where did the rumour come from? And this business of whether Lolly came from Kenya or South Africa – maybe she didn't come from either.'

'Does it make much difference? All these African countries are pretty much the same, aren't they?' Serena said vaguely, turning over Lolly's latest bill from the electricity board.

'Nelson Mandela might have a few words to say on that

subject,' Cassie said, wondering what Serena's IQ was. To say she had the brains of a bandaid was an insult to bandaids. 'The point is, maybe she was hiding from something.'

'And you think it might be this . . . whatever it is . . . which caught up with her the other night?'

'I'm not saying that. Just that you seem to have amazingly little knowledge of your own family. Aren't there any photographs? Or furniture passed down? Especially if your grandparents were dead and Lolly was an only child. People always have things that have been in their families for generations, even if it's an old mug or a wooden box or something.'

'She never believed in weighing herself down with possessions. And she always said she despised the idea of mementoes.'

'Serena, you can't possibly believe that. People like your mother don't live in cardboard boxes: they can't help leaving mementoes. You only have to look around you: you and your sister are going to have more than enough mementoes of your mother from this room alone. The china, and the books, the furniture and so on.'

'Yes.' Serena's brow was wrinkled as she looked round the sitting room. Was she just dim, Cassie wondered, or had she been trained so well by her mother to live in the present that she never thought about the past?

It was half-an-hour later that somebody pushed open the front door. 'Yoo hoo. Anybody home?'

Cassie, who was nearest, went out into the hall. A man in a black suit was standing there. 'Can I help you?'

'Oh, hello. I was passing and couldn't help noticing that there was some activity going on. My name's Lightower, by the way. John Lightower.' He smiled and Cassie was immediately conscious of a surge of electricity, as though he had flicked a switch and accessed a power station.

'I don't believe I've . . .' He took Cassie's hand and shook it heartily, not letting it go at the end of the shake.

'Cassandra Swann. And you are what, exactly?'

His eyes looked beyond her. 'Are you alone?'

'Mrs Smith is here.'

'Ah, she's the one I hoped to see.' He glanced into the sitting room. 'Clearing up, are you?'

'Yes.'

'Serena!' Cassie called up the stairs, not taking her eyes off him. 'There's someone here to see you.'

The man Lightower was moving forward. 'Do I smell coffee?' he said brightly. 'Perhaps I might be permitted a cup.' He walked down the passage and into the kitchen at the back of the house.

'Look, I don't know . . . Serena!' yelled Cassie again.

'Yes?' Serena's voice floated faintly from the loft.

'There's a strange man here, says he wants to speak to you.'

'I'll come down.'

Cassie marched in to the kitchen and stood watching as Lightower spooned instant coffee into a cup he had removed from one of the cupboards, then added boiling water from the kettle. 'Ah,' he sighed pleasurably. 'I could just do with that.' Noticing her hostile gaze for the first time, he added: 'Perhaps I should have explained that I'm attached to St Bartholomew's.'

'Oh?'

'I'm the Vicar.'

'I see.'

'I never met Mrs Haden White, but I knew where she lived. Such a sad death, wasn't it?'

'Very.' Quite apart from the antipathy which churchmen always triggered in Cassie, she was not at all sure that she trusted this man. Something about him did not ring quite true.

Serena came in. Her face glowed at the sight of Lightower. 'Oh, Vicar. How nice of you to come.'

'I was explaining to your friend here that I realised you must be here when I saw the windows open, and dropped in on the off-chance of seeing you. How are you, my dear?'

'Bearing up.'

'A dreadful business.'

'I know.'

'At times like this, it helps to realise that one has friends, Serena.' He took her hand, and put an arm round her shoulders. 'And you know that at St Bart's, we are all your friends.'

'Oh, Vicar . . .' Serena's eyes filled. She leaned her head against his shoulder.

'And now you're clearing up your mother's things?' His eyes darted about the place as though hoping to find something specific.

'That's right.'

Lightower caught Cassie's glance and looked away. He'd already asked that question: she wondered if his talk was mere babble designed to soothe Serena or whether he was really interested in the answer. It was another fifteen minutes before he finally left.

'He's such a dear man,' Serena said, after he'd gone. 'It's a pity that my mother was so dead set against the Church.'

Her and me both, thought Cassie.

'I finally persuaded her to come with me to St Bart's just a short time before she . . . died, which was sad, really, because

149

I always thought that if she got to know John, she might have found him comforting.'

From time to time, as they worked, Serena broke down and wept but she kept her grief to herself, determined not to impose her problems on Cassie. Which was unnecessary, Cassie reflected, since her own heavy-heartedness at the task they had undertaken and the reasons behind it occasionally spilled over into tears. Even though Lolly had not been much more than a near acquaintance, she was constantly aware that, only a short while before, Lolly herself had inhabited these rooms, and – more distressingly – that it was right here that she had met her violent end.

By the end of the day, most of the drawers and cupboards had been cleared and the removable items packed into boxes. Lolly's dislike of extraneous clutter extended to her wardrobe. There were none of those sales bargains which looked so good in the shop and so unflattering at home, none of the ratty cardigans with torn pockets, or pilled sweaters which would do for those days when nobody was expected to call. Apart from a couple of fur coats, which were bagged and hanging in the guest room, Cassie recognised every single item as garments which Lolly habitually wore. She recognised the labels, too: Jean Muir, Bruce Oldfield, Cassini, Hartnell. No wonder Lolly had always looked so elegant. Though some of them had obviously been in Lolly's possession for many years, others were newer: any question there might have been about her income must surely have been answered by the fact that she could afford to buy them. Which put the question of who stood to gain from her death back into the forefront of the enquiries. She would telephone Paul when she got home, explain the significance of those labels, something which his team of male investigators might otherwise have missed.

The appraisers had shown up in time for a cup of tea, and gone about their work. It had already been decided that once the better items of furniture had been removed, cheap substitutes would be found and the house let on a short-term lease. Before they left, Cassie vacuumed the ground-floor rooms while Serena wiped down the surfaces in the bathroom, and arranged the bedrooms. Stripped of Lolly's bits and pieces – her books, her porcelain, the African masks – the sitting room already looked anonymous. Soon someone else would buy the house, would redecorate, bring in their own things, stamp their own personality upon it. For a while, the wistful ghost of Lolly Haden White might still peer between the banisters or from behind the furniture but after a time, even such ephemeral traces of her would have faded, to linger on fragile as an autumn leaf pressed between the pages of a book until it finally crumbles into dust.

Moving Lolly's desk in order to vacuum behind it, Cassie found a couple of screwed-up balls of paper which had evidently been missed both by the police and, presumably, Lolly herself. It wasn't difficult to see why they might have been overlooked: they had somehow become wedged between the leg of the desk and the wall behind it. Curious, Cassie smoothed them out. The two pages constituted a letter, dated several months earlier. The writing was an old person's, faint and quavery, faltering across heavy blue writing paper. The embossed address was somewhere in Henley-on-Thames.

The letter began without preamble.

*Michael, my husband, is gravely ill, and is most insistent that I get in touch with you before it is too late. It has increasingly worried him that he was not more helpful when you first wrote to him all those years ago, and he has asked me to say that he is now willing (in fact eager) to offer any evidence you might require, to pass on such contacts as he still has, and to testify, if necessary, that what you said then was the truth.*

*I want you to know how greatly troubled he has been by what he now considers his cowardice. It would ease his mind considerably if you were to contact him and he has begged me to let you know that if it is of any help to you and it is not all too late, you will not hesitate to get in touch with us.*

The letter was signed in the name of Dorothy Farquharson. Cassie read it twice, and then again, pushing the still-running Hoover back and forth across the carpet in the absent manner of a mother trying to get a baby to sleep.

Secrets. They welled up from the page like a bitter spring, giving off the vinegar reek of ancient rancours. Could it be that the contents of this letter lay behind Lolly's recent disquiet? And how had it got stuck behind the desk like that? She read it once more. *All those years ago . . . what you said then . . . his cowardice . . .* Whatever secrets Lolly had sought to conceal, it seemed clear that in the past few weeks – she looked again at the date on Mrs Farquharson's letter – they had risen from the past and come back to haunt her.

'Cassie.' Serena's voice was faint above the roar of the vacuum cleaner. 'Are you finished?' She was coming down the stairs; another step and she could not fail to see the two pages in Cassie's hand. Cassie thrust them deep into the pocket of her shirt, wondering, even as she did so, why she should be so anxious to conceal them. Serena had already given her permission to look at anything she might find; there was therefore nothing shameful about being discovered with this particular letter. Nonetheless, as clearly as if Lolly had spoken aloud, she had the feeling that the murdered woman would prefer this secret, as all her others, to remain unknown. And for the sake of the relationship, however tenuous and unacknowledged, which had existed between them, Cassie felt that she should try to accede to those unspoken wishes, unless and until it proved absolutely impossible to do so.

'Whimsical, or what?' she asked herself later, sitting up close to the log fire which blazed in the hearth. 'You'll be having visions next, hearing bells.' Nonetheless, as she reread the letter yet again, she hoped she had done the right thing. This was a murder investigation, after all, and the police should be given any and all information which might lead to the arrest of whoever had so ruthlessly stalked and then killed a frail old lady.

However, her mind could not stop turning over the possibilities opened up by Mrs Farquharson's written words. Reading between the lines, it was clear that there had been a scandal of some kind, an unsavoury episode which Lolly had sought to expose, and which Michael Farquharson – and, presumably, others – had covered up. And now the old man was dying and wanted to ease his conscience by coming clean. Where had it happened, whatever it was? Just how many years did *all those years* indicate? Who were these people? Who, for that matter, was Farquharson? Where had he known Lolly? What had happened? There was only one way to find out.

She knew that it was her civic duty to hand the two pages

over to Paul Walsh. This was not a matter for her to meddle
in, nor did she particularly wish to. On the other hand, if this
matter was conceivably linked to Lolly's death then perhaps
she had a greater duty, to a woman who had deliberately
chosen to swaddle herself in silence and must have hoped –
*expected* – that nothing would happen to change that. On the
*other* other hand, however, it was obvious that Lolly had
once wanted to expose whatever event Michael Farquharson
had been instrumental in hushing up. And if by any slight
chance Lolly's killer was involved in that same event, then
she, Cassie, ought to at least give it a shot before passing the
matter over to the police.

She poured another drink. Threw another applewood log
into the flames. Asked herself what right she had to play God
with facts which might help to track down a murderer. She
thought of Bettina Maggs, of Ted Quartermain, even of the
ancient creature swathed in fluffy blankets. Society tended to
sideline people of their age yet, like everyone else, they had
lived and loved, adventured, dreamed. There would be episodes in their lives which they would rather no-one found out
about, even after they were dead. It was only human to
behave occasionally in ways which were discreditable, which
did not fit their own inner image of themselves. Equally, it
must be one of the most human of impulses to rewrite
oneself, as it increasingly appeared that Lolly had done. To
smooth off a corner here, paint over a crack there, buff up the
edifice in an effort to make it look like mahogany instead of
the cheapest softwood. Which of us did not try to present
themselves in the most acceptable light, to engrave upon the
consciousness of those they came into contact with an image
which did them perhaps a little more than justice?

Lolly had taken a somewhat different route in the effort to

recreate herself. Even if Serena couldn't see it, to Cassie it was obvious that she had deliberately wiped out the past. Almost certainly lied about it. Serena must be somewhere in her early forties, Liz Trowbridge perhaps a little older. Was it really conceivable that, thirty-odd years ago, all four of the grandparents, who in the normal course of events couldn't have been much more than fifty or so, would have died? And if she was right in the assumption that perhaps they had not died after all, the very fact they had been deprived of their grandchildren was sad. Whatever the reasons behind Lolly's reticence, she must have considered them pretty compelling.

So all the more reason to see if there was another road to go down, before she went to the police with the letter she had found.

Her diary showed that the day after tomorrow was free. And Henley-on-Thames was not a long drive from here – she had done it in the summer with her godfather, when he came over from France for the Regatta. But how ill was Farquharson? The letter, written four months ago, had made it clear that he was dying: it probably wouldn't make any difference whether she raced down there tonight or waited. She had no idea whether Lolly herself had acted on the letter: if so, would his widow be willing to cover old ground again by talking to Cassie? Surely if she knew that Lolly had been murdered, she would be glad to help.

On that optimistic note, she decided to back-burner Lolly for the time being. Meanwhile, there was Tim Gardiner's latest book – oh Gaahd! – to scan before she next had lunch with him, notes to make for an article she had been commissioned to write for a bridge magazine, a phone call to make to Primula, which would require a considerable amount of sinew-stiffening. She decided on Primula, rather than Hyacinth, as she would then be killing two unpleasant birds with one stone. Thank God there was still some moral fibre left in the bottle: when the whisky was finished, it might be some time before she could afford any more.

'It's Cassie, calling to find out how Aunt Polly's doing.' she said, as soon as Primula picked up the phone. With any luck, the painful cracked nipples would have healed themselves, though that still left the contents of the baby's nappy to be discussed at length. But she'd already eaten her evening's ration of pasta: she could handle full nappies. She hoped.

'We still haven't had the results,' Primula said, managing to make it sound as though in some obscure way it was Cassie's fault.

'I'll go over and see her, if it's of any help,' said Cassie. 'Though Eric said it would be better to wait.'

'Probably.' Again Primula's voice implied that anyone with a drop of decency in their veins would have already been waiting at the hospital when Aunt Polly was brought in for her tests.

'Do you have any idea yet of what the prognosis is likely to be?'

'None at all. We're terribly worried, of course.'

'Of course. And how's Uncle Sam taking it?'

'At least he has his parish work to take his mind off it.'

'You'll let me know if there's anything . . . you know . . . I should know, won't you?'

'Of course.'

'So . . .' Cassie gave a gulp which she hoped was inaudible. 'How's . . .' She couldn't remember the baby's name, nor even its sex. '. . . the baby?' She wished she were a nicer person all round. She summoned up the blood. 'Feeding all right?' The question was above and beyond the call of any duty she could possibly have owed anyone.

A thin wail quavered into the space behind the telephone receiver, like a preparatory Indian smoke signal. 'That's him now,' Primula said.

'Ah.' So it was a he, was it?

In a nanosecond, the wail had developed into a full-blooded roar. 'Look, Cassie, I'm sorry not to be more conversational—'

'That's quite all right.'

'—but it's time to feed little Job . . .'

'Who?' Could anyone seriously have inflicted the name Job on an innocent child? As the daughter of a vicar, Primula must have known as well as Cassie what the name meant. Let alone anticipated all the snide remarks about boils that the child would have to endure at school.

'. . . and you know how twitchy that always makes a nursing mother.'

'Absolutely,' Cassie said heartily, though she had no idea at all. Looked like she'd been reprieved for today.

But as always, Primula managed to have the last word. She gave a little laugh. Her voice was heady with a mixture of glee, contempt and superiority as she said: 'But of course – I forgot, you've never had a baby, have you?'

And before Cassie could point out that Primula knew perfectly well that she hadn't, her cousin had added 'Ciao,' and broken the connection.

Cassie stood staring at the receiver in her hand, lips compressed. She made a fist and breathed heavily through her nose for a moment or two. *One of these days*, she thought. *One of these fucking days . . .*

## ♣ 9 ♣

It was a typical November day: dank and chill, forecasting winter rigours still to come. A thin mist hung over Oxford, beading the naked willows with moisture, clinging to the Gothic ornamentations like insubstantial snow. In the grey light, the college walls seemed more ponderous, weighted with tradition and a kind of oblivious immemoriality. Cassie always preferred the town in this out-of-season state, when the tourists had gone and left it to its melancholy.

From an ancient stone gateway issued a waft of gravitas as three persons in academic dress emerged. They carried books under their arms and spoke earnestly in low tones, heads leaning together. Skirting the small cluster they had formed on the pavement, Cassie overheard snatches of their conversation. '. . . lift passes . . .', '. . . powder snow . . .', '. . . only fourteen and drunk as a lord on gluhwein . . .'

Phew. Sometimes she worried that, in a seat of learning such as this, they might be discussing post-modernism or philosophical niceties. It was reassuring to learn that skiing holidays and the young occupied academics just as much as they did the rest of the population. Although her own prospects for a vacation in the foreseeable future were dim, Cassie felt no envy. She had once gone skiing with her former husband who had booked them in to an hotel in a small Austrian resort. Ten days of humiliation had followed. For her, not for him. There could scarcely have been a square inch of local snow onto which she had not bounced, gaudy as a beach ball in her brightly coloured get-up. Every now and then her husband would sail past with the grace of a Nureyev and give her a wave in which, looking back, she was able to detect the first signs of the incompatibility which would lead to their subsequent break-up. Skiing was an experience she was in absolutely no rush to repeat.

She strolled through the covered market, making for the specialist sausage shop. Sausages were cheap food, even these exotic ones. OK, so they were also fattening, but pasta palls, and sometimes a girl had to let go, give in to temptation. She had read recently that mice fed on a subsistence diet had lived 40% longer than their fatter cousins, thus proving that the way to ensure longevity was to eat 25% less than was needed to sustain life. Something like that. So what? She was about to go in and buy half a pound of the venison and cranberry ones when she caught sight of Hugh Nightingale staring at the buckets of hothouse flowers outside the florist's shop.

'Mr Nightingale,' she called. Maybe he would invite her to lunch with him. Maybe he would install her in a pink-draped flat in North Oxford and shower her with diamonds and maribou-trimmed mules, champagne and oysters, asking only that she kept herself available for him every weekday afternoon.

He turned. 'Hello there,' he said, professional electricity warming his eyes. 'It's Samanth—'

'Cassandra.'

'Of course, Cassandra . . . um . . .' she saw him vainly conjuring up images of river banks. 'Mallard, isn't it?'

'Nice try, Reverend. It's Swann, actually.'

'Ha ha.' His laugh was merry. 'Birds of a feather, eh?' He'd made the same joke at Kathryn's house the other evening.

'Maybe.' Actually, she rather thought not.

He glanced at his watch, a thin circle of gold with red roman numerals to mark the passing of the minutes, each number marked with a gold dot. 'Look. Are you . . .? have you time for . . .?'

'Definitely,' said Cassie, hoping he wasn't hinting his way towards Babylonian excesses in North Oxford.

'There's a place round the corner where they do very nice . . .' He surged forward and she followed. Very nice what?

'Triffic,' she managed.

He climbed some stairs and they found themselves in a Pizza Express. 'Shakespeare is reputed to have come here,' he said in a confidential manner, as though only he, and now she, were privy to this information.

'Surely not.' The idea of Shakespeare scarfing down *Quattro Stagioni* was too bizarre to be worth more than a moment's consideration.

'In one of its earlier incarnations, of course,' he added. 'It's reputed to be the oldest inn in these here parts.' To say the last few words, he adopted a cod-Cotswold accent which made Cassie feel as though steam was about to erupt from her nostrils.

The waitress arrived and they ordered. Working on the principle that Nightingale would be picking up the tab, Cassie went the whole hog, including the dough balls which came as a side order, as well as in combination with various dishes. As they began to eat, Nightingale said: 'I understand there's been a murder in your part of the world.'

'That's right.'

'Nowhere's safe these days, is it?' He hoisted a mouthful of pizza, strings of cheese depending from his fork. 'You somehow imagine that these idyllic little Cotswold villages would be protected from the sordidness of modern urban life, but that's not the case at all.'

'No.'

'Did you know the poor woman?'

'I did. At least . . .' Had anyone really known Lolly? 'I played bridge with her over a number of years. I know one of her daughters reasonably well and I've met the other.'

'I wonder whether it's true, as some theorists have it, that victims, as it were, invite victimisation, whether it be something as – unhappily – everyday as a mugging, or as out of the ordinary as a murder.'

'You can't be suggesting that Lolly was killed simply because she had a victim mentality.'

'Not at all. But if one starts to ask oneself why that victim, why that particular person at that particular time, it's not always easy to find an answer. I worked in a prison for a while, among some of the most depraved men you could possibly hope to meet, and was always astonished at the reasons some of them gave for why they had taken a human life. Obviously there were other explanations, mostly to do with an inability to control themselves, but you'd be surprised how many said things like: "She asked for it," "She wanted me to," "He made me do it." You wouldn't believe how often they expressed it in those terms.'

'But they would, wouldn't they? I've worked inside a prison too, and almost the first thing I learned is that whatever the cons have done, it wasn't their fault.'

'But I'm talking about genuine bewilderment.'

'Sorry, but I'm not going to buy the theory that Lolly *wanted* to be killed. I believe something happened in her life a long time ago, something quite violent, and it finally came home to roost last week.'

He put his head on one side. 'That's very interesting. And on what are you basing that theory?'

'Stuff.' Cassie realised that she didn't want to be discussing Lolly's death with this virtual stranger. She concentrated on cutting her pizza into bite-sized pieces and eating them fairly rapidly, one after another.

'Come, my dear. It must be more than that. You sound as if you have specialised knowledge.'

'Not at all. But I do know that three or four months ago something happened to upset her quite strongly, and I'm convinced that it has something to do with her . . . death.'

'So not only an accomplished cook and expert bridge player, but something of a sleuth as well, eh?'

Cassie tried to remember when she had last heard someone say 'Eh?' and couldn't. In fact she wasn't sure she ever had. She was beginning to think that a slice of pizza could cost more than she was prepared to pay. Nightingale's tone made it fairly obvious that he was the sort of man who appeared to like women but in fact despised them. 'I wouldn't go as far as that,' she said coldly. 'But certainly I think there are things about Lolly's death which make it clear it was something more than merely an intruder who was surprised and took the violent way out. Quite apart from anything else, he'd hardly have pursued her into the garden, would he? I've always understood that professional burglars are a notoriously timid breed, who'll run if you raise your voice.'

'Professionals, maybe. But the opportunistic thief, the

young man high on drugs or drink, emboldened, perhaps by the fact that the person he is robbing is old and apparently defenceless . . . that's when a simple break-in escalates into aggravated assault, even murder.'

'Well,' Cassie said stubbornly, not dead keen on his pomposity, 'from what I know, I'm sure it's bound up with something which happened to Lolly ages ago.'

He folded his knife and fork tidily together in the exact centre of his plate and smiled. 'What a macabre subject to be discussing over lunch. Why don't you tell me something which intrigued me enormously. At that delightful dinner party, Kathryn mentioned that you might be thinking of taking up cooking professionally.'

'Kathryn is prone to exaggeration.'

'Oh dear, What a pity. As a bachelor, I was hoping I might persuade you to come and cater on a few occasions for me. There are people I shall really have to entertain, in my new chaplaincy.'

'It's been confirmed, then?' Clearly, Cassie remembered Lolly's sour voice saying that his appointment was not yet definite.

'Just two days ago. I'm so pleased. Oxford is my *alma mater*, of course, and I look forward to three or four very pleasant years before—' Nightingale broke off.

'Before what?' Had he heard that chaplains at St Frideswide's tended to be elevated into bishoprics?

'Before I'm moved on, I was going to say, but it doesn't sound too good, does it, to be thinking of leaving before I've even settled in?' He smiled again. 'Anyway, I should be so delighted if you would consider my proposition.'

'Proposition?' For a moment maribou-trimmed mules danced depravedly inside Cassie's head.

'About coming to cook for me. You could think about it perhaps and then give me a ring. If you telephone the college, the Porter's lodge will put you through to my office – I can't remember the direct-line number at the moment.'

'It was only a passing thought. Besides, I wouldn't know how to set it up, or what to charge.'

'My dear . . .' He leaned forward, elbows on the table. 'I availed myself of a similar service while I was living in London, and considered their prices fairly reasonable, given that it involved me in nothing more arduous than the choice of wines.' He mentioned a sum per hour which made Cassie gasp. This cooking lark was beginning to sound as though it could be a nice little earner. And it left her free to work or not to work, as she chose. As she grew older, independence increasingly seemed to Cassie to be a desirable commodity. It might mean some lows in the earning graph but it also meant choice, control. The notion of nine-to-fiving it again was one she could hardly bear to contemplate. The odd spot of supply teaching only confirmed that she had made exactly the right decision when she got out of the education system. And if she did as Nightingale suggested, it would almost certainly lead on to other jobs of the same kind. For all she knew, Oxford was full of bachelor dons eager for her culinary services. The more she thought about it, the better the whole idea seemed.

'Let me think about it a bit longer,' she said. She fished about a bit in her bag and found one of her business cards. 'Let me know some time what dates you're interested in. If I do decide to do it, I wouldn't charge London prices.'

'I don't see why not. Oxford's a sophisticated city, after all.'

'Even so.'

★ ★ ★

She took the back roads to Henley. The mist which in Oxford had been greyly dank had turned a hazy blue in the country-side and sat like smoke among the unleafed trees along the ridges. A group of deer stood at the far edge of a damp field, wary, alert for danger. Flocks of gulls scavenged the ploughed furrows, their white feathers soaking up such brightness as there was; although it was not raining, she needed to use her windscreen wipers.

It was difficult to get away from the river. In the summer, she had gone with Robin to the Regatta, enjoying, as she always did, the sight of the English rowing classes at play. Leander had been bursting at the seams with distinguished old buffers in blazers of a garishness scarcely to be believed. There was a large number of bronzed and personable young men in white flannels and navy double-breasted jackets. A river of Pimm's flowed across the bar, the air was full of haw-hawing laughter and old friendships, elegant women in hats sat about with expressions of barely concealed boredom. This was definitely a day for the chaps. Robin, splendid in his pink tie and matching socks, some kind of sporting insignia attached to the pocket of his blazer, had looked particularly macho and virile.

'It's the pink socks,' Cassie had said. 'You can always tell a real man by his socks.'

'Do you think so, dear heart?' Robin waved at some tottering old boy in green and yellow stripes, whose teeth stuck horizontally from his mouth. 'Funny to think I was a real man once. I'll tell you what, though. I'm thinking of doing out the back loo in France in this colour. It'd feel so warm and snug on those cold winter days.'

'Womb pink: very suitable.'

'I prefer to think of it as corset pink.'

Despite the fact that Henley was one of the most famous rowing occasions in the world, she had not seen a race, nor a boat, had scarcely even glimpsed the river apart from crossing the bridge in the car as they drove away.

Yesterday, when she'd dialled the telephone number at the top of the letter she had found stuffed behind Lolly's desk, Mrs Farquharson herself had answered. She'd sounded vague, not quite with it, and after several frustrating minutes Cassie gave up attempting to explain over the phone who she was and why she wanted to drive over to see her, and contented herself with establishing that it would be convenient to drop in the following afternoon.

'Combefield', the Farquharsons' large house, was outside the town, one of several solid Stockbroker-Tudor places set down in tall-hedged suburbia, expensive and isolated from each other by lawns and shrubberies. A burglar's paradise, she thought, despite the heavy alarm box set prominently under the eaves. Once you'd made sure the owners were away and by-passed the security system, you could burgle to your heart's content, confident that nobody would hear you. It would be quite possible never to meet the neighbours unless a conscious effort was made, let alone notice comings and goings.

She pulled into a semi-circular drive, which was surfaced with a mixture of yellow sand and gravel. There were two new cars parked in front of a triple garage, and between house and garage she glimpsed an imposing garden and the netting of a tennis court. She pulled at the iron bell beside the front door. After a while, a middle-aged woman opened it.

'You must be Miss Swann,' she said.

'Yes.'

'Come in. I'm Angela Drew. My mother's expecting you, though she's not too clear why you're here.'

'As a matter of fact, neither am I,' said Cassie. She explained briefly the circumstances of Lolly's death and the letter she had found.

'I would have thought the police would be better placed to handle the matter than you,' said Ms Drew in a nannyish voice.

'I'm sure they are,' Cassie said humbly. 'But I also feel that whatever Mrs Haden White was concerned about should remain her secret if possible. If not, well, naturally I'll go to the police immediately.'

'It's none of my business but you seem to be taking a lot on yourself, don't you? Surely the proper authorities are in a better position to judge the importance of whatever it is than you are.'

'I'll have a better idea of that when I know what it's all about.'

Cassie had not liked to ask about Ms Drew's father. Since the woman had spoken only of her mother, it seemed extremely likely that he had already succumbed to whatever illness he had been suffering from. Certainly, there were no signs of an invalid in the spacious morning room into which Ms Drew showed her. Nor in the large heated conservatory in pseudo-Gothic style which had at some time been added to the room. A number of silver-framed photographs were displayed on mantelpiece and table, some showing children in various stages of development, others depicting an Errol Flynn-type character – Michael Farquharson, presumably – in tropical kit or safari suits. Sometimes he had a woman at his side; sometimes he stood alone or with similarly clad colleagues; in one he was top-hatted and morning-suited, flanked by his family at Buckingham Palace, displaying an OBE.

Stepping through the open doors which led from the first room, Cassie found herself in a large conservatory crowded with arrangements of green plants, tropical trees, hanging baskets, exotic creepers, even a few orchids. Water cascaded gently over a chunk of volcanic rock and into a basin which contained several goldfish. White wicker furniture stood here and there and on a two-seater sofa a still-pretty woman in her late sixties sat at a basketwork table, reading a new paperback novel through a large magnifying glass. Once she must have been beautiful; almost certainly she was the same woman as in the photographs. Thick white hair was piled becomingly on top of her head, and she was discreetly but attractively made up. She wore a thick skirt of black linen and over it, a sweater of soft blue wool.

She looked up as Ms Drew ushered Cassie in. 'I do so enjoy Tim Gardiner's work, don't you?' she said, without preliminary.

'Actually, no.' The response was out before Cassie could monitor it. She felt really mean, having heard often enough from him how poor his sales figures were, and how he was going to have to go back to being a geologist if things didn't pick up very soon.

'Why not?'

'The heroine, for a start. She pretends to be a liberated woman, but she'd never solve a single crime if it wasn't for her boyfriend or whatever he is. And it's all so formulaic: the crime and the endless series of interviews with people and the domestic details of the ghastly woman's life to soften up the whole idea of brutal crime.' Cassie hadn't realised just how much she despised Gardiner's books until she got started.

'But the style: don't you enjoy that?'

'Style's fine, as long as there's some content to go with it.'

'Which detective novelists *do* you enjoy, if you don't like one of the rising young stars of the genre?'

Before Cassie could reply, Ms Drew cut in. 'For heaven's sake, Mother.' She raised her voice. 'Miss Swann didn't drive all this way to talk about crime fiction.'

'What exactly *did* you come about, my dear?' Mrs Farquharson switched from one subject to another with seamless ease. Yesterday she had sounded vague to the point of loopiness; today she was clearly on the ball. It was hard to know if she did this on a regular basis, or whether, like so many older people, she got flustered when she had to talk on the telephone.

'I'll make some tea.' Ms Drew left the conservatory while Cassie recapped the explanation she had just given. 'So I hoped that you or . . .' it was clearly redundant to mention Mr Farquharson '. . . you might be able to give me more information.'

'Such as?'

'For instance, did Mrs Haden White respond to your letter. Did she come here to talk to your husband?'

'Yes. Yes, she did.'

'How soon after you sent your letter?'

'She telephoned the same day she got it. I spoke to her and she seemed very excited indeed at the chance of talking to Michael.'

'Excited?'

'Agitated might be a better word. Or upset, perhaps. Or both. She was crying at one point, I remember. I felt very bad that whatever it was, Michael had waited all this time to help her. 'With any luck I can stop it,' she kept saying. 'I can stop it.' A nice woman, I thought. A proper lady. So often these days—'

Cassie interrupted the ramble as gently as she could. 'Would you be breaking a confidence if I asked you to tell me what exactly it was they discussed?'

'Oh dear.' Mrs Farquharson bit her lip. 'I wish I'd realised what you wanted to talk to me about when you telephoned yesterday. I was having a bad day and what you said didn't make much sense. Otherwise I would have told you that I wasn't in the room when my husband and Mrs Haden White were talking about it. I mean, when she set up her recording machine, Michael asked me to leave. He didn't want me to know about it.'

'Do you know what it concerned?'

'I have absolutely no idea.'

'And I suppose . . . your husband isn't . . .' hesitated Cassie, already sure of the answer.

'He died. Very shortly after Mrs Haden White's visit, as a matter of fact. The matter had been preying on him for years, giving him nightmares, but he would never talk about it. In fact, it was only when he realised that his illness was terminal that he decided he really must make an effort to put things right. As far as he still could, that is.'

'And you have no idea what it was about?'

'None at all.' Dorothy Farquharson smiled at Cassie. 'But whatever it was, Mrs Haden White's visit certainly made it easier for him to let go, when the time came.'

Darn it. Foiled again. 'Can you really tell me nothing about it?'

'Only that it must have been something which happened

before he met me. Because there was certainly nothing for him to have nightmares about after that. I mean, we were together all the time. I knew everything he did, and when.'

Cassie wanted to say that it was a wise wife who knew her own husband, but didn't. 'So where was he before he met you?'

'Out in Africa, in Nigeria. He was a government adviser, you see.'

'Nigeria?' At last. Nigeria wasn't Kenya, or even South Africa, but it provided a hint of connection between Lolly's past and her present. 'What was his field of speciality?'

'He was involved in the biological side of things.' Mrs Farquharson waved her hand about vaguely. Almost visibly, she began to slip away into confusion again, blurring, her outlines seeming to soften in front of Cassie's eyes, her posture drooping. 'Crops and things. You know. Yields. Fields. Circles and so forth.'

'Don't take any notice of her,' said Ms Drew impatiently, coming in with a tray. 'It's word association. She's talking about crop circles now, which is nothing to do with my father. He spent his working career abroad, setting up programmes to improve agricultural production in various Third World countries.'

'Kenya being one of them?'

'Apparently. His first posting abroad, I seem to remember him telling me once.' For a moment, she looked dourly regretful. 'You never ask your parents things, do you? And then when you finally realise what it is you want to know, it's all too late, and they're gone.' She poured tea, handed a cup to Cassie and another to her mother. 'Here you are, Mother,' she said, raising her voice. 'Now be careful. It's scalding hot.' She turned back to Cassie. 'Has she been able to help you?'

Not "my mother", but "she"' Cassie winced inwardly at the depersonalising pronoun. 'I think so. Maybe. Mrs Haden White was also in Kenya – or some part of Africa—' Cassie quickly backtracked, remembering Serena's vagueness about her mother's exact whereabouts, '—at some point in her life, and it could be that the reason behind her murder goes all the way back to then.' She made a brave stab at hiding her frustration. Apart from the single fact, it was beginning to look as if she was going to come up with absolutely nothing.

'I read about her murder in the paper,' said Ms Drew. She shuddered. 'What a dreadful way to die, outside in the cold like that. Or so the papers said.'

It was a detail which Cassie hadn't thought about until now. Ms Drew was right: the cold weather that night made Lolly's death all the more dreadful. And thinking this, another bleak thought occurred to her: the murderer had gone to her house with the express intention of killing her. Why else pursue her outside and down to the end of the garden? 'And your father never talked about anything which happened while he was there?'

'Not really. There was something called the Mau Mau, wasn't there? I gather he found himself in some fairly sticky situations at various times, and witnessed one or two atrocities. But he never ever talked about them to us. Said he preferred to forget. Said we must live in the present, not the past.'

'That's exactly what Mrs Haden White used to tell her own children.'

'Perhaps it's what all survivors say. Perhaps it's the only way to carry on living. I'm sure I've read that those who came out of the death camps after the War dealt with it by pretending it hadn't happened.'

'And I understand that fifty years down the line, those who are left are now coming out and talking about it for the first time. Perhaps it was something of the same urge which led your father to write to my friend.'

'Possibly.' Ms Drew looked thoughtful.

'The strange thing is that he should have kept Mrs Haden White's address all this time.'

'Ah, now that I can be of help with.' Mrs Farquharson swam back into focus, sat up straight again, lifted her cup and saucer and sipped at her tea. 'You see, that wasn't her name when he knew her.'

'But you addressed her as Mrs Haden White in the letter.'

'I know I did. Because we found out who she was now. Not that she wasn't the same person as she was then, of course, but he discovered what her current name was.'

'Do you know how?'

'Oddly enough, he was leafing through one of my women's magazines—'

'I can't imagine why,' Ms Drew interjected.

'—and saw an article she'd written, with a photograph. He recognised her immediately. It was more than a year before he died, wasn't it, Angela?'

'About that.'

'After that, he just went on fretting about it. Seeing her picture brought it all back, whatever it was, and he simply couldn't rest until he got it off his chest. And the only way to do that was to talk to her, do you see? Tell her that she was right all along and he shouldn't have helped to conceal the facts the way he did. Whatever they were. In the end I wrote to the magazine myself and asked them to forward a letter to her, which they obviously did.'

'What a coincidence,' Cassie said, 'to have seen her name in a magazine.'

'I know. Especially since he wasn't the sort of man who normally read such things.'

As though tired of listening to the conversation, Ms Drew got up and crabbily straightened the cushions on her mother's chair, every line of her body radiating discontent. 'It's almost time for your nap, Mother,' she said. A less than gracious hint which Cassie was more than happy to take.

'Nap? I don't want a nap,' said Dorothy Farquharson. 'I'm not in the least sleepy.'

'I'm sure you're tired after your bad day yesterday,' Ms Drew said firmly.

Did she live here, with the old lady, or did she have a home of her own? Was there still a Mr Drew? Not if he knew what was good for him. Cassie put down her teacup, realising she wasn't going to get anything else out of this meeting. Not this time around, anyway. As Ms Drew showed her to the front door, she said: 'Are you absolutely sure that your father left no papers?'

'Papers?' Ms Drew seemed to grow more forbiddingly tall.

'Concerning the matter which was bothering him before his death.'

'Quite certain.'

'And he told you nothing?'

'Nothing.' The woman's manner had grown markedly frosty, though Cassie could see no reason why it should have done.

'Never mentioned any names? Made any references to it?'

'As I said, Miss Swann, none.'

Cassie couldn't bear to let it go without another try. 'Look,' she persisted. 'If you think of anything, however slight, do please contact me again.' She handed over her business card.

Ms Drew frowned at it. 'I shan't think of anything,' she said. 'There's nothing for me to think of. Father never spoke of those times. Whatever it was, he obviously found it too painful to want to go over again.'

'But he did so at the end, didn't he? It was important enough for your mother to write to Lolly Haden White before he died.'

'Yes. But for all you know, he simply wanted to say goodbye to her.'

'We both know,' Cassie said bravely, 'that there's more to it than that.'

'Do we?'

'I'm most grateful to you both,' Cassie said, and had a hard time sounding as though she meant it. Ms Drew bared her teeth in a polite rictus and closed the front door.

So that was that, then. What had seemed a hopeful lead had turned into nothing. But more interesting was why Ms Drew, not exactly a warm person to begin with, should suddenly have started doing icicle impressions. It was after Cassie had asked if Michael Farquharson had left any papers: the negative reaction from his daughter implied that possibly he had but that she was damned if she was going to pass them on to Cassie. Was there a way to make her? Or had the woman already destroyed them and now felt guilty, because of Lolly's murder?

The damp spots of mist on her windscreen had developed into full driving rain which fell heavily from a sky the colour of cardboard. Where the roof of the car met the top of the passenger-side window, there was a damp patch: she suspected that the rust on the roof had become an expensive-to-fix leak. More outlay of funds which did not exist. 'Face it, Cassandra,' she said aloud, to the hum of the windscreen wipers, 'as a freelance bridge professional, you simply aren't hacking it.'

There was always Plan B: the catering idea. Trying not to envisage Aunt Polly's smug Didn't-I-warn-you? face, she drove home planning menus which could be easily prepared in someone else's kitchen. From which it was an easy step towards a fantasy in which one of the bachelor dons, preferably a rich one, introduced by Nightingale, would fall heavily in love with her and, forsaking all others, cleave only to her.

Fat chance.

Yet again, she wondered what could have so troubled Michael Farquharson's conscience that he could not die without sorting it out at the end. Was it logical to assume that it had something to do with Lolly's death? All along, she had known that what she ought to do was simply pass the letter on to Paul and let him take it from there. It was not only the easiest but also the best solution. And Lolly's murder had nothing to do with her, was not her business, even were she equipped to investigate it. Which she most definitely was not.

Instead of forcing her to accept these facts, she found that the indeterminate information gathered in Henley had somehow concretised her feelings and made her more than ever determined to see what she could do before she allowed the police to look deeper into Lolly's private affairs. They could be discreet when they wanted to be. But the case was likely to be widely reported nationally, when and if they found a culprit, and an absolute sensation locally. It was the latter fact which mattered more than the former. For Lolly's sake – or was it for her own? – Cassie knew that she was going to give it just a little bit longer before she acknowledged failure, and handed over to Paul Walsh.

At the junction which led westwards towards her cottage instead of onwards to Oxford, she took the latter direction. Bearded lions often turned out to be tamer than expected.

# ♦ 10 ♦

She was able to park right in front of Liz Trowbridge's house, where a dull light showed between the ill-drawn curtains of the upper bedroom. This evening, there were two bikes padlocked together in the small front garden, instead of just one. Squinting up at the house from her car, Cassie nearly drove on and went home. But there were questions she wanted the answers to, and she could not afford to lose time. The longer she held on to the letter from Dorothy Farquharson, the madder Paul Walsh was going to be when she finally handed it over. She got out, locked the door, walked up the short pathway to the front door, rang the bell. Bearded lions might sometimes be less ferocious than feared, but occasionally they were a damn sight more so.

Someone down the street was playing a saxophone with effortless grace. Did Oxford have saxophone scholars, these days, as well as organ ones? She watched a blurred figure move towards her, light from the kitchen at the back of the house showing that the head almost brushed the passage ceiling. Must be Jan. At least with her, she'd already established some sort of bona fides. The front door jerked open.

'Cassandra Swann, look you,' Jan said, when she saw who it was on the doorstep.

'That's right.'

'Had a feeling we'd see more of you. I told Liz, said you weren't the sort who'd give up easy. You'd better come in.'

'Give up?'

'After the Dragon Lady was murdered – and God knows nobody wants that for anyone, however crappily they've behaved – I knew you'd be round again asking questions.'

'There's clever for you,' said Cassie. 'Is Liz at home this time?'

'At home, but not very approachable. Not even by me.'

'So it's not just me she hates?' said Cassie, following the tall figure down the hall.

'Today, it's everyone.'

The kitchen looked even more garish under electric light, deep reds clashing with strong greens, the huge sunflowers flamboyant against the dark blues and purples, the spots and stripes and stars combining in an epileptic frenzy. Liz Trowbridge was standing by the stove, holding a spill made from a folded envelope in the flame of one of the gas jets. She scowled when she saw Cassie, and lifted the spill to the cigarette thrust between her lips. She stared inimically at Jan, her red hair giving off hostile sparks as she turned.

'It's no use you giving me the evil eye, girl,' Jan said. 'My skin's too thick. And a good thing too, when you're in one of these moods. Now say hello to the nice lady.'

Liz nodded, as she had done at Lolly's funeral. She was wearing spike heels and a very short skirt and looked nowhere near the forty-plus years that she was.

'And pour the nice lady a drink,' Jan went on. 'You're nearer the bottle than I am.'

Ungraciously, Liz found a glass – marginally cleaner than the one she'd been given last time, Cassie was glad to see – and sloshed red wine into it before bringing it over and putting it down on the table.

'Now,' Jan said, not in the least put out by her partner's childish discourtesy. 'What can we do for you?'

'It's really more your affair than mine,' said Cassie hesitantly, speaking directly to Liz. 'But I helped your sister to clear out your mother's house and—'

'She didn't dare ask me, I suppose,' snapped Liz.

'There's surprising, isn't it?' said Jan. 'The way you've been behaving lately, I hardly dare ask you to pass the marmalade. Only pure love's keeping me here.'

'OK, I'm sorry.' Liz's sour features softened a little and she half-lifted a hand in a gesture which a very generous person would assume was apologetic. She looked at Cassie and made an obvious effort. 'Go on.'

'Well, I found this.' Cassie was afraid she was risking a display of outraged temper by indicating that she had held on to the Farquharson letter.

Liz read it swiftly then again, the second time with more deliberation. 'I wonder what that was all about,' she said slowly.

'Don't think me interfering. Or, even worse, mad,' Cassie said. 'But I think it might have something to do with why your mother was murdered. So I'm here to ask if you know anything at all which might conceivably have some bearing on this.'

Liz frowned, thinking about it, her hand tugging at a lock of her auburn hair.

'I know she told you almost nothing about the past,' Cassie continued. 'Lied about your grandparents, perhaps even about your father—'

'*What*?' Liz's eyebrows met ferociously across her freckled nose. 'Lied? What do you mean?'

'I'm sorry. Perhaps I shouldn't have said that.'

'But you did say it. Why?'

'Because when your sister first told me, I couldn't believe – still can't – that all four of your grandparents would have died when you were just children. And your father as well. That's an awful lot of deaths in one family.'

'I always thought that, luv,' Jan said, in her warm Welsh voice. 'It doesn't make sense. One or two of them might have, but not all four.'

'Five,' said Cassie.

'Right. I forgot. Five. There was the da' as well.'

Liz Trowbridge sank down onto one of the bright-painted wooden chairs and clutched at her neck. The gesture was more poignant than melodramatic. 'I always wondered,' she said hoarsely. 'Always wondered why we were different from everyone else, why there wasn't any family. No cousins or aunts or grannies, none of that. She just said they'd died. In a plane crash, she said. I asked her once. I said, all of them in the same plane? And she said Yes, that's right. I knew it was odd. And I can see now that you're right. She was lying. She must have been.'

'Some of them, maybe,' Jan said softly. 'But surely not all.'

'Was she running away from something?' asked Cassie. 'Or hiding? She went to such lengths to destroy the past that it must have stemmed from something more than just a desire to forget.'

'Was it this?' Liz tapped the Farquharson letter, which she still held.

'It seems possible. It looks as though she wanted to publicise whatever it was but got no joy from people like Michael Farquharson. Perhaps she was being threatened over it. Perhaps, because she'd got you and your sister to look after, she decided the best thing would be to drop out of sight, and simply start again from the beginning with a new identity. Her very own witness-protection scheme.'

'There's a scenario for you,' said Jan.

'It would explain things to a certain extent,' Liz said slowly.

'Who's got the power to bring that much pressure to bear on an individual?'

The three women stared at each other. 'A government?' said Cassie.

'A white supremacist government?' said Jan. 'Remember how Harold Wilson was so paranoid about BOSS?' She smiled kindly at the younger Cassie. 'The South African Bureau Of State Security. Wilson was convinced they were out to get him.'

'You think something similar might have happened to Lolly?'

'I've no idea,' said Liz. 'It doesn't seem to tie in with what I knew of my mother. On the other hand, she could be amazingly strong, almost ruthless, when she wanted to be.'

'Kind of hard on the rest of the family, though, if she felt it necessary to cut herself off completely from them,' Jan said.

'How do we find out any of this? How can we prove it?' said Cassie.

'There may be nothing to prove,' said Jan. 'Best give it to the police. Fascist pigs or not, they've got the organisation to cover the investigation of this sort of thing.'

'Except,' said Cassie stubbornly, 'there was something more to it, something she didn't want people to know. And I don't believe it was necessarily because she was afraid. It was because she was ashamed.'

Liz was frowning again. 'Do you seriously think there's a chance my father is still alive? I'd give absolutely anything to . . .'

'Get real, girl,' Jan said. 'How can either of us possibly answer a question like that?'

'No, but *do* you?'

'Anything's possible.'

'We could find out,' said Cassie. 'There must be papers. Wedding certificates. Your birth certificate. Don't they have to give the father's name? When you got married, you must have had to produce a birth certificate. Wouldn't that say where she came from, who her family was?'

'Yeah,' said Liz, thinking back. 'There was some trouble about the birth certificates, I remember now. Both for me and for Serena. Was it something to do with being born out in Africa? Had they been destroyed in a fire? I can't remember. She had to apply for new ones for us both.'

'Didn't they give your father's name?'

'Is it possible that they didn't?' Thinking back to things she had tried to forget, or possibly never known, Liz's forehead wrinkled like rhinoceros skin. 'I was rather dozy in those days or I'd never have got married in the first place, let alone to Larry. Could she possibly have put down "father unknown" on it? I'll look it out tomorrow and let you know.'

'Wouldn't you have questioned her about not knowing who your father was?' asked Jan, disbelievingly.

'We'd been conditioned not to ask questions for so many years . . . you can't imagine how little you query when you're repeatedly put off.'

'Serena thought your father was a high-powered business man,' said Cassie.

'No. Definitely not. Something . . . arty. That's all I can

come up with. I remember that sometimes he was away working.' Liz shrugged defeatedly. 'But maybe none of it's true. Maybe everything she ever told us was a lie.'

'What about your early years. Were you really out in Africa or is that something else she made up?'

'I think we must have been. I remember a black butler in a white jacket. And a nurse who used to cuddle me. The house was always dim, with the windows shaded, but there was this blazing light outside, and huge blossoms everywhere. But there was all sorts of tension all the time. I remember it . . . the feel of it. The air thick with it.' The lines on her face began to smooth out as she gazed past the present to a time forty years ago when she was still a little girl and her troubled middle-age was then as distant as a star.

'What about your father? Any memories of him?'

'Just a presence. I remember my sister lying in a crib and me staring down at her, and my parents – I suppose it was them – shouting somewhere behind me. I thought it was probably because of Serena. My mother, yes, I remember her shouting that it was disgusting and shameful. I thought she meant the baby.'

'Perhaps he'd got her pregnant again already.'

'You've never told me any of this, girl,' said Jan.

'I haven't thought of it for years and years.'

'What happened after that?' asked Cassie.

'Living in England, I think. We came on a plane, my mother and the baby and me. I think we lived in a London flat for a while. I remember going to school or a playgroup. And my mother always writing things: letters, mostly, talking on the phone, trying to make people do something for her. And she cried a lot. And then we came to Larton Easewood. After that, things were much simpler. We went away to school, to university, got married, got—'

'—unmarried,' said Jan. She reached over the table and took Liz's hand in hers.

'It's perfectly possible that her name wasn't even Haden White,' said Cassie.

Liz thought about it. 'We've been Haden White as long as I can remember. Except . . . it was something slightly different when I was really small.' She gave a half-smile. 'Remember how almost the first thing you learn is your name? I used to spend a lot of time with the servants, whenever Mother was away, and I remember standing looking up at them saying over and over again: 'My name is Elizabeth Angharad White.'

'I hadn't realised we had Welshness in common,' Jan said.

'I was called after my grandmother, apparently.'

'If your surname was White,' said Cassie, 'that would mean that your father was called White, wouldn't it?'

'You'd think so. Except I'm beginning to realise that almost nothing in my life was what it appeared to be.'

'You implied that your mother went away quite a lot.'

'Yes. She did. Working for her newspapers.'

'And your father, too?'

'Yes. Until he went away for good. Which must have been shortly after Serena was born.'

'Did Lolly ever let her guard slip? Ever say anything, however insignificant it might have seemed, about the past, what she did before she had you?'

'Never.'

'Not once?'

Liz screwed her face up into an ugly contortion of wrinkles. 'She was a straight newspaper reporter at some point. And then a feature writer. She also acted as a local stringer for one of the South African dailies. The *Johannesburg Star*, would it have been? Some quite big paper. And Reuters came into it somewhere, I'm sure. I don't know how I knew that – maybe I just made it up. But I definitely have these vague impressions.'

'That could be helpful. This was presumably before she started working for the fashion magazine.'

'That was in England. I do remember, when I was still quite young and we were living in London, that she was always drawing women in dresses, like the ones you get on the front of dress patterns, thin and elongated. She used to give me crayons and paper and I'd draw ladies in frocks too. Was she designing the patterns, or writing copy for articles? I honestly don't remember. If I ever knew.'

Cassie looked again at the letter. 'What did she tell you about your father?'

'Nothing.'

'Didn't you ever ask?'

'We asked, all right. Both of us. But she just shut us up. She had this way of lifting her eyebrow which made you want to get the hell out of there. She was pretty intimidating in those days.'

'So what changed?' Jan said drily.

'But when you were older,' said Cassie, 'didn't you ask more forcefully?'

'*I* did. Over and over again. Told her it wasn't fair, that she had no right. Serena just gave up. She did tell me that my father was a failed whatever it was he was.'

'You thought he was something arty,' said Jan. 'Do you mean a ballet dancer? A writer? A calligrapher? A painter? Maybe that's why you took up with me, because I'm one too.'

'I told you: I don't know.' Liz stood up on her spike heels and moved restlessly about the kitchen. 'It's all so many years ago and she just put up a stone wall to any of those questions. But if I find out that all along I had grandparents, I shall be . . . oh *God*, I'll be angry.'

'Let alone a father.'

'Yes. Especially that.'

'If she *did* lie, maybe your father's still alive,' Cassie said. 'And if he is, then we ought to be able to find him.'

'Even if he's still a failure,' said Jan.

'I don't care about that,' Liz said. 'I really don't.' Tears came into her eyes. 'If I discovered that all these years, she's deprived me of . . . of . . .'

It did seem monstrously cruel, if it were true. 'I have no basis for thinking that she did,' Cassie put in hastily. 'It just seemed too much to believe that he too was dead. You know?'

'I know.'

'Somewhere,' Cassie said, 'there must be papers. There have to be. Even your mother couldn't have hidden everything. These days, human beings can't exist without documentation. So where are they? Does she have a safety deposit box? And if so, where's the key? Or did she have some close friend who kept them safe for her, and if so, where's the friend? I mean somewhere, there must be documents. Perhaps she also left an account of this incident or whatever it is which Michael Farquharson was involved with.'

'And this letter . . .' Jan pulled the blue pages towards her, '. . . the wife says here that he's willing to help prove whatever it was; he must have had something which could be helpful. So might your mother have had.'

'I went to see his widow this afternoon,' Cassie said. She

explained the results of her visit. 'But I know that woman was concealing something. She got very shirty indeed when I suggested that her father might have left anything which could be useful. But if it was some old scandal he was going to help your mother reveal, he couldn't have been much help unless he had proof, could he?'

'Same goes for the Dragon Lady,' said Jan. She caught Cassie's eye and said: 'Just because she's been murdered, I'm not going to go all soft and gooey about her. She behaved shittily to Liz and me and that's all there is to it.'

'Why don't you stay to supper?' Liz said suddenly.

'That would be great.' Cassie envisaged some rib-sticking stew, with a crock of boiled potatoes glistening with butter, home-baked rolls, perhaps. A big salad.

'We're only having pasta pesto,' Liz continued, 'but we'd be glad to have you.'

Cassie tried not to groan. She was prepared to bet that the pesto would come out of a jar. 'How very kind,' she said. At least someone else would be paying for the pasta. 'I'd love to stay.'

Back home at Honeysuckle Cottage, she sat down with a pen and some paper and wrote down what she had actually discovered about Lolly Haden White.

*Africa, probably Kenya.*
*Husband 'something arty'.*
*Straight news reporter*
*and fashion journalist?*
*Scandal*

The list was pitifully short. At the moment, the best lead

seemed to be the husband. Dead or alive.

Or Michael Farquharson. If she was right and somewhere he had left documentary evidence of whatever it was, she ought somehow to contrive to get her hands on it quickly, before the dour Ms Drew destroyed it. If she hadn't already done so.

Another thought came to her. Farquharson's obituary. With an OBE to his name, he might have been considered worthy enough to have merited one in the national papers, but if not, the local rag would certainly have written him up. It might help to establish what his link with Lolly had been. She'd check that tomorrow.

Lolly, too, must somewhere have concealed her own papers. It was simply a question of finding out where they were. Using the Trowbridge/Thomas telephone, she had rung Serena from Oxford to ask if there had been any keys on Lolly's chain which were unaccounted for, but Serena had said there were not. Those for her car, her house, front and back doors were there: that was all.

Cassie went to bed but could not sleep. Working on the presumption that there were papers, then it seemed likely that there were at least two possibilities. The first, that there was indeed a safety deposit box somewhere, in which case they were simply looking for a key. The second, that the box itself – or container of some kind – was hidden somewhere in Lolly's house. Given Lolly's nature, Cassie felt sure that she would keep her proof, her documents, near at hand, rather than in some anonymous storage vault where they would not be under her control. If so, where might that be?

In her mind's eye, she walked through the rooms of Lolly's house again. Between them, Serena and she had effectively got rid of almost every piece of paper there, and they had both scrutinised those which Serena had taken away. So nothing there. The box – if it existed – was disguised or hidden among the ordinary objects still left in the house. Would the efficient Lolly have made contingency plans for what might happen if she were taken ill or, as had so tragically occurred, died? Or had she not thought that far ahead? And if she had, what would she want to happen to her story if she died: did she simply hope that it would die with her, or did she still want it told?

And why the hell did it matter so much? Given what she had learned from Liz, Lolly's so-called strength of character was beginning to degenerate into Gestapo-like cruelty. She appeared to have ditched a husband, kept two daughters entirely ignorant of their background and family ties, lied over and over again. Nothing – certainly not some old scandal – could be worth causing the kind of distress Liz Trowbridge had demonstrated at the faint possibility that there was a family out there whom she had never been allowed to know. Even, perhaps, a father. Lolly was proving to be an unlikable character.

And yet it was impossible not to admire her indomitability. She had not allowed circumstances to beat her down, until that final fatal blow. Cassie pulled the covers restlessly about. It would be so much easier if she had some inkling of what the matter concerned. It was as though all the traces were being carefully wiped away, like chalk on a blackboard. She frowned up at the ceiling: Dorothy Farquharson had spoken of Lolly's tape recorder: where was that? She had certainly not seen one during her exploration of Lolly's drawers and shelves. Had Serena?

She sat up, excited now. Could it be that Serena had simply packed the machine in with other objects she didn't wish to leave in the house? If so, the tape might still be in the machine. She glanced at her clock. The digital figures told her it was seven minutes past one: far too late to telephone the Smith household. It would have to wait until the morning.

She spent the rest of the night alternately dozing and imagining some punk ignoring the Neighbourhood Watch stickers to break into Serena's neat house in order to steal whatever resaleable objects he could find, including the tape recorder. Assuming Serena had it.

She did. At seven o'clock the following morning, Cassie was ringing her doorbell. Scarcely bothering to apologise for the earliness of the call, she said to a dressing-gowned Serena: 'Did you by any chance find a tape recorder among your mother's things?'

'One of those tiny hand-held ones. Yes, I did, actually.' Serena pulled at the belt of her robe and shivered. 'Come in, Cassie, for goodness sake, before the heat goes.'

In the kitchen, two teenagers were eating toast and marmalade. Both of them wore headphones and swayed to invisible music as they ate. Recognising her, the older of them made a half-hearted attempt to rise to his feet but Cassie put a hand on his shoulder and pressed him back down. The younger simply stared, his mouth open to display a complicated structure of wire and steel attached to his teeth.

'I've told you before,' his mother shouted, competing with whatever was pounding his brain to pulp, 'you shouldn't put your brace on until you've had breakfast. Now you'll have to go upstairs and take it off and clean it again before you go to school.'

She turned back to Cassie. 'Bringing up two boys with a husband who's away most of the time isn't easy, believe me. And when he's home, he tends to spoil them more than he should. Which I can't blame him for really, since he sees so little of them, but it does make it more difficult when he goes away again. Still, I suppose they're—'

'The tape recorder,' Cassie said. 'Where is it?'

'In one of the boxes we brought back from Mother's house.'

'Is there a tape in it?'

'I don't know. I didn't—'

'Can I look?'

'All the boxes are stashed out in the garage.' It finally dawned on Serena that Cassie was excited about something. 'Why do you want it?'

The elder boy took his headphones off. 'You talking about Gran's recorder?' he said.

'That's right.'

'But . . .' He faltered as Cassie turned a cold eye on him. 'Don't you remember, Mum? I asked if I could have it?'

Cassie's high hopes were fading rapidly.

'Did you?' Serena asked vaguely.

'Yeah. And you said I could so I took it.'

'Where to?' rapped out Cassie, feeling for the first time in her life some sympathy with the KGB interrogators.

'School.'

'Why?'

'I wanted to record old Chilly Bum—'

'I presume you mean Mr Chillington,' said Cassie, who, thanks to her supply teaching at the local comprehensive and the fact that he played bridge, knew the headmaster quite well.

'Yeah – doing his nut in Assembly.'

'Is that all, Nick?' his mother asked sharply, sensing something under his bravado.

'No,' Cassie said. 'No. You didn't.'

'Didn't what?' His face assumed a mixture of unease and embarrassment. He twisted in his chair.

'You didn't record over the tape already in there, did you?'

'What else,' his mother said accusingly. 'What else were you recording?'

'Just a few things.' Nick glanced at Cassie and then back to his mother, as though wondering which of them was going to be the less dangerous to deal with.

'What things?' demanded his mother.

'A sexy chat line, I should think,' Cassie said. She might not be a mother but her stints with the education system had taught her all she ever needed to know about adolescents.

'Chat lines?'

'Miss Payne, is it?' Cassie said, addressing Nick. 'Bottom marks given to naughty boys sort of thing?'

'*What*?' His mother's voice was thick with outrage. 'If that's what you've been up to, my lad, I'll belt you and no mistake. And so will your dad, next time he's home.'

'If he's recorded over that tape, don't bother his father, I'll belt him myself,' said Cassie. 'Hard.' She glared at the squirming boy. 'You could be impeding a murder investigation.' Too late she remembered that it was his own grandmother who had been killed.

Nick's eyes watered. 'I didn't know, did I?'

'No, you didn't. And if you put in a fresh tape, it doesn't matter. Did you?'

He kept a wary eye on his mother. 'Yes. We went over to Danny's house and—'

'Where's the old tape, the one that was already in the machine?'

'In my desk at school.'

'Sex lines!' said his mother. 'But you're only fifteen.'

'You're sure it's in your desk?' Cassie said.

'Yes.'

'And you didn't record over it?'

'No. I thought Mum might ask about it and I was going to just put it back in if she did.'

'Very sensible,' said Cassie. 'Look.' She turned to Serena, whose expression was fairly indicative of one in the grip of agitated incredulity. 'If it's all right with you, Serena—'

'Chat lines, indeed. I'll give him sexy chat lines.'

'—I'll drive Nick to school . . .' Catching sight of the boy's agonised look, she amended her words. '. . . I'll wait for him at the school gates, and Nick, you go in as soon as the school bus drops you off and bring it out to me. All right?'

'Yeah.'

'You do that and I'm sure your mum will forget about the other thing.' She glanced at Serena's furious face and hoped she had enough powers of persuasion to make this promise come true.

She sat outside the school for nearly twenty minutes before Nick Smith's school bus arrived. Because she did not want to waste gas, she had switched off the engine and by the time the bus showed up, she was halfway through the metamorphosis from woman to iceberg. He glanced over at her car and she managed to raise one frozen arm and give him a thumbs-up sign. Thank God some atavistic sense of survival had prompted the lad to switch the tape in the recorder for a fresh one before dialling Miss Payne or her colleagues. With any luck, she would have a complete recording of the interview which had taken place between Lolly and Farquharson, and a number of things would be made plain. Including, perhaps, the reason behind Lolly's murder. She wondered whether Serena would so willingly have allowed her to appropriate the tape if she had not been completely distracted by evidence of her child's burgeoning – or, for all Cassie knew, already burgeoned – sexuality.

Ms Angela Drew was perfectly right. Cassie was willing to concede that her behaviour was not only high-handed but could be construed as obstructing the police in the performance of their duties. She figured that as far as they were concerned, another hour or so before they got the tape wasn't going to make any difference to their murder enquiry. If she decided to hand it over at all, that is.

She saw Nick appear at the school gates, pause for a moment to speak to another boy, and then come hurrying over to her car.

'You're sure that's the right tape,' she said, rolling down the window and taking the recorder from him.

'I think so.' He cast an uneasy glance over his shoulder, in case any of his friends caught him talking to a woman who wasn't his mother.

'Let's just check it out, shall we?' Cassie pressed the button and a panting voice said:

'My legs are open, they're ... mmmh ... wide open, I'm touching myself now ... mmm ... can you imagine how excited I am, oh God, all wet and glist—

Nick blushed fiercely. 'Must've got the wrong tape,' he mumbled.

'Then bloody well go and get the right one,' said Cassie. 'I'll hang on to this one until you come back.'

'For fuck's sake,' Nick said under his breath, too quietly for Cassie to accuse him of swearing in front of her but loudly enough for her to hear. He chased off again. It was another ten minutes before he reappeared, by which time

Cassie's right leg had gone completely numb with cold, and her teeth were beginning to clatter together like a frozen xylophone.

Nick handed her another tape and she put it into the recorder and pressed the button again. This time she heard the unmistakable sound of Lolly's voice saying, through tinny static: '. . . but it was after that, wasn't it?'

It was enough. 'OK. That's the one,' Cassie said. 'Thanks.' She started to roll up the window.

'Hey. What about the other tape? Can I have it back?'

'Certainly not, you frightful little beast.'

'You're not . . .' His face went white. 'You're not going to give it to Mum, are you?'

'I might.'

'If you do, I'll kill myself.'

'In that case, I'd better just give her back the recorder when I've finished, and keep the tape.'

Relieved, he stepped back from the car window. 'Going to listen to it yourself, are you?'

'Cheeky devil,' Cassie said. She made as if to open the door and come after him and he sprinted away from her, grinning over his shoulder.

The recorder lay on the passenger seat like a bomb. Once she had played it, she would be on the other side of mystery. Once knowledge has been granted, it is not possible to give it back, to resume ignorance. Certain matters would have been revealed and she would have to act upon them.

The sound of Lolly's voice, however brief, had also unnerved her. She was dead now: why not let her rest in peace? Whether or not the police found her killer was, to a certain extent, immaterial. Nothing would bring her back. She thought of Lolly in her Chanel-style suits of rich tweed, her silk blouses and immaculate shoes. She remembered the fur coats, once, presumably, worn with élan and then, when the wearing of animal fur became unacceptable, zipped into plastic bags and left to await rehabilitation. Cassie still had Gran's old fur, though for different reasons. It smelled nasty, particularly if the wearer became too warm, when the smell clung like bindweed. There had been occasions when Cassie had attended functions in what was definitely an aura of eau de goat's bottom, rather than the expensive French pong which Robin kept her supplied with. But Lolly's furs had been altogether higher quality: one was mink, the other fox. She tried to imagine Lolly in Gran's poor old musquash, and failed.

At home, she held the recorder in her hand for a while. What secret was going to be revealed. Nerving herself, she finally rewound the tape and set it to play.

Some electronic crackling. A cough which sounded as though it came from the roof of the Farquharson house rather than in the room. A couple of bumps. Then Lolly's voice. She was – had been – a professional journalist: she knew how to handle the machinery of her trade, so both voices were for the most part perfectly audible if not always completely clear. Listening, Cassie found herself reliving events which had taken place over thirty years ago but which still had the power to cast a cold shadow across her heart. What the two voices said to each did not always make perfect sense to her: they were talking about events with which both were familiar and were able to use conversational shorthand rather than exposition. Nonetheless, Cassie thought she could piece together enough of the story to understand why Farquharson could not die at ease until he had made some attempt to put things right, why Lolly should have gone to Henley as soon as possible after receiving his letter, why she should have felt bitter about the fact that no-one showed any interest in the results of the bizarre and ugly bargaining to which she was a witness. How either of them thought that anything could be done at this stage it was difficult to imagine. There were maddening gaps in the story, of course. Both protagonists were old and, in one case, failing. They mumbled, forgot things, talked over or contradicted each other, repeated themselves. In spite of this, enough of the essential story came through for Cassie to put together a complete narrative.

Was it evidence? Was the tape conclusive or informative enough to prove anything? Could anything be done about it now? More importantly, did those silent unreported screams of long ago lead inexorably to Lolly's death? Cassie didn't know. There were few names on the tape, and those there were were unfamiliar and unsubstantiated. While Farquharson unburdened himself of long-held shame, Lolly kept saying that it didn't matter if he couldn't remember exactly, she had everything written down, all she needed was for him to corroborate the facts.

Which he did.

The only problem was that there weren't nearly enough of them for Cassie.

# ♥ 11 ♥

Cassie spent the afternoon packing and dispatching. Over the last few days, Bridge The Gap had been experiencing a miniboom as the Christmas season approached. Deliberately she kept her mind blank, concentrating on parcel tape, address labels, invoices and order forms. Somewhere deep down, below the level of the here-and-now, she was aware that her unconscious mind would be working on Lolly's story, refining it, elaborating it. She knew, too, that when she next came to pull it out and expose it, nothing would have changed. It would remain what it had been when she first listened to it: a horrifying tale of expediency and betrayal.

Pulling out into the lane, she drove to the Post Office in Bellington to send off her parcels. The queues were long: people were stocking up on stamps or sending presents to far-flung places. Cassie found herself stuck behind an old lady in a coat which smelled of mothballs, who was sending dozens of cards to relatives on the other side of the world, each one needing to be separately weighed and stamped. She tried to be tolerant but failed. By the time the grandson in Sierra Leone and his cousin in Papua, New Guinea, the granddaughters in Auckland, the five great-grandchildren in Toronto and the daughter in Osaka had been processed and there were still another dozen of cards to be dealt with, Cassie was beginning to sigh and tut, inaudibly at first and then less so. The old lady took no notice, continuing to dole out her envelopes to the postmistress one by one.

The result was that darkness had already fallen by the time Cassie was ready to set out for home again. Passing through Frith, she saw lights on in the Dower House and, on impulse, pulled up at the front door. As she rang the bell, she asked herself what she thought she was doing. From past experience, she knew that most encounters with Charlie Quartermain were liable to irritate, if not thoroughly enrage her. And there was the humiliating memory of their last meeting still flushing through her brain like a defective toilet system. But however annoying or embarrassing it might be to see him again, anything was better than going back to the cottage and facing the story which waited for her inside the tiny amplifier of Lolly's hand-held recorder.

Hearing footsteps on the other side of the heavy oak door, she braced herself for a dose of over-the-top ebullience.

''Ello, darlin',' Charlie bellowed, opening the door. Before she could take evasive action, he had swept her off the ground as though she were carved from polystyrene and was holding her against his massive chest in a boob-crushing hug.

'Put me down, Charlie.' Did he not remember bursting in on her and Paul Walsh, about to engage in carnal knowledge of each other?

'How're you doing, girl?'

'I can't bloody *breathe*.'

'What?' He squeezed her even tighter and buried his big face in her hair. 'Gawd, you smell good.'

'Get off.' Ineffectually, she brushed at him. 'You're suffocating me, for chrissake. Let me go.'

After planting a sloppy kiss on her face, he did so. 'Dad's in the lounge,' he said. He beamed at her, but, with a pang which cut across her heart like a lightning flash, she could see that he had by no means forgotten the circumstances of the last time he had seen her.

Well, it wasn't her fault. If he insisted on bursting into people's houses without warning, what else could he expect? Seeing her sour expression, he put a giant finger to his mouth in a parody of contrition. 'Oops. Pardon my French. Shouldn't say lounge, should I? S'pose I've got to get used to calling it the drawing room.'

'What does it matter?' lied Cassie. God, she was *such* a snob. 'It's the same room, whatever you call it.' Surreptitiously she rubbed at the wet mark on her cheek where his lips had touched it, as he led the way into the room.

Ted Quartermain was sitting in front of a blazing fire of logs. 'Hello, Cass,' he said, getting to his feet and giving her a nod. 'This is a bit of all right, isn't it?'

'It certainly is.' Since her previous visit, heavy curtains had been hung from brass rods, the broad oak planks had been polished to a rich gleam. A large oriental rug was complemented by several smaller ones. The overall effect was one of elegance and comfort. For a moment, Cassie felt a pang of envy. More than envy: the certain knowledge that if she wanted, all this could be hers. But before the thought could become more than fleeting, she remembered that there was a serpent in this Eden. A large serpent, uncouth, hairy, big-bellied. She shuddered inwardly. Fancy reaching up to pick an apple to find Charlie grinning down from the branch on which it hung, offering all kinds of temptations. Freedom from penury, for one. Ownership of this beautiful house. A fridge full of food. A terrific sex-life . . . her smile wavered.

The sooner she wiped that disgraceful episode from her mind, the better. It had been once-in-a-lifetime, never-to-be-repeated, out-of-the-ordinary. It would not happen again. Ever.

'Drink, Cass?' Charlie asked.

'Gin and tonic would be great,' she said, unwisely giving him the full hundred-watt gaze to make up for the treachery of her thoughts.

'Cassie,' he said, his voice rough with an emotion she wished he didn't feel. He took a step towards her then glanced over at Ted, who was watching them both with an interest which made no bones about being prurient. He cleared his throat. 'Ice and slice with it?'

'Yes, please,' she said, trying not to wince.

When he'd gone, Ted leaned his big body towards her. He shifted his teeth about inside his mouth like a wad of tobacco and said: 'My boy's hard, Cass.'

She stared at him in astonishment, thinking for a wild moment that this was an announcement of sexual arousal. 'What?'

'Hard,' repeated Ted. 'I brought him up that way because softies get stamped on.'

'Do they?' This probably wasn't the time or place to point out that according to the Quartermain mythology, as reported by Charlie, Ted had been Down Under, shagging everything that moved, rather than rearing his offspring.

Ted reached for her hand but was too far away to get hold of it. 'Don't stamp on him, Cass.'

'If only he wouldn't always—'

'He'd kill for you.'

'But I don't want him to,' said Cassie. Had Charlie been coaching Ted in this line of sentimental twaddle on the off-chance that some time he'd get the opportunity to come out with it? 'There's enough violence in the world already, without Charlie adding to it.'

'I'm an old man, but I'd give my left nut to see my boy happily settled before I pass on to a better life than this,' Ted said piously, raising his eyes heavenward.

It didn't seem like much of a bargain. Before Cassie could say so, she heard the tinkling of glasses outside in the hall. 'I know he's not been educated like wot you have,' began Ted, as his son came back into the room. 'But—'

'That's me,' said Charlie cheerfully. 'The School of Hard Knocks, followed by the University of Life.'

'I'll tell you one thing,' Cassie said.

'What's that, then?' He handed her a heavy tumbler with ice-cubes banging gently against its sides.

'You didn't get your degree in originality.'

'Kill for you, he would,' said Ted, in a heart-rending quaver.

'I'll bloody start with you, Dad, if you carry on like that.' Charlie slopped his drink down the front of his shirt as he made an expansive gesture. 'But he's right: give me a mountain and I'll climb it for you, Cass. Give me an ocean and I'll swim it for you.'

'If I ever find myself in possession of either, I'll be straight round.'

'Lovely way of speaking,' said Ted. 'Hasn't she, son?'

'For God's sake,' exclaimed Cassie. 'If you two don't stop it, I'm leaving.' Somewhere deep inside her head, she heard Lolly's voice again, describing murder and bloodshed, cruelties beyond comprehension. 'Tell me,' she said in desperation, 'about the Christmas thing – pageant or whatever.'

'Extravaganza, if you don't mind. That Craufurd fellow's

definitely coming. In fact, he said he'd come down beforehand, have a quick run through with his mate Ken. They thought they'd do "Underneath the Arches", give the old dears a treat, Flanagan and Allan in fur coats. If we can find any.'

'You could borrow my Gran's old one.'

'Could we? That's nice.'

'And if that's no good, I know where I might be able to get a couple of others,' Cassie heard herself saying, before she could stop herself. Because there were Lolly's coats, as well, if Serena would be willing to lend them. Gran's would be big enough for Craufurd, and one of Lolly's might do for the other man, whom she vaguely remembered as a little old fellow who looked as if he was descended from a long line of capuchin monkeys.

'Mega,' said Charlie.

'How's the "Daisy, Daisy", number going?'

'Phwooar!' said Charlie. 'Them Sixth Formers from the school don't half look a treat. Wouldn't say no to a look inside *their* bloomers, I can tell you.'

'Oh, God,' said Cassie, rising from her seat. 'Do you always have to be so incredibly sexist and vulgar?'

'Does the Pope shit in the woods?'

'What?' Even for Charlie this was obscure.

'Don't go,' Charlie said. 'Please.'

'Watch it, then.'

'Did I tell you Madonna turned us down?'

'I was afraid she might.'

'Thought I'd ask Demi Moore instead.'

'Might have more luck there, Charlie.'

'Tell her about the other chappie,' said Ted. 'The Yank.'

'Oh yer, there's that Scott Lyall.'

'Scott Lyall?'

'Turns out he's going to be in London during that week and he's promised to come down, lend a hand.'

'Do you mean *the* Scott Lyall? The film-star?'

'That's the one.'

'How in the world did you manage to get him to come?'

'Bit of luck, really. Turns out he's a college friend of that Yank who's taken over Kathryn's scholarship. Quinn Macfarlane. So when Quinn heard about it, he give Scott a bell in the States and asked him.'

'And he said he would?' asked Cassie.

'Just like that.'

Cassie looked at him admiringly, wishing she could stop feeling that she had done him wrong. 'You really are amazing, Charlie.'

'Yer, well . . .'

'Think of the publicity. I should think you'd make enough money to refurbish not just Chadwell Court, but all the other residential homes in the Cotswolds as well.'

It was late by the time she got home. Despite residual embarrassment, she had accepted Quartermain's invitation to stay for supper, even though it meant that the two of them had cooked it together, moving about the kitchen in an awkwardly cosy intimacy which she was not anxious to cultivate. After the expansive warmth of the Dower House, Honeysuckle Cottage seemed small and cramped. It was also extremely cold, since part of her economy drive meant that she kept the central heating turned off for the greater part of the day. Shivering, she moved the philodendron which was cashing in its chips on the hearth, lit a fire, poured herself a large brandy and then looked at the tape recorder which lay on an arm on the sofa. For most of the day she had tried to put it out of her mind. Now, she could no longer avoid thinking about what had happened on an African afternoon years ago, when seven people had lived, and twenty-seven had dreadfully died. Even with the imaginative leaps she had been forced to make in order to fill in some of the blanks, even granted that some parts of the story could only be pure speculation, all too clearly she had been able to piece together from the conversation between Lolly and Michael Farquharson a story which still resonated with horror . . .

. . .It was early evening when the call came. 'You've been bitching about wanting to do a man's job,' came the hostile voice of her editor. 'Well: you've got your chance.'

Twelve hours later, Lolly was in a hotel in the eastern region of Nigeria. Her editor on the Nairobi paper for which she worked wanted her to cover a massacre by one of the warring sides in what was a sudden flare-up before the disastrous civil war that later ensued as Biafra tried to proclaim its independence. She had flown to Lagos, then made her way to a small town whose name she couldn't even determine exactly. She knew she had only been given this opportunity to prove herself because the war correspondent of her newspaper had been taken ill, his deputy had broken a leg and there was no one else to call on. Normally sidelined into Women's Issues, whether they were fashion or cooking, or human interest stories, she had suddenly found herself plunged into covering an event which was to shock the world. And, more importantly, into finding a way to put a new twist on it since, through no fault of her own, she was the last reporter to arrive.

She was determined to do well, despite the appalling

conditions. Communications were difficult: the telephone system was out of order for most of the time and all the local drivers had already been bribed by the other representatives of the press to take them to the site of the slaughter. Standing irresolute outside her hotel in the stifling heat of early afternoon, she caught sight of a boy on a cart. She shouted, ran after him. She showed him money. She pointed in the direction she believed the massacre had taken place, found herself miming, horribly, people being killed, people dead. His eyes filled as he nodded and indicated that she take her place beside him. He flicked the reins across the haunches of an ancient donkey, which set off at tortoise speed. Twenty-two miles outside the town, her editor had said. At this rate, they wouldn't be there until well after dark and by then, all the other reporters would have filed their stories and be sitting back in the hotel bar. He'd done it deliberately, sent her off on this wild-goose chase, just to show her she wasn't up to it. Nonetheless, now that she was here, she was determined she would give him a story which would make him take her seriously.

The boy veered off the road and headed into the bush. He wailed in what she assumed was sorrow for the horrors she would eventually have to face, and from his wail came the beginnings of her story. She could feel it forming inside her head, a tough story, but a compassionate one, the sort that only a woman could have written. A prize-winning story. The afternoon advanced, in a haze of sun, flies, the stink of something rotten carried on the wind, the jerk of the cart as the donkey plodded through dry soil, the soft harsh cries of the boy.

Sooner than she expected, she could make out roofs ahead, a white wall, some thorny green bushes. She heard a noise like a choir humming. Ahead, on the reddish earth, she saw the first body. It was a woman, lying face up, legs spread, blood dried between them. Her belly had been slit from throat to crotch and her internal organs pulled out to lie in dark dry strings across her torso. The woman had no arms, and only half a head; the rest of it lay nearby, under a thick coating of black flies. Lolly gagged, put a hand on the boy's arm, indicated that they must stop. She got down and stumbled away to throw up, pressing a hand against her chest, unable to block out the image though her eyes were closed. This was the test; she mustn't fail it. She took out her camera and photographed the body, the pieces, while the boy sat on the cart, staring off into the distance. When she was ready, she climbed up beside him and they set off once more. As the white building came nearer, she realised that it was some kind of mission-house: there was a stocky bell-tower showing above the walls, and the roofs of a number of low buildings.

By then, they had passed other bodies: mostly women and children, but a few men as well. Their limbs were bloated, mutilated. It was clear that most of them had died horribly, tortured, raped, then hacked to death. The boy had jumped down at one point, to stand beside the corpse of a girl of about twelve. Lolly could not bring herself to take note of what had been done to the child, but as the boy knelt beside the body, beating his chest, sobbing, she took photographs, her throat thick with nausea. She understood this must be part of his family, his sister perhaps, his cousin. Also, that this was not the first time he had seen her dead body. By now, she had realised that he had not taken her to the killing fields where the other reporters were gathered. This must be a smaller local massacre, and she was the only person here to record it. She knew then that her editor had been right all along: she couldn't handle this horror.

They reached the open gate of the mission. All round it were more bodies, and the unbearable noise of the flies, loud as an orchestra. She could hear voices coming from a little chapel, the sound of an organ, people sobbing. The boy stopped his donkey and sat, staring at nothing, traumatised. Calling out, she stumbled into the chapel. After the fierce sunlight, the place was dark, but stretching away from her she could see several primitive benches, a cloth-covered trestle serving as an altar, candles burning, a wooden cruci-fix. There was a robed man in front of the table, on his knees, holding his arms up towards the cross. Five people sat watching him, their backs to her. A sixth, a woman, pressed the keys of a table-top harmonium.

The sound of her footsteps was loud. The six people leaped up, clutching each other, gasping. Even in the gloom, their terror was palpable. They were all white. The robed minister got up and came towards her. 'Who are you?' he asked.

'I'm a reporter,' she said. 'What on earth happened here?'

'Isn't it obvious what happened?' he said angrily. 'Are you blind? Or just so callous that horror makes no impression on you?'

'I've seen the bodies outside,' she said. 'But who killed them? Who's responsible?'

He looked at her for a long minute, weighing her up, taking decisions. Then he said: 'If you've come from the town, you'll need a drink. I suggest we go back to the hall and we'll try and tell you what happened.' He turned to his tiny flock. 'I don't know about my friends here, but I still haven't really . . . taken it all in.'

There were murmurs of agreement, a muffled exclamation at remembered atrocity. She heard the whispered name: 'Edith!'

The priest did not want to talk about personal details. Far more important than names and addresses, he said, was the tragic slaughter which had taken place and which he hoped she would broadcast to the world. It appeared that a small group of rebel soldiers had become separated from the main army and had then stumbled across the isolated little mission in their attempt to rejoin their comrades. There were visitors staying, one of them from London, representing a government department, one who was ill and had been left there to recover, the others a young couple travelling cross-country in a jeep. There was himself and his two assistants. There had also been a number of local people who were taking shelter: the rebels were known for their brutality and they hoped for protection from the people at the mission.

'The soldiers showed up last night,' he said. Wearily he brushed a hand across his forehead, focusing back on the horrific events of the past few hours. 'About a dozen of them, under the command, if that's the word, of their sergeant. They wanted food, they said, then they'd be on their way to join up again with the army.'

That was fine, he had told them: the mission turned no-one away and though there was little food, they were welcome to share it. Unfortunately, they had found the fairly extensive stores with which the mission was stocked in order to cope with emergencies. These included a case of whisky. They became drunk, started molesting the women, both white and black, then grabbed Edith, one of his lay assistants, and the sergeant and some of his men had raped her, despite his own attempts at intervention, while they had been forced at

212

gunpoint to watch. After a while, they had taken her away to continue their brutalisation of the poor woman. They could hear her screams for what seemed like hours. He had helped the others to hide, but when the rebels had finally disposed of Edith their blood was up, they wanted more; they wanted sex and death. They turned on the locals, herded them outside and began systematically to abuse and then kill them. The terror went on through the night. When dawn came, they had gone, mercifully sparing the whites.

'We buried poor Edith's body,' the clergyman said. He was young, his face haggard. He was obviously exhausted.

'*You* did,' said the harmonium-player, who, along with the others, had listened to this recital. She looked white and ill. 'I couldn't have borne to do it. None of us could. Only you.' Around her, the others sat dazed, moaning, nodding occasionally in agreement.

'She was always such a help to me,' murmured the minister. 'I would never have managed to run this place without her.'

Already Lolly could see that it was a different story from the one her colleagues were pursuing further north, that though there were fewer deaths, it was all the more appalling because it was the more encompassable. She asked if she might take pictures.

The priest looked round at the others and then, over their murmurs, said: 'We have no objection. If you think it appropriate and you can bear to. Perhaps out of this evil will come some good.'

'And your full names,' Lolly said. She got out her notebook. 'Perhaps I could talk to you individually, later. Get your stories.'

'We are not the important ones here,' the cleric said.

'Those poor butchered people out there are the ones who matter.'

'But if the international community learns about this horror, they may be more inclined to intervene, try to stop it happening again. I know there's been something much worse than this, but precisely because this was on such a small scale, I think it will move people more.'

'Even one death is too many,' said the priest. 'But I'm sure I speak for all of us when I say that we don't want *our* photographs taken. *We* are not the victims of this tragic event. And we certainly don't wish to talk to you until we've buried our dead. Our . . .' His voice shook slightly '. . . our friends.'

'Edith . . .' whispered the harmonium-player, staring at nothing. 'If you'd seen . . . It was so . . .' Her words dropped into silence.

Outside the walls of the mission, they dug graves, little more than shallow pits in the dry earth, bodies buried in groups. Apart from the clergyman, the survivors moved like zombies, gagging and gasping as the full extent of the horror became obvious, their faces twisting at the sight of each fresh corpse. It was obvious that the rebels had enjoyed their bloodthirsty work, had been ingenious in the methods employed to dispatch the helpless victims. The boy had stood apart, watching them.

The cleric moved among them, comforting. A hand on a shoulder, a swift embrace, a soft word: they seemed to take strength from him. Apart from the harmonium-player, it seemed that none of them had met him before yesterday, yet they leaned instinctively towards the healing he offered them.

Much later, the grisly task done, and night fallen like a blanket, food was provided from what the rebels had left. None of them had much appetite, but all recognised that they had to eat something. By now, Lolly had been able to make some distinction between the group of assorted strangers. The harmonium-player was Janice, a theological student who had taken a year off her studies to come out and help in the mission. One of the men was Michael, an agricultural adviser, who was surveying the area for the Government, advising local officials, trying to set up self-help programmes which would make more effective use of the available farmland. The other, Ken, was a member of a theatrical touring group which had been on its way to the university at Ibadan, and had stopped in the town to give an open-air performance of *Hamlet*. He had been taken ill and had been dropped here in a state of delirium by his troupe: he was still weak and debilitated, unable to do much digging, though he tried. Edith, it appeared, had been an SRN, the only form of medical aid for miles around. The young couple were graduate students from Cambridge, Viv and Nick, on a working vacation.

After eating, Lolly slipped outside into the darkness to smoke a cigarette and think about the form her interviews would take. These were people in the grip of horror: she couldn't just barge in with insensitive questions or she would end up with nothing. She became aware of a voice whispering at her from the dark. 'Missy. Missy.'

'Who is it?' she asked softly.

'Here, missy.'

For a moment, she hesitated. One of the rebels, returned for more slaughter? Someone from the town who would rob and possibly murder her? She thought of her editor, of her story, and slowly walked towards the voice: it was the boy. He took her arm, led her behind the chapel.

'Listen,' he said. In reasonable mission-school English, he

told her that he had survived the massacre, he had been there but by pretending to be dead, had later been able to run away. It wasn't like the priest said, he insisted. The soldiers had not found the stores: the priest had offered them whisky in exchange for the lives of the Europeans. It had been his idea, it had not come from the soldiers. 'He was afraid,' said the boy. 'Afraid he would die.' One of the white women – the one called Edith – had protested, and had been murdered by the sergeant, after he and several others had raped her, in front of her colleagues. The clergyman had done nothing. None of them had. After she had finally died, the soldiers looked around for more victims and the clergyman had told them to take the sheltering locals and leave the white people alone. His authority was such that the soldiers agreed to this. Also, said the boy, perhaps they were ashamed or even frightened by the possible repercussions of killing a white woman. The other white people were so terrified that they would be the next victims that they had not said a word, not tried to stop the locals being led out, even though they must have known what would happen to them, that they would be systematically tortured and killed. The boy's sister and mother had been among them, and his baby brother. When the soldiers had left, he had made his way back to the town, but most of his family had run into the hills to wait until this new trouble was over.

'The priest did nothing?' Lolly said.

'Nothing.'

'Nor the others?'

'Not after the first one was killed.'

'He said they were forced at gunpoint to watch her being raped.'

'They did not have guns,' the boy said.

'And the others just let the natives – the local people – be taken away?'

'It was his idea. He offered the whisky. He said they could take the others if they left the white people alone.'

The story was far worse than Lolly had feared. Yet she knew instinctively that it was true. She had already wondered at some of the details of the priest's story. For instance, there did not seem to be any shortage of food, though he had implied that the rebels had taken it all. How likely was it that the English people would have survived unhurt unless some kind of bargain had been struck? And why were the survivors so obviously under the thumb of a man most of them had never seen before?

She asked the boy if he knew the cleric's name, but he shook his head. He had attended the school here for a year or two, while his father could spare him, but that had been under the old priest. He had left before this new one came; he had never spoken to him until the reports of the rebels coming into the area drove his mother to take them to the mission-house for protection.

Then he was gone, his dark shape in the darkness suddenly no longer there. At the same time, she heard the clergyman's voice. 'I thought I heard you talking to someone,' he said.

'No.'

'I could have sworn . . .' He peered about but there was nothing to see. 'So . . . how are you going to present our story to the world?'

'I'm going to tell the truth,' Lolly said.

'Ah. The truth.' He asked if he could have one of her cigarettes. 'There are so many truths, are there not? So many ways of presenting facts.'

'Some things are absolutes, surely.'

'Are they? There are always weighings up, balances, to be taken into account. Things are so seldom black or white. And there are so many shades of grey.'

'There is also something called selling out,' said Lolly, unable to listen to him in the light of what she knew.

'Profit and loss, setting one thing against another. Who is to say what is ultimately right and what is wrong?' He must have been fifteen years or more younger than she was, but he sounded infinitely older and vastly more cynical. She had already noted the way he seemed to mesmerise the others: she was in danger of being mesmerised herself.

'If you can't judge that, then you've lost an essential piece of your soul,' she said sharply.

'Or perhaps learned that even souls can be traded,' he said.

'No.'

'Who can be sure?'

They were silent for a moment. Then he said: 'I think it would be better if you left us, as soon as you can. The people indoors . . .' she heard the rustle of his sleeve as he pointed back over his shoulder, '. . . are traumatised by what has happened to them, what they have witnessed: they find your presence disturbing.'

'Have they said so?'

'They are worried about what you will say. They have miraculously been preserved from slaughter and now they look for another kind of preservation – self-preservation.'

'That's disgusting.'

'But very human.'

'What about you yourself?'

'Me? My mission is to save others, not myself.'

She wanted to cry out, to denounce, tell him that she knew what he had done. She kept her voice cold. 'I meant, do you find my presence as disturbing as you say the others do?'

'I am disturbed by very little,' he said, and even in the darkness, she knew that he smiled. 'It is for their sake, not mine, that I urge you to leave.'

'And if I refuse?'

'It would be better if you did not.'

Was there a threat behind his words? Lolly thought so. He offered to drive her to the town, and although she did not say so, she found herself suddenly frightened. She was afraid that he had overheard the boy's accusation and that he intended to kill her if she persisted in trying to get her story. It would be easy for him to dispose of her. One more body would mean little when there were so many others. He would only have to alter his story slightly for the authorities, add a second white woman's murder to the outrage of the first. He would bury her near the remains of poor Edith, and that would be that. Her family would institute enquiries, her editor would send someone to investigate but by then it would be too late. There would be nothing to prove that she had not been butchered by the rebel soldiers, along with the others. A breeze sighed across the compound: it smelled of smoke and dust and some night-blooming flower. She was conscious of a passionate wish not to die, not yet, not while she still had stories to tell.

She dissembled. 'How far away is the town?'

'Ten or fifteen miles from here.'

'Can I stay here for the night?'

'Of course.'

'Then I'd be grateful for a ride in the morning,' she said.

When they had retired to various parts of the mission, she slipped out of the place with her bag and began to walk. She had lived too long in Kenya not to be afraid of the African night and the predators it concealed, but this time it was

human predators she feared, not animal. She listened for a
car, knowing he would come after her if he realised that she
had left. After she had walked some four miles or so, she
heard the creak of the cart and saw the boy loom up against
the night sky.

'I knew you would come,' she said.

Her editor laughed at her. 'Twenty-seven bleeding corpses?'
he said. 'There were three thousand just down the road.'

'The point is that they were sold for seven whites,' Lolly
said. 'Surely that's just as bad. Worse, in some ways. They
raped and killed a white woman. There's got to be a story in
that.'

'Oh, dear. Oh dearie me.' He tipped back in his chair. 'I get
it. One white bint being knocked off is worse than the
slaughter of three thousand innocent kaffirs, is it?'

'I didn't say that.'

'Maybe not.'

'I didn't *mean* that.'

'But that's how it's going to come across. Now, if you can
get corroboration of any of this, we might have something
going. But . . .' He looked down at the impassioned story she
had worked on for the past thirty-six hours. '. . . Boys
appearing and disappearing in the night, your "feeling" that
there was something odd, a sense that this bloody sky-pilot's
story didn't hang together. Is that all you could get out of it?
Not even a name?'

'If I can get it confirmed by the participants, will you print
it?'

'I might.' He squinted at the typescript again. 'It wouldn't
be a half-bad story if there was the slightest evidence to
support it. Shame you didn't get the God-botherer's moniker,

or anyone else's for that matter. Pity you never made it to the flaming massacre you were sent to cover in the first place.'

'It can't be too difficult to find out where this mission is.'

'Where was it, then, this place you say you went to?'

'I don't know. About ten miles from the town.'

'Which friggin' town?'

'The one nearest to the airstrip.' But even as she said it, Lolly knew that she'd been guilty of the worst journalistic crime of all: not getting the facts. It was because of the girls, Liz and Serena; she had been worried about taking off, just leaving them behind without a chance to explain where she was going or when she'd be back. She was often away, but always with warning. This time, she'd had to leave before they were up, before she'd had time to prepare them. She had worried about it on the flight to the main airport at Nairobi. She knew she could fill in some of the blanks: the name of the town, the area and so forth. But not to have taken down names was ridiculous. She started to explain how the priest had refused her access to his people, had withheld his own name, had said that such detail was unimportant in the larger scheme of things, and then fell silent.

Her editor was right. She couldn't do a man's job. She was better sticking to the usual women's-page stuff.

Later, through phone calls, she was able to establish that the agricultural adviser from London was called Michael Farquharson. She wheedled an address in Buckinghamshire from the department responsible for his presence in Nigeria. She wrote to him, saying that she wanted to publicise the story, and got no answer, wrote again, with the same result. She telephoned, and was told he was not available. She tried to contact the Cambridge couple, Viv and Nick, but without their full names it was impossible. She tried to find out who Ken was, which theatrical troupe he had been a member of, but again had no success.

'Somebody must know who these people are,' she said to her editor.

'It was your business to find out,' he said.

'Can't you see that it's a cover-up? They were all in it together.'

'Prove it,' was all he said. 'Bring me evidence that'll stand up in a court of law to say that any of this happened and I promise you I'll print the story on the front page.'

Her marriage broke up. It had been coming for a long time, but even so, it was a shock when her husband finally asked for a divorce, saying he had met someone else. She was all the more humiliated by the circumstances. He told her that if she asked for alimony or child support payments, he would fight it and the details would be blazoned across the head-lines. To protect her daughters, she accepted his terms, hating him for imposing them. Bitter, humiliated, degraded, she returned to England, cut herself off completely from family and friends, began to make a new life, set about earning enough money to keep the three of them. Gradually time and detail overlaid her burning sense of the injustice and horror of the story which had never been fully told. However, she never lost her feeling of shame that those seven people at the mission, under the leadership of the cleric, had got away with cold-blooded murder and she had done nothing about it.

And then, three or four months ago, a number of events had occurred. In separate encounters, she told Farquharson, her path had crossed that of two people who had been present at that scene of carnage out in Nigeria. Although she didn't elaborate on the tape, she mentioned that there had also been a more personal encounter, which had little bearing on that matter but nonetheless brought back memories of that troubled time, thus adding to her sense of confusion and disorientation. After so many years, she had thought that perhaps the feelings of inadequacy and horror she had felt then might have diminished but they had not. Then out of the blue, the letter from Farquharson had arrived and she had determined that, however late it was, she should try once more to bring to justice the people – the person – responsible for that outrage.

Cassie stopped the tape and got up to pour herself more whisky. The fire was burning brightly but she still felt cold; she held her hands close to the flames, seeking warmth, of any kind. She knew already that, once she restarted the tape, Michael Farquharson's thin, well-bred voice would immediately chime in, protesting that he too had never been able to get the incident out of his mind, that the shame he had felt at allowing the priest to make that monstrous bargain – 'our lives for theirs' – had never left him. He would explain that he had retired to his room almost as soon as he had arrived at the mission, in order to type out reports on the small manual typewriter he had with him, that he had arrived in the hall a few minutes after the rebels had grabbed the brave and luckless Edith, and that he had taken some time to understand exactly what had happened. At this point, his voice would break, and Lolly would murmur, though her words would not be comforting. Her disapproval of Farquharson's refusal to get involved all those years ago, when it had mattered so much, came through strongly.

Cassie sighed. She knew that, on the tape, Michael would then give Lolly the names of the actor and the young couple

– Nick the husband, had died in a plane crash in Brazil, but Viv Parfitt still lived near Cambridge. Would tell her that Janice had married a theological student and moved to Devon. Would apologise, yet again, for his refusal to cooperate when Lolly had originally contacted him. 'I couldn't bear to bring it up, even to myself,' he would say. 'I could never talk about it to anyone, not my wife, nor my children. I tried to write it down once and tore it all up. That I could have been party to such an appalling . . .'

Lolly would tell him that she had quite by chance seen the actor, though he was not aware of her, and that she also knew the clergyman. 'Between us,' she'd say, 'we could at least do something about him.'

And Farquharson would feebly agree that the Man of God – the words spoken with a terrible irony – was the one responsible, that though the others were guilty of weakness and cowardice, it would never have occurred to any of them to come to such a frightful agreement. 'Our lives were saved at the expense of theirs,' he would say, over and over again, 'Our lives for theirs,' and his voice would eventually die away on the whirring tape, ephemeral as smoke.

Cassie realised she had been holding her breath, tensing herself against yet another repetition of the ugly tale. What she found most frustrating was the fact that throughout the long conversation, neither of them had mentioned the name of the clergyman responsible for it all. Farquharson said somewhere on the tape that he knew the whereabouts of some of the other participants in the scene, that he would pass them on to Lolly. Cassie was convinced that if she could only find out who these people were, they would be able to throw further light on a connection between the minor and yet so significant massacre of thirty years ago and Lolly's recent death. But it was the man at the centre, the bargaining priest, who was the most important. He must have known the people concerned more intimately than anyone else and if she could only talk to him, she might have precisely the evidence she needed to give to Paul Walsh. She couldn't help reflecting on the parallels between Lolly's impotence then and her own impotence now, when the badly needed proof simply wasn't forthcoming.

Perhaps the better way to approach the problem was to come up on it from behind. It looked like one of those difficult hands when the bidding has been ambitious rather than precise and yet, once the cards have been laid down, the tricks are there to be taken, with a lot of skill and a little luck. Instead of trying to follow the track from then until now, perhaps she should concentrate on now. More exactly, she should concentrate on what had happened in the past few months. On the tape, Lolly had mentioned it more than once. 'I encountered the past,' was the emotive phrase she used, her white African accent strengthened by feeling.

Did it have anything to do with the episode at Serena's house? Cassie thought back to what she'd been told about it. Lolly had been sitting at the supper table. The television set had been on, showing some kind of comedy programme, and she had suddenly started shouting, had fallen back in a faint or something similar. But she had said her path had crossed that of two people from that time: what precisely did she mean by the phrase? Literally come face to face with them? Or simply had them brought to her attention? Seen them across a crowded room or passed them in the street and recognised them? Was that feasible, after so many years? She wondered how she could find out what Lolly had been doing recently, where she had been, whom she had met. She remembered that it had been during the same period that Lolly had come with her to play bridge at Chadwell Court and been distressed by something.

And, with the ease of an ice-cube slipping from a warmed refrigerator tray, she remembered Ken. Ken, the travelling player who'd been forced by illness to stop off at the mission. Was he, could he be one and the same as Kenneth Langdon, the old actor with whom the comedian Robert Craufurd had agreed to do a turn at Charlie's Christmas spectacular? Could it be that simple? She tried to run through the events of the afternoon at Chadwell Court, but it had all been so under-stated that she had barely taken enough note at the time for there to be anything to recall. It had been teatime, she remembered. They had gone into the dining room where various residents were seated at tables, and been given a cheery introduction by Matron.

'This is Agnes, our piano player, and this is Jimmy, who's a whizz at Racing Demon, isn't that right, Jimmy, a proper little devil, he is, and this is Annie One and Annie Two, we call them that to distinguish between them, don't we, dears? And this is our Star, Kenneth Langdon, I'm sure you remember the name, don't you, ladies, appeared in – what was it, Kenny: *Rainbow Over Suez*, and *A Row of Tents*, then went over to Hollywood and made a real name for himself playing English toffs, like Ronald Colman or David Niven, quite a feather in our cap to have him with us, and this is Deidre, who writes the sweetest poems about animals, don't you, love? . . .' and on and on.

Kenneth Langdon. Cassie stared into the dying flames of the fire. She still had to work out the connection between

Lolly and whatever it was that she had seen on the telly at her daughter's house. But meanwhile, it was at least possible that the old boy in the high-backed chair with his arthritic hands lying on his lap had the key to all this, or, if not the key, then at least part of the combination number which would release the secret which lay behind Lolly's death.

## ♠ 12 ♠

'It's so nice of you to come, Miss Swann; I know Kenneth will appreciate seeing you,' the Matron at Chadwell Court Residential Home for the Elderly maintained firmly.

'I wouldn't bank on it.' An elderly woman sped past them as they stood in the wide hallway. It was rather how Cassie herself felt.

'What?' Matron stared after the rapidly vanishing wheelchair. 'What did you say, Agnes?'

The wheelchair executed a 180-degree turn and raced back to them, pulling up with a screech of rubber. 'Ken. Don't know if he's up to visitors. He's been having his nightmares again. Wouldn't appreciate seeing Father Christmas in fishnet tights today, if you want my honest opinion.'

'Why wasn't I informed?' said Matron.

'The staff's probably got better things to do than come running to tell you every time one of the prisoners has a bad dream.' Agnes grinned at Cassie. 'Anyway, at our age, is there any other kind?' Under her back-to-front baseball cap, earrings shaped like bunches of grapes hung from earlobes as yielding as blancmange. She wore a purple-mauve shell-suit which precisely picked up the colour of the grapes, with lipstick and eyeshadow to match. She reversed away from them, tilted on the rear wheels of her chair.

'Thank you, Agnes. But I'll take Miss Swann down to Ken's room, just in case.'

'Don't blame me, that's all I ask.'

'You'd never believe she was eighty-four, would you?' Matron said, not altogether approvingly.

'Has she ever thought of entering for the veteran Olympics,' said Cassie.

'She'd win, if she did.'

'Tell me, Matron, am I right in thinking that Mr Langdon was out in Nigeria for a while, when he was younger?'

'Indeed so. He toured the country with a group of actors, putting on Shakespeare in small villages and so on. What the local inhabitants made of it, I don't know, but I suppose it's all cultural, isn't it?'

'That would depend on your definition of culture.'

'I suppose it would. But certainly Ken spent some time out there. As a matter of fact, it's that part of his life he has the bad dreams about it. I don't know what happened because he never talks about it, but the poor man's been suffering terrible nightmares in the past few months. Something must have brought it all back.'

'Whatever it was.'

'Exactly.'

Another figure approached them, skirts swinging, high forehead shining beneath the unforgiving overhead lights designed to eliminate shadows which might cause the unwary old person to trip and fall.

'Ah,' said Matron. 'Good morning, Vicar.'

'Mrs Albeury.' The clergyman stopped and smiled at them both. 'And Miss Swann. A double pleasure.'

'Mr Lightower is our house chaplain,' Matron said. 'Such

a source of strength and comfort to our little family here.'

Cassie tried to drag her eyes away from his and found that she could not. They were blue eyes. Electric drill kind of eyes. Eyes which told her she was a highly attractive woman and were he not a man of the cloth he would be pretty damned interested.

'Cassandra is so kind. She's come to visit poor Kenneth,' said Matron. 'Wants to ask him about the past, isn't that right, Miss Swann?'

'Sort of,' said Cassie.

'Ken's a particular favourite of the Vicar's.'

'Such an interesting old gentleman. Some of his theatrical reminiscences are hilarious.' The Vicar laughed in retrospective appreciation. 'I've known him for years.' At one level, both he and Matron were behaving like characters from a *Carry On* film, she booming, he beaming. But the Vicar, Cassie would have sworn, seemed to playing a part while Matron couldn't help it.

'Where did you meet him?' asked Cassie.

Both Vicar and Matron looked at her in some surprise, though it didn't seem to be a particularly odd question. It was, nonetheless, one to which she would have liked the answer. 'When I was working overseas, as it happens,' said the Vicar.

'Which bit of overseas?'

Vicar and Matron looked at each other this time. 'I really can't remember,' said Lightower. 'Why do you ask? Are you a close friend of Ken's? A relation, perhaps?'

'Not really.' Cassie did not want to admit that she didn't know the old boy at all, had, indeed, only clapped eyes on him once, when she came with Lolly to play bridge here. Looking at the light reflected off the clergyman's forehead, she tried to remember if he had been around when she had brought her bridge team into the home, earlier in the year. She had come here today in the hope of discovering that recognising Kenneth Langdon had been one of the factors in Lolly's marked distress. But perhaps she was barking up the wrong tree. Perhaps the person Lolly had seen here, and recognised, was Lightower, not Langdon.

On the tape recovered from Serena, Lolly had spoken of two recent encounters, not just one. But even if Kenneth Langdon proved to be the actor struck down with illness who had been present at the mission, it was surely far too much of a coincidence that the local vicar should also turn out to have been present at the outrage, perhaps even been responsible for it. Or would it? A man who had behaved with such hard-headed expediency might well wish to keep tabs on those who had witnessed his shameful pact with the devil, if only to ensure that they didn't reveal the truth of what had happened.

Studying him in the cold judgemental light from the ceiling, she wondered if he slept easily at night. Also, whether she was building hypotheses from suppositions based on nothing more substantial than conjecture.

Mrs Albeury looked at her watch and said: 'But we must get on, mustn't we? I'm sure you're tremendously busy, Vicar. You too, Miss Swann. I know I – ha, ha! – am. Let's—'

'How well do you know Ken?' interrupted Lightower. He turned his eyes on her again and turned the dimmer switch to bright.

Cassie blinked. She didn't have time to prepare a lie. 'Um . . . I don't, actually. Matron introduced us last time I was here bu—'

'In that case, may I enquire why you've come to see him?'

'It's to do with something which happened a long time ago,' Cassie said. 'You know about the murder of Mrs Haden White . . .'

'Yes, indeed . . .'

'. . . and I have reason to believe that Mr Langdon just might be able to throw some light on something which could prove to be relevant to that death,' said Cassie. Damnation. If the Reverend Charisma was by any chance involved, he was in a prime position to assume that she was too, however vicariously.

At her words, the blue eyes – or was it simply her overactive imagination? – hardened. 'A poor old man in a home for the elderly? Involved in a murder? How very bizarre,' he said.

'There you go,' said Cassie. If he *did* know something, he was not going to be content to leave it at that. He would certainly make some excuse to meet her again, to pump her, find out exactly what she knew.

'Come along,' said Matron. 'Let's go and see if Agnes was right about Ken.'

Walking down the corridor, Cassie looked back. Lightower was watching them. More accurately, watching her. The blue eyes crinkled smilingly at the corner and he gave her a little wave. Strive as she might, it was impossible not to feel a shiver climb down her spine as though descending a ladder into a cold dark cellar.

It turned out old Agnes was right. When they reached Kenneth Langdon's room, he was in bed flat on his back but with his head turned towards the wall, sleeping noisily. An aide was tidying up his room, straightening the dozens of framed photographs which stood on the broad windowsill, all of them showing Langdon in his glory days. Shaking hands with Princess Margaret, embracing Richard Attenborough, standing with a group of faces which were all instantly recognisable as former – or even current – icons of the British theatre. In one photograph, he stood in boxer's pose, clutching the similarly raised arm of what was unmistakably Robert Craufurd, although Craufurd's hair had not yet turned white, and his face was still unlined.

'I don't think we should wake the poor dear, after his bad night,' said Matron, *sotto voce*. 'I'm awfully sorry. Would you mind coming back another day?'

'Is there any time in particular that's best?'

'Whenever's convenient, really. Though it might be better, to save a wasted journey, if you telephoned before you came.'

'I'll do that.'

Cassie was disappointed. No question about it. But she could try again tomorrow. Or the next day. Kenneth Langdon didn't look as though he was going anywhere. In fact, he didn't look as though he had the physical stamina to sit up, let alone put on a fur coat and battered hat and sing 'Underneath the Arches' with Robert Craufurd. She walked back to the entrance and shook the Matron's hand. The Vicar was just driving away in a dark green Land Rover. He gave her the little wave again, but this time he did not smile.

Since she was psyched up for visiting the elderly, Cassie decided to drop in on Mrs Maggs on her way back to Honeysuckle Cottage.

The old lady was delighted. 'How nice to see you,' she exclaimed when Cassie, having knocked at the door of her room, came in. 'And how very kind of you to visit me.'

'There's nothing kind about it,' said Cassie. 'I was looking forward to talking to you again.'

'And I you, my dear. Particularly since this appalling

murder. I feel so frustrated, unable to find out what exactly happened, and nobody seems to understand that I want to know, not from prurient curiosity but because I was a good friend of Lolly Haden White's. Perhaps her only one – she didn't make friends easily – but the two of us were much of an age and came to live in the village at roughly the same time and had children at more or less the same stage.'

Cassie tried to repress unworthy thoughts about casting bread upon the waters and having it returned to her an hundredfold. 'I can tell you the facts, as far as I know them,' she said, and proceeded to do so, though because of her conviction that Lolly had secrets she wanted kept, she did not touch upon the more intimate details she had begun to uncover.

Bettina Maggs had no such scruples. 'How very odd,' she said thoughtfully.

'What is?' Cassie said, quivering like a greyhound.

'This business of the grandparents and father all being dead.'

'Why?'

'I remember commenting once on the fact that she didn't seem to have any family to help her out with bringing up the girls. I said that surely their father could take them for a while in order to give her a break, even if he'd married again and got a new family to look after.'

'What did she say to that?'

Bettina frowned. 'Perhaps I've got it wrong, but I seem to recall that she burst out laughing in a rather unpleasant fashion and said that that was most unlikely. And that anyway, although his parents would be glad to take the girls, she didn't want them to have anything to do with his family, or him. I thought it was monstrously unfair of her, but it wasn't my place to say anything and besides, Lolly could be formidable at times.'

'I knew it,' Cassie said. 'I knew that they couldn't all have died.'

'*Her* parents had, I believe. She told me that they'd been involved in a car crash out in Kenya and her father had died instantly, her mother a few weeks later, from her injuries.'

'Someone told me that her mother had once been the teacher – or the headmistress – at the village school in Larton Easewood.'

'Not *her* mother, *his*.'

Cassie felt like someone who for days had been chopping their way through jungle undergrowth and then had suddenly reached a clearing. 'His? The husband's mother? Are you sure?'

'That's what Lolly said.'

'Which means she could be checked out.' Cassie couldn't keep the excitement from her voice. With his mother's name to hand, it ought to be possible to find Lolly's husband, supposing he was still alive.

'Absolutely.'

Cassie stood. 'If you don't mind, I'll leave now and see what I can find out.'

Bettina Maggs clutched herself and said: 'It's a terrible thing to say, with poor Lolly dead, but this really is most interesting. You *will* let me know what you discover, won't you?'

'Count on it.'

The school playground was quiet, though a certain amount of chaos seeped through the walls of the Portakabins which had been erected to soak up overspill from the school building itself, an unreconstituted Church of England primary school of vaguely ecclesiastical design. It was a miracle that it still existed, when so many of them had been shut down or centralised by mergers with bigger and more impersonal schools miles from where any of the pupils lived.

Cassie went in through a gothic-style porch and found herself in corridors even shinier than those at Chadwell Court. The smell hit her like a punch on the nose. Hot bodies, gym shoes, disinfectant, disillusion: she recognised it immediately. She'd been there, done that, paid her dues to the education system, and never been so happy as the day she finally left, thanks to her godfather's generosity in offering her Honeysuckle Cottage to live in.

Breathing shallowly, she made her way to the secretary's office. 'I'm so awfully sorry to bother you when you must be absolutely up to the ears in school stuff,' she said, laying it on with a trowel: no school secretary worth her salt would ever admit to having time for anything, even in a small country school like this one.

'How can I help?' The woman behind a file-laden desk stared up at Cassie through thin-rimmed glasses.

'I'm trying to find the names of teachers – or head teachers – who were here thirty or forty years ago.' It had seemed a simple matter of checking records on the way here. Now, she saw that it was fairly unlikely that she'd find anything at all.

The secretary seemed to agree. 'Thirty or for – that's a long time ago. I don't know where I'd start looking.' She glanced at the filing cabinets which stood ranged along one wall. 'I mean, we probably do have a record, but I don't know where I'd look it up.'

'Would the current head teacher know?'

'She might. She's fairly new, though. But the one before

her was here for years. Mrs Madingley. She might have more idea.'

'Where is she?'

'She went to live in Bournemouth, I believe. Hang on, and I'll find her address for you.'

After some scrabbling about in the filing cabinets, designed to demonstrate efficiency hampered by overwork, she scribbled on a bit of paper and gave it to Cassie. 'As I say, she'd probably be more help to you than I could.'

In other words, pass the buck, thought Cassie.

She drove on home and hit the phone as soon as she had got through the door, dialling the number in Bournemouth. A firm but elderly voice answered. 'Heather Madingley here.'

'Is that the same Mrs Madingley who used to be headmistress of the primary school in Larton Easewood?'

'It is.'

'Oh, hello. My name's Cassandra Swann . . .' Cassie lumbered into an edited explanation of why she should want information about former teachers in a village primary school, without making any reference to Lolly's murder.

'The person you want is Commander Ruthven Gowrie.' Mrs Madingley spoke with the brisk efficiency of her kind.

'And he is?'

'A retired naval man. Lives in Larton Easewood. In The Stone House. He's something of an amateur historian and he's been working on a history of the village for a number of years. If there's anything you want to know, he'll have a chapter, or at least a footnote, on it. I know for a fact that he's written about the school.' Her voice changed to that of someone embarrassed at taking a liberty. 'May I ask what it's in connection with?'

'I'm trying to track someone down and the only clue I

have is that his mother once taught at the village school in Larton Easewood.'

'And you are what – connected with the police? An investigation agency.'

'It's a private matter.'

'I'll tell you what. Why don't I call Ruthven for you? I know him well and he might respond better to a friend than a complete stranger.'

'That would be very kind.'

An hour later, Mrs Madingley rang back. 'I knew Ruthven would come up trumps. Since you weren't sure whether the person was one of the teachers or the headmistress herself, and the period was quite broad, I was expecting some difficulty, but the dear Commander had the names of the entire school staff ever since its inception following the Education Act of 1870 at his fingertips. They were stable times, of course: staff didn't change, and primary school teaching was an acceptable occupation for a woman, particularly after the First World War. I can offer you a number of names covering the period you mentioned: shall I dictate them to you?'

'That would be—'

'Go and get a pen, my dear, so you can write them down.'

Amazing. Even across the distance between Bournemouth and Honeysuckle Cottage, Mrs Madingley could recognise the sort of disorganised person who wouldn't have pen and paper to hand. Cassie obediently found something to write with and returned to the phone.

Mrs Madingley began dictating. At the seventh name, Cassie stopped her. As soon as she heard it, she knew that this was the one she was after. 'This Grayson person: that's Miss, is it, not Mrs?'

'That's right. Most of the headmistresses, as opposed to the teachers, were unmarried.'

'This lady was there for ten years: what happened after that?'

'Ruthven didn't say. But then I didn't ask him.'

'I guess what I really want to know is whether she went on to get married and if so, to whom.'

'I'll ask Ruthven. Is there anything else you'd like to know about her, while I'm at it?'

'Any information at all would be useful.'

'Miss Grayson is definitely the one you're interested in, is she?'

'For the moment, yes.'

'Would you tell me why?'

'Her first name was Angharad,' said Cassie.

It was not a common name. Coupled with the fact that Liz Trowbridge had been named after her grandmother, a grandmother who was believed to have taught at Larton Easewood School a number of years ago, it seemed reasonably conclusive proof that Angharad Grayson had been the mother of Lolly's former husband. If the Commander knew whom she had married, that might produce a name for Liz's and Serena's father, and Lolly's husband. Which meant that it might be possible to find out who he was and whether he was still alive.

And, if he was, whether he was involved in some way with Lolly's death. On the tape, Lolly had said that she had had a personal encounter recently: perhaps out of the blue, she had come across her husband again. There must have been compelling reasons why Lolly had chosen to live in obscurity after the breakdown of her marriage: it was possible that he had threatened her or her children and seeing her after all this time, discovered that none of his anger against her had died. Possible, but unlikely. They had gone their separate ways more than a quarter of a century ago. Their children were grown. They themselves were elderly. No-one could nurse a grudge for so long and still find it red hot and murderous. Or could they? She wasn't much good at grudges herself, because after her first flash of rage or resentment, she tended to forget what she was supposed to be grudging about.

She was making a cup of coffee when the telephone rang. Liz Trowbridge said: 'I was right. I checked my papers and she'd put "Father unknown" on them.'

'So not much help there.' Cassie didn't say she was on the trail of Liz's unknown father even as she spoke.

'She actually put "father unknown", even though she was married to him,' Liz said, her voice rising in outrage. 'God, she must have hated him. In effect, she simply wiped him out of her life – and ours.'

'What do you think he'd done, to make her do that?'

'Nothing. The . . . *bitch*.'

'Was he violent?' Cassie hoped she would never have had cause to talk about her own mother with such hatred.

'I don't remember it, if he was. And I was certainly old enough to be aware of raised fists and screams and so on.'

'Perhaps his violence was more subtle.'

'I don't think so. I think it was her who caused the trouble, not him. I have these memories of him as someone very laid-back and easy-going. Someone,' Liz said wistfully, 'who laughed.'

There were worse things to deprive a child of than laughter. Nonetheless, Cassie could share Liz's sentiments. After the warmhearted years she had spent with her dad and her gran in the Bricklayers' Arms, the effect of the joyless life in the Vicarage with Uncle Sam and Aunt Polly had been like stepping into an arctic waterfall. 'Apropos of nothing much,' she said, 'what was your mother's maiden name?'

'Just a minute . . .' Liz shuffled papers about at the other end of the line '. . . here we are. Dolores Mary Crawford.'

'Crawford?'

'Yes.'

'How's that spelled?'

'The normal way. C-R-A-W-F-O-R-D. Why?'

'Just for a minute there, a wild surmise flashed across my mind.'

'Do I get to hear what it was?'

'No. You'd think I was really stretching if I told you.'

Which, in fact, she had been. Crawford was not an uncommon name. And it was difficult, if not impossible, to imagine a link between stiff-necked journalist Dolores Mary Haden White and camp actor Richard Craufurd. Even if they had shared the same surname, rather than merely variants of it.

She spent the afternoon giving bridge classes on three sides of the county. By the time she got home, she was more than ready to accept Kathryn's invitation to share fish and chips with her and Giles, this being the night of the week that the mobile chippie van hit Frith. When she got home, reeking of malt vinegar and hot fat, there was a message from the Commander on her answering machine.

She called the number which had been left on the tape.

'Ruthven Gowrie here,' a voice announced clippedly.

Cassie explained who she was and that she was returning his call. At once, the voice said: 'White. Angharad Grayson, former headteacher, married a man called William Anthony White. Some kind of civil servant, attached to the Foreign

Office. Colonial administration. That any help to you?'

'In as much as anything is. Thank you.'

'My pleasure, ma'am. If I can help in any other enquiries, do telephone me. Haven't much to occupy myself with these days, to tell the truth. After an active life, it comes as a bit of a shock, quite frankly.'

'What does?'

'The way they sideline you, once you reach a certain age, as though you suddenly lose control of your mental and physical faculties. As though you're some old donkey put out to pasture, fit for nothing. Why I took up writing the history of Larton Easewood, frankly. Give myself something to do.'

'If I need any more information, I'll be on to you like a shot.'

'Good show.'

She was saddened by the wistfulness which lurked behind the words.

# ♣ 13 ♣

Lolly was growing visible now, the jigsaw pieces of her personality beginning to fit together, to make up a picture. There was the unhappy marriage to a man called White, son of Angharad Grayson and William Anthony White, who was some kind of colonial administrator. There was the ambition to make it as a reporter. There were the two children and the frustration of having a terrific story to tell to which no one would listen, since she could not get the necessary factual corroboration. And later, after the marriage break-up, there were the lies told, the facts concealed, the deliberate falsification of records, the building of a new life.

Why? This was the central fact about which it was impossible even to theorise. What on earth could have made Lolly dig herself into a Cotswold village like a fox going to earth? Frustrated, Cassie struck the table with her fist. Was it merely habitual circumspection which had led both Lolly and Farquharson to refer to 'my husband', or 'the priest' in their taped conversation? They had spoken readily enough of the others: Ken, Janice, Edith, Viv and Nick. But for some reason the two other key players in the tragedy had been left unnamed. Perhaps neither of them knew the clergyman's name. Perhaps Lolly, woman of her generation, preferred not to refer to her husband by his name to someone who didn't know him and whom, by then, she herself scarcely knew.

Reading through the information she had noted down, Cassie could see ample reason why Lolly might have felt overloaded. In the four or five months prior to her death, her daughter Liz had left her husband, an event which old-fashioned Lolly would find troubling. Guilt-inducing, too, since she herself had been through a broken marriage. In addition, Liz had come out as a lesbian, something which Lolly, judging by her homophobic remarks at Natasha's bridge evening, found particularly difficult to handle. At more or less the same time, Michael Farquharson's wife had written to her from Henley, reviving memories which had never been exorcised. If Cassie's conjectures were right, she also met up again with Kenneth Langdon when she accompanied Cassie to Chadwell Court Residential Home to play bridge, another entirely fortuitous reminder of the traumatic and unresolved past. Equally conjectural, but nonetheless possible, she might have recognised John Lightower, having reluctantly accompanied Serena to the church where he was the incumbent.

At least one of these hypotheses could be checked. Cassie picked up the phone and dialled the number for Chadwell Court. She recognised Mrs Albeury's booming voice, identified herself, asked if she could come and visit Kenneth Langdon that afternoon.

'Oh dear,' Matron said. 'I'm afraid not.' She coughed.

'No? When, then?'

'I'm very sorry, Miss Swann, but poor Ken passed away during the night.'

'Oh no.'

'Sad, isn't it?'

'Kenneth Langdon is dead?'

'We're all very shocked, as you can imagine. At least it was a peaceful end. He ate his supper as usual, watched a bit of telly – that programme with his friend on it, Robert Craufurd, which was nice for him – and then just went to sleep and never woke up. It's how we'd all want to go, given the choice.'

'I suppose it is.' Cassie was more interested in trying to assess the implications of this latest death than in contemplating her own, quiet or otherwise.

'As I say,' said Matron, 'it was quite peaceful. But even so, a bit of a surprise. We'd had no idea that he was so frail.'

'And it was definitely a natural death?'

There was a startled pause. Then: 'Of course it was. He died in his sleep. What on earth are you trying to suggest? That we're in some way responsible? That we neglected poor Ken? I can assure you, Miss Swann, that that was not the case.'

When she was finally able to reinsert herself into the conversation, Cassie soothed and reassured. But, putting down the phone, she felt like someone who had touched an electric fence. This was too much of a coincidence to be acceptable. She thought again of the Reverend Lightower and his velvet-swathed Black & Decker eyes. He was the right age. He had admitted working overseas. For someone who'd never been there before, he had seemed very familiar with the layout of Lolly's house. He said he'd known Ken a long time, and agreed that he took a particular interest in the old man. Might that interest not have something to do with the fact that Kenneth Langdon could spill the beans on Mr John Lightower if he so wished?

A bad thought struck her. By her own boldness in stating that she wished to question the ancient thespian, had she precipitated the poor old boy's death? She desperately hoped not. But nonetheless, could not help wondering how Lightower had done it – *if* he'd done it. With a pillow? She must find out if he had been in the home last night. And also get a straight answer to the question about where he had met Kenneth Langdon. '*I really can't remember*,' he had replied, when she asked him yesterday. It was such a pointless lie, when it was common knowledge that he'd been out in Africa. So why the obfuscation? She wondered where she could get a copy of *Crockford's*, the ecclesiastical equivalent of *Who's Who*. It ought to tell her the details of his clerical life before he fetched up at St Bart's.

There was another point to consider: both Lolly and Michael Farquharson had referred at different times to the charisma of the clergyman in charge of the mission: Lightower might not look like much but he certainly had enough personal magnetism to wipe the contents off several tons of floppy disks.

There were other questions she wanted to ask, too. Like, who would Charlie get as a substitute for the 'Underneath the Arches' number? And would Robert Craufurd bother to come to the Christmas spectacular, now that his old chum had died? She reached again for the telephone, and called Directory Enquiries. An extra-terrestrial sort of voice gave her the number she wanted and she dialled it. After a number of rings a woman answered: 'Parfitt here.'

'Viv Parfitt?'

'Yes.' There was irritation in the voice, as though it should be obvious to even the meanest intelligence that it was Viv speaking, rather than another Parfitt.

Cassie introduced herself. Mentioned Lolly Haden White and Michael Farquharson.

'I've never heard of either of them,' said Ms Parfitt, evidently a woman in a hurry. 'What exactly do you want?'

'Nigeria,' said Cassie. 'Forty odd years ago. You and your husband Nick were travelling cross country and stopped at a Church of England mission-house. There was a terrible massacre.'

There was a long silence. Then Viv Parfitt said: 'What is this? What are you after?'

'Just want to get the facts,' Cassie said.

'Oh, please. I'm not that naïve. Are you trying to blackmail me?'

'Have you something to hide?'

'Look, I don't know who you are or what you're trying to do, but my conscience is entirely clear. Nick and I got caught up in tragic events which were . . . were entirely outside our control. We had . . . we weren't in any way . . . it really . . .' The briskness gave way to silence.

Cassie let it hang.

'It was, in any case, a long time ago,' said Ms Parfitt, rallying. 'A very long time ago.'

'And I'll bet,' Cassie said softly, 'that not a day has gone by without you thinking of it, remembering how you buried those stinking corpses, hearing Edith's screams all over again, every day of your life.'

'Who *are* you? How do you know so much about what happened?'

'I'm someone who wants to see justice done.'

'Isn't it rather late for that?'

'Is it ever too late? Besides, two people have been murdered in the past week,' said Cassie, stretching the possibilities with more confidence than the facts at her disposal warranted.

'Murdered?'

'Almost certainly because of their connection with what happened out in Africa.'

Viv Parfitt gasped. 'But it was nothing to do with us.'

'No woman is an island, as I'm sure you're aware.'

'It was pure chance that we were there.'

'Don't tell me you wouldn't be happy to see someone pay for what happened to those poor people.'

'Certainly I would, but—'

'Who were sacrificed, after all, to save you.'

'Oh God,' Viv said. There was another long pause. 'But we weren't the ones who struck the bargain.'

'Did you protest?'

'After what they did to that poor girl? Of course we didn't.'

'Edith,' said Cassie. 'The only one with the guts to stand up against the soldiers. The only one who tried to prevent it happening.'

'Oh God . . . what they did to her,' choked the woman on the end of the line. 'I can't bear even to think about it.'

'If you helped me, it might go some way towards easing your conscience,' Cassie said quietly. 'You know as well as I do that it was a shameful and appalling episode.'

'Is that Jan?'

'Who?'

'Janice. Is that you? Is this some kind of vile stunt you're trying to pull?'

'Janice lives in Devon.'

'Not any more. Not since her husband moved to – where was it – somewhere near Cheltenham, that part of the world.'

Jan. Janice. Both names had resonances which Cassie could not explore at the moment. Not while Viv Parfitt hung like a landed fish on the end of her line. 'Do you remember

the newspaper reporter who arrived at the mission the morning after the killing?'

'Is that who you are?'

'No. But I'm speaking on her behalf. Look, Ms Parfitt, I've
no wish to disturb you, or to bring back memories I know
you'd much rather forget. All I want from you is the name of
the man we both know was really responsible. The horse-
trader. The one who set profit against loss, who made a
bottom-line decision with people's lives.'

Viv Parfitt exhaled a long sobbing breath. Swallowed.
Gave a tug to her thoughts which was almost audible.
Eventually she said: 'If only I knew. I've tried all these years
to remember, but neither Nick or I knew what his name was.
Everyone called him Padre, so we did too.'

'Padre.'

'Not much use to you, is it?'

'Not much.'

'We talked about it a thousand times, Nick and I. What we
ought to do. The man was a priest, for God's sake. Supposed
to be compassionate, loving. He just sold those poor people
for us, seven of us for nearly thirty of them. What kind of a
deal is that?'

'You mean it would have been better the other way round?'

'The mathematics of it . . . seven whites for twenty-seven
blacks. It was utterly shameful. There were little children
there, old women . . . He herded them out like cattle. There
was a girl who looked back at me as they went, a beautiful
little thing who . . .' Ms Parfitt's voice broke. 'I will never,
never . . . And the terrible thing is, that we let him do it.'

Cassie said nothing. How would she have behaved in similar
circumstances? Just as cravenly? In any case, was there anything which could have saved those people? Perhaps the Padre

had been right, and it was better to save seven than none.

'This may sound completely hypocritical,' Viv went on, 'but many times I've wished we'd died then, too. We were just as much to blame, really. Maybe if we'd all said something, stood up to them, the way that Edith girl did . . . It altered things between Nick and me, you know. We stuck together because we were unworthy of anyone else, we deserved each other. We never had children. I've had several nervous breakdowns; Nick never did anything with his life after that, although he'd just got his D.Phil. – which is why we were on holiday in the first place. To celebrate. He was so brilliant, too – he'd been offered a fellowship at his old college, but he never took it up.'

'If it's any consolation – and I'm sure it's not – yours weren't the only lives ruined.' Cassie thought of Lolly's two daughters, robbed of their family, perhaps of their father, because of one man's brutal bartering with human beings. She thought of the old man who had died last night.

Which reminded her. Excited, she said urgently: 'There was an actor there, at the mission.'

'What about him?'

'Do you remember what he was called?'

'His name was Kenneth Langdon.'

'Ah.' Jubilation filled her. This was confirmation at last. The first solid piece of evidence that she had to connect with Lolly's death.

'We saw him again several times over the years, in comedy films and the like. Bad ones. On the TV, sometimes. And he was in one of those farces which people seemed to like in the old days – *A Row of Tents*, it was called. It had that actor in it, the one who's such a hit these days: Robert Craufurd.'

'I know who you mean.'

'Nick and I waited at the stage door afterwards, but then we thought: what would we say to Ken? What is there we could possibly have said? So we just went home.'

'Kenneth Langdon is one of the two people I mentioned who've recently been murdered.'

'But who'd want to kill him? He must be an old man. We all are. Old, I mean.'

'I think someone was afraid he was going to speak up about things which that someone wants kept quiet. Which is why I'm ringing you.'

'Jan might know.'

'Janice, do you mean?'

'Yes. She was a music student: she was out in Nigeria doing VSO work, I believe.'

'Do you have her address?'

'No. And I don't know what her married name was, either. Or there was that government man, Michael Farquharson.'

'You said you'd never heard of him.'

'I lied. When you mentioned his name, I was afraid. I knew . . . it finally was about to burst.'

'What about Farquharson?'

'Nick and I were in the same field, so we got on well with him. Saw him a couple of times after we all got back to England. But there was always this . . . *thing* between us. We couldn't ever forget it. So we didn't keep the relationship going.'

'I'm afraid he's dead, too.'

'Not . . .'

'No, not murdered. He had cancer.'

'I'm sorry to hear that.' A long pause. 'I'm sorry about everything, really.'

'If I can identify the priest, the clergyman, whatever, would you be willing to confirm that he was the one who offered those people in exchange for you?'

'We were all guilty.'

'But some are guiltier than others.'

'I'm not sure I can accept that. But I'd be prepared to stand up and admit that I was there with him. To take some of the blame. Yes. I would like to do that. For Nick's sake as well as for my own.' More silence. 'He was drunk when he crashed his car. He was an alcoholic.'

'I'm sorry.'

'I don't know why I'm pouring all this out to a complete stranger.'

'Perhaps you needed to.'

A sigh as light as a soufflé came down the line. 'I haven't spoken of this to anyone, ever: I'm glad to have the opportunity.'

'I could come and visit you.'

'Please don't. It's so much easier to talk to you like this, disembodied, than it would be face to face. And such a help. Since Nick died, it's become more and more of a burden. When there were two of us, we were able to share it, but now . . .' Three heartbeats of silence went by, then Viv Parfitt went on: 'It's not so difficult to keep a secret when it's to do with personal privacy, or to protect someone, but when it's something which conflicts with your moral sensibilities, with your perceptions of right and wrong, of self, then it grows unbearable. So thank you, whoever you are, for listening, and please count on me to back up anything you want to reveal.'

The links were growing stronger. Kenneth Langdon had been positively identified. If only she could find out the name of the troublesome priest. She thought of Janice, the music student. And then of Liz Trowbridge's lover. She was the right age. Could it be . . . but no. That Jan Thomas was one and the same person as Janice the harmonium-player would be too much of a stretch for anyone to believe in. And yet, coincidences do happen. In real life they happen a lot. And it would explain Lolly's over-the-top reaction to the woman. Not homophobia but distress at seeing her again, and in such a situation.

Resonances. There was another Janice on the scene: Janice Frankum. If you were going to suspend disbelief once, you might as well suspend it twice. And while there was no reason on earth to suppose that Janice Frankum had the slightest connection with Lolly or Africa or, indeed, the harmonium, it could not be gainsaid that she had arrived on the local scene at the same time as Lolly had started acting oddly. Perhaps she had been a contributory factor.

Without hesitation, Cassie reached for the telephone once more then put it down while she searched her files for Janice Frankum's address and phone number. There were various approaches she could take. She could be subtle; she could be direct. Direct was often best. When Janice picked up the phone, she said: 'Hi, it's Cassandra Swann here.'

'Who?'

'Cassie Swann. We played bridge at Natasha Sinclair's house the other—'

'Oh yes, I remember. The big girl, is that right?'

Fuck you, too, Cassie thought. 'I was wondering whether you'd ever been in Nigeria,' she said coldly.

'What an odd question. Why do you want—'

'Have you?'

'As it happens, yes.'

'How long ago?'

'Years and years. Before you were born, I should think.'

That won't put you back on my Christmas card list, thought Cassie. 'Did you play the harmonium while you were there?'

'Play the what?'

'Harmonium.'

'Look, do you have an alcohol problem? I couldn't help noticing that you and that other girl – Petra, was it? – weren't stinting yourself the other night. You personally had at least six glasses of Chardonnay, to my certain knowledge.'

'Are you trying to avoid answering my question?' Christ: no wonder nobody liked this woman. Fancy counting how many glasses of wine a complete stranger drank at a party. And what was it to do with her, anyway?

'Not in the slightest. Just wondering why you should think I ever played the harmonium.'

'So you didn't.'

'Never.'

'Ever work for the VSO?'

'I was in Nigeria with my parents – my father was a naval attaché – for about eight months before he was posted to Singapore.' Janice spoke as though through gritted teeth, her exasperation clear. 'I was sixteen at the time, and at boarding school here, but I went out there in the Easter holidays. All right? Does that satisfy you?'

'Not quite.' Defeated but determined, Cassie pressed on. 'Did you ever meet the Vicar of St Bart's while you were out there?'

'John Lightower?'

'That's the one.'

'No, I did *not* meet John Lightower, as far as I recall. Nor any other clergyman. My parents weren't churchgoers.'

'I see.'

'Anything else you want to know? What my mother's

maiden name was? Whether I'm an undischarged bankrupt? What my golf handicap is?'

'That's all.' Cassie put the phone down.

Janice Frankum didn't sound like the Jan she was after.

Which left the more problematic Jan Thomas, friend and partner of Liz Trowbridge. A woman with both the opportunity and the ability to kill Lolly. A woman with a motive. But – Cassie paused with her hand on the receiver – what motive, exactly? Even if she were to crack under the pressure of Cassie's remorseless questioning and admit that she'd been glued to a harmonium since she was a child, what would it prove? Why would the harmonium-playing Jan want to murder witnesses to the Nigerian atrocity, especially after so much time had elapsed? If Jan Thomas had a motive at all, it was much more likely to be the hope of gaining financially by Lolly's death, via Lolly's legacy to Liz, or the desire to save Liz from further distress caused by Lolly's unabashed loathing for sexual deviancy. And the police would have checked that out already.

She picked up the telephone again, and dialled Chadwell Court. Put through to the Matron, she produced a cod-Mummerset accent, lowered her voice and said: 'Oi'm ringin' on behaalf of Mr Chaarles Quartermain.'

'Ah.' Matron sounded delighted. 'And what can we do for him?'

'He's just heard the news 'bout Kenneth Langdon . . .'

'So sad . . .'

Would Quartermain's Devonshire secretary say 'he'm be'? She thought not. '. . . And he's wonderin' 'bout the Christmas entertainment.'

'You know what those showbiz types always say?'

A number of clichés sprang to mind. 'Whass tha', then?'

' "The show must go on." That's what he would have said. Ken was such a trouper, I know he would hate to think that his death should cause the entertainment to be cancelled.'

'Oi don't think there's any question of tha',' said Cassie. 'But Mr Quartermain was real upset when he were told. Said he hoped it were a quiet death.'

'Yes, indeed.'

'Benefit of clergy an' tha'.' Cassie said encouragingly, since Matron was declining to volunteer the details.

'He can rest assured on that score. Ken was visited by Mr Lightower just as he was going to sleep. The Padre assured us that he saw him drifting off himself and crept out of the room so as not to disturb him.'

'Who did?' Pulses thudded behind Cassie's ears.

'The Vicar. The Reverend Lightower.'

'You called him the Padre.'

'That's right. One of our residents, Colonel Forster, started it when he came here, and in the end we all adopted it.'

'Whoi'd 'e do tha', then?'

'I've no idea. It's the normal Army usage, isn't it? To call the chaplain Padre?'

'Aar. Well, Oi'll be glad to pass that information on to Mr Quartermain.'

'He's such a sweet man, isn't he?'

'Adorable.'


Every time she thought she had started up a hare, it turned into a field-mouse. Hearing the Vicar referred to as Padre, for a moment there she had truly believed that she had finally pinned him down, could prove that he was the man who all those years ago had traded seven people for twenty-seven. Yet Matron's explanation could not be argued with. Nothing could be more logical than that a military gentleman in a nursing home should address the resident clergyman as Padre. Which did not remove suspicion from him entirely, of course.

So where to now?

As if in response, a shadow darkened the kitchen window and Paul Walsh came in through the back door, ducking under the trailing strands of ivy, making God-it's-cold-out-there noises as he stood smiling at her.

'Paul!' She got up and walked round to stand with her body pressed against his, wondering why her heart leaped up when she saw him when, if the truth were told, she hardly knew this enigma of a man and what she did know, scarcely approved of.

He kissed her. 'I'm on duty.'

'So I can't tempt you by showing you my knickers.'

'You could try, but I'd have to report it.'

'How about coffee: is that allowed?'

'I think so.'

When they were seated on either side of the table, she said: 'Shoot.'

'What do you want to know?'

'Guess.'

'OK. Yes, I love you.'

'Anything else?'

'We're still trying to trace Mrs Haden White's husband. So far, there's been no record of his death, so we're working on the assumption that he's still around somewhere. And by the way, she made some pretty shrewd investments: if he *is* still alive, and knew what she was worth, he could have a damn strong motive. Since there's nothing to show that they ever divorced, if he turns up, he could stand to cop the lot.'

'He refused to support her and the children when he left her,' Cassie said. 'So she cut him out of her life. If he is the killer, I wonder how he found her again.'

'Probably sheer chance. There's a lot more of that around than people believe. She's in London, at the theatre, strolling down the Strand, bumps into him. She sees his name in the papers and decides, after all this time, to get in touch.'

'Not Lolly.'

'She goes to a party and, surprise, surprise, he's there too. It could have happened thousands of different ways. And once he's found her again, and discovered how well she's done, he begins to plot her murder. Obviously,' Paul said, 'it must have happened fairly recently.'

'Like in the past three or four months.'

'That's about the time scale we're looking at, yes.'

'It's when she started to go funny, too.'

'Which bears out my theory. While we try to find him, we're continuing to eliminate the obvious suspects. We've cleared the older daughter and her partner: they were both at a Parents' Evening at their school and then went out with some of the other teachers to have an Indian in Bellington. The party didn't split up until well after 1 a.m., by which time the poor old lady was dead.'

'What about the younger daughter?'

'She doesn't have an alibi, but she doesn't strike me as the sort.'

'I thought it was cop shop lore that the more harmless they look, the more likely they are to have done it.'

'You've been reading too many detective stories. Mrs Smith's far too mumsy to go out leaving her children alone in the house. I suppose she *could* have done it – slipped across the road when the kids were asleep and bashed her mother's head in – but what motive would she have? The husband makes good money and so does she. The house isn't mortgaged; they're neither of them into gambling or drink or drugs.'

'Who else are you looking at?'

'I'll be frank with you, Cass. We haven't got a clue about who it could have been. Not a clue. Every lead we've followed so far – except for the husband – has turned out to be a dead end. All the fingerprints in the house have been accounted for, including yours, except for one set, and that doesn't have to be chummy's, it could have been the guy who came to fix the central heating. Nobody's reported any sightings of strangers lurking that evening, or cars which no-one recognised. It's not going to be an easy one, I'm afraid.'

He looked so dispirited, that for a moment she was almost tempted to tell him what she had discovered about the African connection, about Lolly's virtual disappearance when she returned to England and the distance she'd put between herself and her family. Then she remembered Lolly herself, her fierce privacy, the effort she had made to reinvent herself. She thought, too, about the indignities of old age, treated as no more than an object to be moved about at someone else's will, stripped, scrubbed, polished and fed, no longer a sentient being, inanimate. She thought of Commander Ruthven Gowrie, his occupation gone. Of Bettina Maggs, cheerful in her despair. All of them clinging, against the battering of society's desire to tidy them away, to the remains of their selves. For all Cassie knew, the African business might have no connection at all with the case, might be no more than a creel full of conjectural red herrings. If she had one positive piece of proof . . . but she didn't, beyond the connection between Lolly and Kenneth Langdon. She could hardly be accused of withholding evidence. For the time being, she determined to go on keeping Lolly's secrets.

Paul Walsh really was on duty, so apart from a couple of lingering kisses and an exploratory fondle or two, he did not stay long. When he had gone, Cassie wheeled her new bike out of the shed-cum-garage and cycled down to Frith, with the intention of dropping in on Charlie, to tell him about Kenneth Langdon's death.

He opened the door to her. He seemed less than enthusiastic at the sight of her. 'Hi,' he said.

'What did you say?'

'I said "hi".'

'That's all?' Something was wrong. She peered beyond him into the spacious hall. 'What's going on, Charlie?'

'Nothing.'

'Can I come in?'

'Uh . . .'

She pushed past him into the house. She could hear Ted talking to someone in the drawing room, laughing his phlegmy laugh. She stopped. 'You've got company. I'll go.'

'Well . . .'

She had never seen Charlie nonplussed before and found it rather sweet. Teasing him, she said: 'Any chance of a drink before I go? I promise not to stay long.'

'I suppose . . .'

She pushed open the drawing-room door. There were three people in there. As well as Ted, there was Petra Lewis. And someone else, a man whom she could not have failed to recognise unless she'd been living down a well for the past twelve months. He came forward with his hand outstretched.

'Hello. How very very nice to meet you,' he said. 'I'm Robert Craufurd.' As if she didn't know.

Cassie took his hand. Did he already know about Kenneth Langdon? Was that why he was here? 'How do you do. I'm Cassandra Swann.'

'Spinster of this parish,' said Charlie. 'But don't blame me.'

'Such a pleasure, Cassandra.' Craufurd switched on a practised smile and switched it off again before it could do anything more than elongate his lips. 'I must say, Quartermain, old son, what with Miss Lewis and now Miss Swann, you've some ravishing females concealed about your person. What're you running here, a harem or something?'

It was the kind of remark which would normally have had Petra asking where the sick bags were kept but now she simply laughed, a tinkly silvery unPetra-like laugh which made Cassie wonder if she'd been drinking.

Cassie bared her teeth. 'How are you, Petra?'

'Brilliant,' said Petra. She'd definitely been drinking. 'Charlie's always such a generous host, aren't you, darling Charlie?' Only she said 'darlie Charling'.

'Yer.' He cast an uneasy glance at Cassie.

'Are you staying long?' Cassie asked Craufurd.

'Got to get back to London tonight,' he said. 'But Charlie suggested I pop down and visit, just run over the arrangements for the Christmas, my dear, Extravag*anz*a.' He did his Harry Walkinshaw bit, and Ted guffawed sycophantically. 'Thought I'd drop in on my old mate, Ken, too, while I was here.'

'Could I use the . . . uh . . .?' Cassie said to Charlie, who was standing awkwardly beside her.

'Course.'

'Would you mind showing me where it is?'

'But you—' He stared at her, then, seeing her expression, switched from yokel to on-the-ball mode. '—this way please.'

Outside in the hall, Cassie said: 'You obviously don't know that Kenneth Langdon died last night.'

'No. Oh no.' Charlie's big face drooped. 'Oh Lord. What happened?'

Cassie explained.

'Somebody'll have to tell him.' He nodded at the closed door of the drawing room.

From the other side of the door came peals of girlish glee. '*You'll* have to tell him,' Cassie said firmly. 'How long's he been here?'

'Came for lunch.'

'He'll have to know.'

'Yer.'

He looked so crestfallen that Cassie said: 'All right: I'll do it.'

'Thanks, Cass.' He turned and grasped the brass door handle.

'What's *she* doing here?' They were the last words Cassie had intended to produce but they popped from her mouth with the alacrity of woodlice scuttling from beneath a turned stone.

'Who?'

'Who do you damn well think?'

'She stopped by.'

'Does she make a habit of it?'

'She's been here before,' Charlie admitted unwillingly.

'And you're always such a *gen*erous host, darlie *Char*ling.'

'Cass . . .'

'Would you climb a mountain for *her*, Charlie? Or swim an ocean?'

'*Course* not.'

'Have you – you know – been to bed with her?'

He looked confused.

'Don't bloody well answer that.' Cassie said. She went back into the drawing room, telling herself that she did not feel in the least hurt, that Charlie had a perfect right to screw whomever he wished, just as she did. She smiled at the assembled company then rearranged her features into solemnity. 'I'm afraid there's been a bit of a setback for the Christmas show,' she said.

'Oooh,' screeched Craufurd, all camp attention. 'Don't keep us in suspense, dear heart.'

'One of the old folk at the home died last night.' She looked at him directly. 'I'm really sorry, Mr Craufurd, but they found your friend Kenneth Langdon dead this morning.'

The actor stared at her, his features doing a slow dissolve from facetious to appalled. 'Oh no. How too ghastly.' He put his hands to his face. 'Poor old Ken,' he murmured brokenly.

The trouble with actors was that it was almost impossible for their behaviour to appear spontaneous. Having simulated grief of anger or amusement on screen or stage, any observer found themselves mentally evaluating the performance when they came up against the real thing. Or was Cassie just more cynical than most? Craufurd certainly did good distress. Perhaps he was genuinely moved; Cassie couldn't tell.

'I'm sorry to be the one to tell you,' she said awkwardly.

'For a small place, we certainly have our share of sudden death.' Petra turned to Craufurd. 'Only last week we actually had a murder.'

'In an idyllic spot like this? How terrible. Who was it?'

Was that a hint of tears on his cheek?

'Someone Cassie and I often played bridge with. Which somehow makes it all the more dreadful, doesn't it, Cassie?'

'Much worse,' agreed Cassie. She was trying to decide whether she liked Craufurd or whether he was a posey old queen. Or both. Also, who exactly was it that he reminded her of. Or was it simply that everywhere he went, he carried with him, perforce, his *alter ego*, Harry Walkinshaw, OAP, sixty-eight and still going strong?

'And the police still don't seem to have the vaguest idea who killed Lolly.' Petra turned to Cassie. 'Or has your boyfriend finally made an arrest?'

'Who do you mean?' Cassie asked coldly.

'That policeman you go around with.'

'Did you say Lolly?' Craufurd's body assumed a pose of actorish curiosity, arching itself into a question mark. 'What an odd name.' He brushed a hand across his eyes.

'It's short for Dolores,' Cassie said.

'Dolores. How very Forties.' Shifting about on the sofa he was sharing with Petra so that he could look more directly at Cassie, he added. 'And you say this poor woman was murdered?'

'That's right.' Cassie gave him the details.

As though he were a dog emerging from an icy pond, Craufurd shook himself. Transmuted into an alternative persona. 'God *knows* what it says about the human race,' he said campily. 'We're all so *ghoul*ishly fascinated by violent death, aren't we? *Do* tell me more. How long had this woman been living here? Did she have family? Children? They must have been *dev*astated, poor things.'

'She'd been here a number of years. And there are two daughters.'

'Two daughters, hm? And no father?'

'The father's supposed to be dead,' Cassie said. 'That's what Lolly told people, though we're beginning to wonder if it was true. Her elder daughter, in particular.'

'And where would she be living now?'

'In Oxford. She's Head of Drama at one of the local schools.'

'Drama?' said Craufurd. 'I suppose she has her own family to sustain her in this *grievous* loss. A husband? Children?'

Cassie always felt as if the piss was being taken when people used such phraseology, but the actor seemed perfectly serious. 'Sort of.' She didn't feel it was her business to parade Liz Trowbridge's private affairs in front of this stranger, even if he was interested enough to ask.

'Odd that there's no apparent motive for this poor woman's murder.' Craufurd continued. 'No sexual assault. Nothing stolen. Remind me not to move down here, sounds horribly dangerous.' The talk of murder had obviously disturbed him. He looked over at Charlie, and with an effort, switched back into actorish mode. 'Charlie, old boy, I think I shall have to make my adieux, if you don't mind. Apart from anything else, I really ought to pop along to this nursing home place and pay my last respects to poor old Ken before I leg it back to Town.'

'Want me to drive you? You could leave your car and I'll bring you back here, afterwards.'

'Wouldn't hear of it, old boy. Don't worry about me, I can find my own way. You stay and look after your guests.' He turned to Cassie. 'It's been most interesting, Cassandra Swann,' he said. 'I look forward to meeting you again when I come down for Quartermain's pageant thingie.'

'So you're still on for that, are you?' Charlie's big face broke into a grin.

'Gave you my word, old boy. All I need now is a substitute for poor Ken. But leave that to me: I'll find someone suitable.' He shook his head sadly. 'I can't believe he's died: we've been friends for years, and now he's gone.' He glanced round the room. '*And all our yesterdays*,' he declaimed, '*have lighted fools the way to dusty death*.'

'Lay on, Macduff,' said Charlie.

Craufurd straightened his shoulders, touched his hair again, relaunched himself into campness. 'Lay on indeed, dear boy. The younger the better. As a matter of fact, Kenneth and I did the Scottish play together once, Down Under. He played Banquo, I gave them my Macduff. And, to be honest, anything else they wanted. Ooooh dearie me, those Ozzie types, in*sat*iable, they were.'

Ted's lip curled. Cassie left.

She had cycled almost as far as the main road when a car pulled up alongside her. 'Miss Swann,' the driver called from his window. It was Craufurd.

'Yes?' She wobbled slightly, trying to avoid a couple of waterlogged potholes in the road.

'This woman who teaches drama at a school in Oxford . . .'

'Liz Trowbridge? What about her?'

'It occurred to me that it might be fun if she had a pupil who could take the part that poor Ken Langdon was going to do. After all, this is a local entertainment and—'

'I'm sure the old people would rather see someone professional, if you could find someone at such short notice. And Oxford's hardly local.'

His grey Volvo crept through the dusk, keeping pace with

her. 'Nonetheless, given the connection with this poor murdered Mrs White, it might be a sort of memorial.'

'Except none of them had ever heard of her.'

'But they knew Kenneth Langdon.'

'What's that got to do—' Cassie wrested the handlebars round to avoid hitting what might have been a dead cat lying in the road. 'Look, do you mind if I . . .'

'At the very least, it'd be backup, just in case I can't find one of my colleagues willing to take the part.' His white hair gleamed at the car window. 'Television is so demanding, as I'm sure you're aware.'

'Why not a drama student, then?'

'God preserve me from drama students,' he said richly. 'What about this Miss . . . wotsername? Trowbridge? . . . taking the part herself.'

'Nothing, I suppose. Except she's a woman.'

'I'm not prejudiced, dear, though some of my best friends are. Could add a certain piquancy to the number, don't you think? And it would save me all that phoning around if she'd be willing to lend a hand. She's in North Oxford, I think you said.'

'East, actually.'

'Got an address?'

Why was the man so persistent? 'Yes, but I'm not sure I should give it to you.'

'Dear heart, the lady has nothing to fear from me. I'm not in the least straight, I promise you.'

It might do Liz Trowbridge some good professionally to make the actor's acquaintance. She might even be annoyed if she discovered that Cassie had refused to give her address to a man who might be in a position to further her career in some way. You never knew what could come of it. Cassie

gave him the address, which he repeated a couple of times
before thanking her and speeding off, sending a wave of cold
water over her feet. Dammit. She must remember to ring Liz
as soon as she got home, to warn her that Robert Craufurd,
no less, might arrive at her door any moment, demanding that
she don a stuffy fur coat and sing 'Underneath the Arches'
with him.

# ◆ 14 ◆

Paul Walsh's face floated through her sleep. Bothering her. Admonishing. Or challenging. Something said during their conversation – was it by him, or her? – buzzbombed her brain with the irritating persistence of a bluebottle but she couldn't isolate what it was. Don't think about it. Turn. Shift. Get up for a pee. Ignore it and eventually it would settle long enough for her to swat it. Something else was bothering her – an out-of-place remark, a misplaced object? – buried deeper, no more than a shape beneath the surface of her thoughts. That, too, would make itself known eventually.

She got up early and went down to the kitchen to make tea. There was a ratty chunk of bread left in the stoneware crock; that was it, breakfast-wise. She scraped the lichenlike rings of mould off the crust, sliced it sideways to make two pieces and stuck them in the toaster. Hadn't she read recently that eating mouldy food caused cancer? Grimacing with distaste, she ate the toast and stared out at the winter drizzle which softened the skyline beyond the back hedge and added a varnished look to the graveyard garden. The leaves of the hollybush beside the converted barn which was now the head office of Bridge The Gap had an inimical slick to them which made her feel reluctant to venture out into the wet chilliness in order to open up the office and start the day's work of dealing with correspondence and dispatching the orders which continued – thank God – to come in with every post. One of these years, she and Natasha might even be able to draw a salary.

At nine thirty, Hugh Nightingale rang from his mobile phone; he would be passing nearby tomorrow morning and wondered if she had made any decision about cooking for him and some guests one evening next week, in which case he'd like to drop in and discuss the menu with her. It was difficult to give him an answer. The job would pay well. It would also bring some much-needed glamour and excitement into a life which on this grey morning seemed about as close to not worth living as she cared to get. Nonetheless, she had not yet made her mind up about whether she wanted to take on a new responsibility and was about to turn him down when she produced a tiny burp. This reminder of the bread she had been forced to consume for breakfast – it was that or starve – stiffened her reluctant sinews. She reminded herself that there was an added bonus: once he was in the house, she would be able to quiz him about his friend, John Lightower.

'What sort of time?' she asked.

'Elevenish? I'm on my way to have lunch with some old friends.'

'Good. We can talk over coffee, if you don't mind instant, which is all I've got.' She wondered if she dared ask him to bring in a fresh loaf or a packet of Digestives, but decided that given the shortness of their acquaintance, that would be going too far.

She had scarcely replaced the receiver when the telephone rang again. This time it was Brian Edgecombe. 'Remember I said we should have lunch some time?'

'How could I forget?'

'I'm off to Cornwall in a couple of days' time, so how about making it tomorrow?'

She thought quickly. If she survived until tomorrow, if Nightingale arrived on time and their discussions were fruitful – which meant she would definitely have to make up her mind about taking the job before he got here – then that would pan out well. 'Sounds terrific.'

'I'll come and pick you up in the motor. Nothing fancy, mind. Just a pub lunch. Us pensioners can't afford luxuries like you young folk, we've got to keep an eye on the future.'

'Don't give me that crap, Brian Edgecombe. I saw what you put in your basket at the supermarket.'

'Got to keep up my strength, you know. I'm not as young as I was.'

'Who is?' she said. 'Why are you going to Cornwall?'

'Always wanted to go there.'

'Will you be there on your own?'

'Since you mention it, no.'

'What've you been up to, Brian?'

'What happened was, I met this very nice woman, widow of a friend of mine, as a matter of fact. And turns out she's keen on Cornwall, too. So we decided to go together. Drive down, share the cost of the petrol, that sort of thing.'

'Separate rooms, Brian?'

'That's my business, young lady.'

'Won't your wife be jealous if she gets to hear of it?'

'She'll hear of it, don't you worry. I'll make sure of that.'

'Sounds to me like you're just using this poor widow for your own ends.'

'One last shot for my generation,' he said, enigmatically.

'Is that your own line, or did you steal it from a presidential campaign?'

'Of course, if you'd come with me, I'd ditch the widow quicker than you can say "pension book".'

'Shame on you.'

Over a mug of coffee, she glanced at the paper. Recently there'd been a spate of cases involving children; abductions, murders, sexual abuse. She considered herself fairly tuned in to her fellow humans, even if she didn't like a lot of them, but the mindset of someone who could mistreat, at whatever level, a helpless child, was incomprehensible. Which was how she hoped to keep it. Understanding is supposed to lead to forgiveness but there were some crimes which were unforgivable. She turned the pages of the newspaper. It was pretty much the same old stuff as usual. Wars. Politicians. Celebrities getting married or divorced. A really useful article on Yuletide gifts for under £100.

The phone rang again. A frail voice identified itself as Dorothy Farquharson. 'I've been going through my husband's things and I've found some papers which might be of interest to you,' she said. 'If you're still interested, that is.'

'Believe me, I'm interested,' Cassie said.

'I was wondering . . . are you free this afternoon? It might be as well if you picked them up as soon as possible. I don't know why, but my daughter seems to object to any mention of her father at the moment.'

Or any sign of independence in her mother, Cassie thought. 'I'll set off in the next half-hour,' she promised.

'Don't be late. I don't wish to behave in a deceitful fashion, but my daughter will be away until this evening and whatever she says about it, I'd like to feel that Michael's worries were sorted out, even if it's too late for him. He died before he could send these things to Mrs Haden White, and though she rang up and even came here once, Angela wasn't very nice to her.'

'I see.' Poor old lady: her future looked bleak if the bitchy daughter was going to be in charge.

'I'd be much happier if I could somehow put things right by giving the papers to you.'

'I'll see you soon,' Cassie said. Never mind the cost of the petrol. She'd just have to break into her emergency funds, i.e. the five £10-notes she kept rolled up in an empty plastic container which had once held Oil of Evening Primrose capsules.

Before she left for Henley, she found a copy of one of Tim Gardiner's books which had been signed but not dedicated. Dorothy Farquharson would probably appreciate it a lot more than Cassandra Swann ever had.

Driving through the shut-down countryside, she wondered why a daughter should treat her own mother with such contempt. Perhaps as a mother, Dorothy Farquharson had been neglectful in some way, and this was her reward. But she hadn't struck Cassie as that kind of woman. Quite the opposite, in fact. She was of the generation where women dedicated their lives to their families, always there, always caring. Whereas someone like Lolly . . . There was something detestable about the fact that Serena should feel guilty about weeping for her dead mother, as though feelings must be suppressed at all costs. Aunt Polly had brought Cassie up to feel the same, but the training had not, thank God, taken. At least Lolly's own lack of emotional input hadn't – as far as Cassie had been able to judge – harmed Serena's own mothering instincts.

Aunt Polly must be thought about, try as she might to

avoid the subject. When she got back, Cassie determined to go through the motions: telephone Eric, act concerned. Not that she wasn't concerned – of course she was. But only as she might be for any human being waiting to hear whether they were going to die from cancer. Anything more personal was difficult. It was impossible to dredge up any weight of grief for a woman so contained, so emotionally cold. So bloody *damaging*.

Best not to continue down that route. Instead, she tried to work out what exactly it was that was bugging her about the conversation she'd had with Paul. The significant words hovered clearly, just at the edge of her mind, but refused to come into focus. Something about . . . Or was it . . .? '*Too mumsy*,' Paul Walsh had called Serena. Too mumsy to kill Lolly. This was not a mother who would allow her children to play outside on the street, or stay out late without adequate precautions or leave them alone at night. Cassie's hands began to sweat. With sickening clarity, she realised why it had been nagging at her. Serena could have done it, he'd said, she *could* have done it – but what motive would she have? And yet, days ago, Serena herself had supplied a clear motive.

Rain spattered the windscreen as Cassie tried to remember the exact words spoken. When she'd first become alarmed about Lolly's state of mind and had gone to visit Serena, Serena had said that putting her mother into a home would not be an option, since it would cost far more than she and her husband could afford. She had added that her marriage was going through a rocky patch and that her husband had said he wouldn't have Lolly to live with them, that if push came to shove, Serena would have to choose between them. No prizes for guessing which one she'd go for. If that wasn't a motive, what was?

And who would find it easier to kill Lolly than Serena? She only had to make sure her children were asleep, then slip round the corner and across the green. Lolly, half-dozing over a book in the sitting-room, would have heard the knock and enquired through the door who it was. 'Only me, Mother,' Serena might have said, 'just popping in for a quick coffee, it's been a hard day at work and the children have been playing up all evening, I need to relax.' Something easy and natural along those lines. And then, while her mother was plugging in the kettle or looking for the biscuit tin, Serena had crept up from behind and tried to strangle her. Lolly had broken away. Perhaps tried to calm her daughter down. Reason with her. If that strange cry on Cassie's answering machine telephone was indeed Lolly, it would mean she'd somehow found a chance to get to the telephone. It would also explain why she had called Cassie rather than her own daughter. But Serena, knowing that her mother was behaving more and more oddly and seeing the ruin of her marriage lying ahead of her, had only been delayed in carrying out her plan, not deflected from it. Perhaps she'd gone on to accuse Lolly of denying her and her sister of the things that children need: family, demonstrations of love, warmth. Wound up, she'd attacked again, chasing Lolly out into the frosty garden, catching up with the old woman and strangling her, stowing her body behind the garage. Then she would have slipped back home across the green, let herself quietly into the house, and gone to bed as usual. In the morning, she would have telephoned her mother's house several times then alerted the police when Lolly didn't answer the phone, though knowing all the while that her mother was dead.

God, how horrible. Perhaps the reason Serena had wanted

Cassie with her when she cleared up her mother's house was not sorrow, but guilt. Fear that Lolly's ghost might rise up and point a condemnatory finger at her. She remembered Serena's madly nodding head, and how she had thought then that there was something slightly out of kilter about her. Because you'd have to be off-balance to kill your own mother, wouldn't you? Had Lolly known, or at least suspected, that her own daughter harboured murderous thoughts towards her? Probably not, otherwise she would never have let her into the house so late at night.

The more she thought about the scenario, the more obvious it seemed. How could she have missed it? Even though it felt like a betrayal, she would have to tell Paul, since it was highly unlikely that Serena would have spoken so frankly to the police about her family circumstances. After that, it was up to him to follow it up. She thought about Michael Farquharson's papers. If Serena had killed her mother, they no longer had any bearing on Lolly's death. Still, it would be satisfying to clear up the loose ends at last.

She was back in the cottage by whisky-pouring time. Dorothy Farquharson had been touchingly grateful for the book and, in exchange, had handed her a plastic Tesco carrier. 'I'd love to invite you in for coffee,' she said wistfully, 'but I daren't, in case Angie comes back early. It would never do for her to find you here.'

'All right. But I'll come and visit you soon,' Cassie said. 'I'm quite often in this direction.'

'That would be lovely,' said Mrs Farquharson brightly. She touched the photograph of Tim Gardiner on the back of the book. 'Not as good as Raymond Chandler, is he?'

'Tell me who is,' said Cassie.

'But better looking.'

'If you like that kind of thing.'

'I do,' Mrs Farquharson said fervently. 'Very much indeed.' Almost immediately, she faded; her shoulders started to hunch, her still-pretty face to fold in on itself, as though she had taken her teeth out. 'Don't tell Angela, though,' she whispered, as if afraid her daughter might otherwise accuse her of gross impropriety. She gazed wistfully at Cassie then went inside. But before she closed the door, before Cassie had taken a step towards her car, she had come back onto the step. 'I'd so much rather have given Michael's things to you,' she said, 'than to that clergyman.'

Cassie whipped round. 'What did you say?'

'He tried to bully me. Just like my daughter does.'

'Which clergyman? What was his name?'

'He didn't even tell me. Such discourtesy. He came to the door, said he'd met Michael years ago in Africa and was writing a book about that time, that he'd spoken to Michael on the phone and been promised his papers. Such lies.'

'Are you sure they were lies?'

'Of course they were. I said I didn't remember him telephoning and he said he'd done so several times over the past months. In the weeks before he died, Michael couldn't have answered the phone, he was far too weak. And after that, he was dead. So this clergyman must have spoken to me and I certainly don't remember anyone asking for those papers, apart from yourself and Mrs Haden White.' She gazed vaguely at the shrubbery which separated the house from the road. 'It's particularly disconcerting, don't you find, when those you expect to be morally pure prove to be quite the opposite?'

'Oh yes. It seems to make the sinning doubly sinful.'

Mrs Farquharson nodded, went back inside the house and closed the door.

The clergyman. John Lightower! If Mrs Farquharson would identify him, she'd finally have the proof she needed to place him right there, at the centre of Lolly's drama.

Cassie emptied the contents of the carrier bag onto the carpet in front of the hearth. They were fewer than she had expected. Some cheap notebooks with red covers, some letters, a list of addresses in crabbed writing, a few yellowed newspaper cuttings. Both the notebooks had the word Kenya written on the first page, but when she thumbed through them, Cassie saw that these were no more than working notes, probably taken in the field, to do with water tables and local use of fertilisers, cash crop percentages, population figures per square mile, agronomic equations. None of it seemed remotely interesting, let alone to have any connection with Lolly.

The letters were more interesting. Dated more than thirty years ago, they were from Kenneth Langdon, from Viv and Nick Parfitt, from Edith's parents. From a woman called Janice Millington. Somehow Farquharson had tracked them down and then asked them if they knew the name of the clergyman in charge of the mission and they had all told him that they did not. Had this been before or after Lolly had written to him and he had rejected her? After, probably, his conscience perhaps stirred by Lolly's questions. And yet, although he had most of the information Lolly so badly needed, he had not got in touch, had still hesitated until it was almost too late. Why? Fear of exposure, of the press, fear of losing his job, fear of having his friends think less of him, of seeing disillusion in his wife's eyes? Or perhaps because of the difficulty of facing himself each day in the mirror. It was over, done with, nothing could bring those poor people back, or change the course of events. Better to leave it lie.

Cassie looked again at the letter from Janice Millington. The others had written long letters expressing a desire to keep out of it, but passing on names where they knew them. Janice had not.

'*I don't want to think about what happened out there,*' she wrote, curtly. '*It was too horrific, too horrible. We have to go on living our lives. Please don't contact me again.*'

Her address was printed at the top of the writing paper; Farquharson had crossed it out, fairly recently by the state of the ink, and added a new one. So despite her rejection of his enquiries, he had kept tabs on her. By an annual phone call, perhaps, and then one day the new owners telling him she'd moved, giving him her new address, her phone number.

But there was still no mention anywhere of the name of the cleric who had struck that infamous bargain. What lay behind the constant omission? Was it carelessness, coincidence, coercion? Not one of the people who'd been present at the time seemed to know what he was called. She went through the other papers. The cuttings were from newspapers in South Africa but there was nothing useful. Janice Millington looked like being her very last hope of identifying the man. After this, she could not see where else to go in her search.

But perhaps it no longer mattered. Thoughtfully, Cassie lifted the phone and dialled the number. It rang five times and then a man's voice said: 'This is the Millington residence. I'm afraid neither of us are here to answer your call, but if you'd like to leave your name and phone number, we will get back to you as soon as we can.'

'My name's Cassandra Swann, and I'd like to speak to Mrs

Millington,' said Cassie. She gave her phone number. 'It's a matter of some urgency.'

She was conscious of let-down. If Serena was responsible for her mother's death, then Lightower couldn't be. So even if Janice Millington could confirm his presence at that massacre, it wouldn't implicate him in Lolly's murder. Which was just as well, really, since the only motive she could come up with would have been flimsy, no more than a desire on his part to keep the incident in Nigeria quiet. And his involvement in *that* was still pure supposition on her part.

Aware of creeping exhaustion, she remembered that she had been going to try to identify Lolly's husband. How was she to achieve that? And what did it really matter – except to his daughters? It was another thing Paul Walsh could handle, since he had all the resources necessary to follow him up, especially with the new information she'd obtained from Farquharson's papers and Ruthven Gowrie's research. She'd call him in the morning. Tell him everything she had found out.

Meanwhile, she was going to go to bed early with, in the absence of anything more exciting, a good book.

# ♥ 15 ♥

'Paul? It's me.'

'Hello, me.'

'Listen: perhaps I should have told you this before, but it only occurred to me after what you said about her having no motive.' Hurriedly, guiltily, Cassie stumbled through the reasons why Serena had to have been the one who killed Lolly Haden White.

Walsh listened in silence until she had finished. Then he said: 'Haven't you got a friend who writes detective stories?'

'Tim Gardiner? Yes . . . why?'

'Ever thought of taking up writing fiction yourself?'

'In other words, you don't agree with me?'

'In other words, darling, I know for a fact that Mrs Smith couldn't have killed her mother. She's got an alibi.'

'What kind of alibi can a respectable wife and mother have at one o'clock in the morning?'

'Think about it.'

Cassie frowned. 'You mean she . . . she wasn't alone?'

'I'm not going to break any confidences, Cassandra. But if you were an attractive woman of forty-odd, with a husband who's away most of the time, you might not have been alone either.'

'Serena's got a lover?'

'My lips are sealed.'

'I'm absolutely staggered.'

'Love's old sweet song.'

'That's that, then.'

'It is rather, isn't it?'

The news was so startling that Cassie found herself numbly replacing the receiver without giving Paul the rest of the information she had for him. She couldn't even decide whether to be relieved that Serena was innocent of murder or disappointed that the bright image Serena presented to the world was tarnished.

One thing was clear. Serena's alibi pushed John Lightower back to the front burner. If she could just place him definitely at the mission, it would provide a clear motive for him to kill Lolly. She went through the sequence of events which would have led up to the murder. Lolly goes to Chadwell Court with Cassie, recognises Kenneth Langdon as the actor who was present during the massacre and goes back some time to visit him (this could be checked up, but she was prepared to bet that Lolly had gone to see him again). This is disturbing enough for her, but then Langdon identifies the Reverend Lightower as the clergyman at the mission. She breaks a longstanding habit and goes to church with Serena, recognises the man despite the time which has passed since she last saw him, and has to decide on a course of action. Eventually she contacts him, tells him she knows who he is and asks him to come to see her to discuss it. He does so, she threatens to expose him unless he – what? Resigns from the Church? Whatever, she effectively is going to ruin his career, so he kills her. End of story.

284

At eleven, she reluctantly pushed her chair back from her desk in the office and picked up her umbrella. Early morning drizzle had turned into pelting rain; it was now distinctly colder than it had been. Dashing across the space between cottage and barn, she pushed open the back door, cursing as freezing raindrops from the hanging ivy strands fell down her neck. Inside, she filled the kettle and plugged it in, listening out for Hugh Nightingale's arrival. He was late. She walked into the sitting room and peered out through the rain-slicked windows but could see nothing. The stone walls emanated damp: she was afraid to touch them in case water immediately gushed from them. It had happened once when Uncle Sam took her camping with her minuscule cousins. How was she supposed to know that if you touched canvas, it would let in the rain? She'd never been in a tent before and, following that experience, had prayed that she never would be again.

By the fireplace, a miserable pot plant turned beseechingly in her direction and she went back into the kitchen, found a jug and gave it some water. It shuddered, like someone knocking back a double shot of slivovitch. Several of its desiccated leaves tumbled to the ground, but then it rallied, straightened its vegetative shoulders, took on a new lease of life. She regarded it without enthusiasm. She'd never wanted the darn thing to set up housekeeping with her in the first place, hadn't personally bought a houseplant in years, but people kept on giving them to her. Previously, she had thought their motives misguided but kindly; now, looking at the sad *tetrastigma*, she wondered if in fact her friends and family were nothing more than a sadistic bunch of plant-haters, who knew that to give Cassandra Swann a pot plant was to condemn it to a lingering death.

Where was Nightingale? If he didn't come soon, she
wouldn't have time to talk to him before Edgecombe arrived
to pick her up for lunch. As if in answer to her thought, there
was a knock at the front door. She opened up. Nightingale
was standing in the porch, shaking out an umbrella while
beyond him, rain drummed down from a darkly waterlogged
sky. Under his mud-splashed cassock, the cuffs of his black
trousers were soaked.

'I didn't hear you arrive,' she said. Behind him, no curve of
shiny wet car roof showed over the top of the hedge. He
probably drove one of those fancy roadsters which were so
low-slung they were barely higher than the kerb.

'In this damn rain,' he said, glancing up at the sky, 'you
wouldn't hear a herd of elephants arriving.'

'True.'

He stepped into the hall, apologising for the lateness of his
arrival, and thrust a bag into her hands. 'I hope this'll make
you more inclined to forgive me.'

She peered inside. Coffee beans, a box which obviously
held cakes, a piece of Stilton, a fresh loaf of walnut bread,
some unsalted French butter. Not her first choice, but who
was she to quibble? 'Goodness, how amazingly kind of you.'

'I was in the covered market and bumped into a colleague,'
he said. 'He wanted to discuss some urgent bit of college
business and I couldn't get away, which is why I'm so late.
So I bought peace offerings, in case you were cross.'

'How could I possibly be?'

Cassie led the way into the kitchen and ground some of the
beans, put them into her cafetière and added boiling water.
She opened the box: it contained four patisseries, including a
crescent-shaped one studded with almonds. Her favourite.
She smiled at Nightingale. 'Thank you *so* much.' She felt

ashamed of her previous lukewarm reaction to him. How could he have known that she adored absolutely anything that tasted of almonds? Apart from cyanide.

'My pleasure, my dear. Besides, I do have an ulterior motive.'

'Oh?'

'I'm really hoping that you'll agree to cook for me next week. I've already invited the guests, and if you let me down, I'll have to take them to a restaurant, which won't be nearly as much fun.'

They discussed it for a while. Eventually Cassie agreed, for a sum far larger than she expected, to produce a four-course meal for Nightingale and his seven guests the following week. Or eight if she wanted to join them? His eyebrows arched enquiringly.

'I'd much rather stay out of sight in the kitchen, if that's all right.'

'Whatever you say,' he said. 'I'm just delighted you've agreed to do it.'

She tried to think of a way to bring John Lightower into the conversation without making it too obvious. 'You must be glad to be so near your old friend and colleague,' was all she could come up with.

'Which old friend is that?'

'John Lightower.'

'I don't think I'd describe him as a friend,' Nightingale said, frowning slightly.

'I understood you trained together.'

'We did, but that hardly qualifies as a reason for friendship.'

'You mean you disliked him?'

'I wouldn't go that far.'

'What do you think of him?'

'My dear Cassandra, you can hardly expect me to gossip about my colleagues. It would be most indiscreet.'

'Do you like him?'

'Since you ask, no.'

'Why not?'

'There's something . . . I don't know . . . rather ruthless about him. And the way he fixes you with his eyes. Very compelling, I'm sure, but a little scary, wouldn't you say?'

'Do you think he's capable of violence?'

'What a strange question. Tell me why you ask it.'

'Do you know where he was in Africa?'

'In Africa?' Nightingale touched a finger to the scar which ran down the left side of his face.

'I understood he'd worked out there for a while.'

'I believe he did, now you mention it. But I should emphasise that I hardly know him. It's more than thirty years since we were at Wycliffe Hall and our lives have taken vastly differing routes since then. But I seem to remember that he went out to run a small Church of England mission in Africa somewhere, almost as soon as we were ordained.'

She tried to stop the excitement showing in her eyes. She poured him coffee, pushed over the plate on which she had put the pastries, keeping the almond one on the side nearest to her. 'Could you find out exactly where it was?'

'If it was absolutely necessary, I suppose I could. These things aren't exactly secrets. Why don't you ask him yourself?'

'I could do that.' Why not, especially if she took Charlie Quartermain with her, to repel any murderous reaction the question might provoke? 'I was interested to hear that you were originally an accountant,' she said.

'Why should you find it interesting?'

'I suppose because it seems such a switch, moving from love of Mammon to love of God.'

'I'm not sure that training as an accountant necessarily implies a love of money. More a love of order, or equilibrium, I would have said. But I take your point: God and money are the two greatest impulses of the human psyche. We're all ruled by one or the other.'

'What about love?'

'Ah. Love.' Nightingale stared at the built-in dresser of stripped pine which took up the wall behind Cassie's head. 'Love,' he repeated.

'Commitment to another. However you define it, I believe you know what I mean.'

'God and Mammon both require a genuine commitment of the heart. Perhaps when you speak of love, you refer to something quite different – what our American cousins so often call "lurv". The physical chemistry which can ignite between a man and a woman? Is that what you mean?'

'Actually, I meant the kind of love which men like yourself are supposed to be brimming over with. Love for their fellow human beings.'

'I would hardly have chosen this profession had I not loved my fellows. And gone on loving them, despite their manifold efforts to make me wonder whether they are, in fact, lovable.' He fingered his dog-collar, sipped his coffee, said: 'This is wonderful. Especially on a cold wet day.'

The telephone rang. She thought of letting it click onto the answering machine. He saw her hesitation. 'Don't mind me.' He glanced at his watch. 'Perhaps I should slip away.'

'No. I'll tell them to call again.' She pushed back her chair and ran into the sitting room. 'Cassie Swann.'

'This is John Lightower, Miss Swann.'

Her heart began to thud. He'd walked right into the web she had spun for him. 'How can I help you?'

'I understand from Natasha Sinclair that you and she are partners in a bridge company. My mother is a keen bridge player and I thought you might have something in your show rooms which would make a suitable Christmas present for her.'

'I'm sure we have.' He probably didn't even have a mother. In the kitchen, Nightingale was scraping his chair along the kitchen floor, as though he was getting ready to leave.

'Would it be convenient for me to call this afternoon?' Lightower continued. 'I'm making parish calls and should be in your vicinity at about tea time.'

'Splendid,' she said, falsely bright. She'd have to make sure someone else was here, Big Charlie Quartermain, if possible. Or Paul Walsh, complete with handcuffs. 'See you then.'

'I look forward to it.'

I don't, she wanted to say.

Back in the kitchen, she found Nightingale looking out of the window. 'I'd better be on my way,' he said, not turning back to look at her. 'I'll see you next week.'

'Fine. If any last-minute problems come up, I'll call you, otherwise—' The telephone rang again. 'Sorry . . .'

'Answer it,' Nightingale said brusquely.

She did. 'Hello?'

'My name's Janice Millington,' a voice said. 'You left a message asking me to call.'

'That's right.' Why did the wretched woman have to call now, with Nightingale obviously becoming increasingly edgy about getting to his next appointment? She didn't want to alienate her prospective employer before she'd even taken on the job. 'Look, can I call you back?'

'What does it concern? Who are you exactly?' The voice was no more than mildly curious, even faintly amused. 'Have I won the pools?'

'It's about something which happened a long time ago,' Cassie said. 'In Nigeria.'

'Nigeria?'

'Yes. But why don't I—'

The battening-down was almost audible. 'I don't want to talk about it.'

'I'm simply trying to tie up some loose—'

'I said I *don't* want to *talk* about it.' Janice Millington's decibels revved suddenly, moving rapidly from repressed to out-of-control.

'That's fine,' Cassie said soothingly. She was uneasy about the fact that Nightingale could hear every word she herself was saying, and quite a bit of Mrs Millington's side of the conversation, too. 'All I wanted to find out from you was—'

There was a kind of sobbing pause, so long that Cassie began to wonder if the woman had simply put down the phone and gone into another room. Then, quite unexpectedly, she spoke again, her tone reasonable: 'I think if you'd been there, you would have done as I did.'

'Believe me, I'm not standing in judgement over—'

'There were drunken soldiers with blood all over their clothes.' Janice's voice rose. 'I was twenty-one.'

This was obviously a deeply disturbed woman. Cassie could hear Nightingale shifting about in the kitchen again. It sounded as if he was opening drawers. Damn. She should have left this call for the answering machine, rung the woman back later. 'I know it must have been the most terrible—'

'Terrible? It was a nightmare, the worst you could imagine. Edith, my best friend, lying dead on the floor with blood coming from between – they'd beaten her first, used their knives, sticks pushed up . . . bottles . . . it was – and Hugh standing there with his face slashed, bleeding, it was—'

'Who?'

'Hugh. The Padre. Hugh Nightingale.'

'Nightingale?' whispered Cassie. Oh, my God. What a complete and utter idiot she had been. She glanced over her shoulder. Nightingale was leaning against the door jamb, watching her.

'One of the rebel soldiers had practically sliced off the side of his face. He was covered in—' Suddenly, the woman lost it. The words poured out of the receiver, an endless guilty stream. 'How dare you, how *dare* you telephone me out of the blue and accuse me, *accuse* me of standing by and doing nothing, when there was nothing I *could* do, absolutely nothing, it was . . . if he hadn't done what he did, we'd *all* have been dead, there was nothing we could have done to save any of those people, nothing at all, do you hear, absolutely *nothing*.' She was raving now, shrieking at the top of her voice, pouring out stuff which, it was easy to guess, had been festering inside her head for thirty years.

Cassie hung up. Slowly she turned. Nightingale was at her shoulder now. He only had to reach out a hand and he would be able to grab her neck. Instead, he smiled a little. 'So it looks as though you know all about it,' he said.

'I've known for some time.' Cassie hoped her voice was not as shaky as it felt. How could she have been so stupid as to overlook him? Why hadn't she considered the scar on his face, the fact that he had worked abroad? Why had she concentrated on John Lightower when someone like Nightingale was just as obvious a suspect? He was the one Lolly had seen and recognised when she went to Matins with Serena, not Lightower.

How was she going to get away from him?

'Did Mrs Haden White tell you?' He asked.

'No. She didn't tell anyone.'

'She tried to.'

'She did at first, but nobody would cooperate with her. Nobody would identify you, give her a name. Some of them didn't know it anyway. The others, I imagine, were too ashamed to want to be associated with what happened. Or perhaps you'd intimidated them, reasoned with them, pointed out that seven people saved was better than no people saved, that it was better for all your sakes to hush it all up.'

'If the story had come out, it would have ruined me. Besides, I've made up for it since. I've been able to serve God through my vocation, I've done a great deal of good, both in this country and abroad. Had I just stood there and let them kill us all, think of the waste. Farquharson, doing tremendous work in the fight against starvation and disease. Kenneth Langdon, bringing pleasure to thousands through his work. Nick and Viv Parfitt—'

'Not such a success story there,' said Cassie, playing for time, wondering how she was to get out of this. 'Neither of them did anything after that except stumble through their lives until one of them killed himself with alcohol. And what about Lolly, whose life was one long unfulfilled promise? And Edith, dead. Or Farquharson, haunted for the rest of his days. Was it really such a good bargain?'

'Surely you would agree that the end can sometimes justify the means.'

'Bad means can never be justified,' said Cassie. Behind Nightingale, the grandfather clock struck the quarter-hour. There was coldness in the pit of her belly. She knew she was going to die unless help came soon. He had something in his hand, though he held it hidden against his jacket.

'I cannot agree with you there. I made a decision, weighed one thing against another, chose what I thought was the best way forward.' He seemed desperate to justify himself.

'An accountant's decision. A balance-sheet decision.' She tried to envisage his coldly handsome face covered in blood, the cheek slashed, the dead woman raped and mutilated at his feet.

'If you like.' Nightingale began to laugh. 'Why you should have thought John Lightower capable of such judgement,' he said, 'I really can't imagine. He always was a plodding fellow. Which is why he's still in a dead-end place like St Bart's, while I—'

'Should eventually get a bishopric,' said Cassie.

'Precisely. Despite the efforts of people like Mrs Haden White to prevent me from doing so. And now you.'

'Did you kill her?'

'She was threatening to go to the college authorities, to write to my bishop, to Canterbury. What else could I have done? After all the years I've put in, to lose my just reward at the end of it . . . She had some absurd notion of expiation. Expiation? For what?' The expression on his face was almost comic. 'She must have been crazy.'

'No,' Cassie said. 'I don't think she was.'

'You sound as though you agree with her.'

'Of course I do. I can't possibly say what I'd have done, faced with a similar situation, but I'd like to think that I would at least have behaved like Edith, rather than the rest of you.'

'Those were extraordinary times, Cassandra. Actions are taken in such circumstances which, looked at rationally later, can have no rational explanation. Certainly I can't say that what happened out there at the mission was what I would have chosen, but I'm not going to spend the rest of my life beating my breast about it.'

'Any more than you will about killing Lolly. Or me.'

'You do see, don't you, that I have no choice?' He came towards her, then tripped over the footstool which had once been Gran's, knocking his forehead against the rough stone walls of the chimneybreast.

'I don't see that at all,' said Cassie, quickly moving towards the sofa. The longer she could keep him away from her . . .

'But you're bound to spill the beans, aren't you?' He stood upright, touching the small cut on his forehead, looking at the blood on his fingers. 'And even if nobody believes you, it will stick, my reputation will be lost.'

'Too right,' Cassie gabbled, trying to keep him talking while she thought up a means of escape. 'Even if you . . .' she gulped, '. . . do kill me, there's a tape, too. Or didn't you know that?'

His composure wavered. 'A tape? Where?'

'You don't seriously think I'd tell you, do you?'

'A tape.' He tightened his mouth, thinking about it.

'Anyway,' she pressed. 'How do you know someone won't have seen you coming here?'

'I have a perfectly good reason to be in the area since I'm on my way somewhere else.'

'Somebody may have noticed your car parked outside my gate.'

'But it's not, my dear. I left it in a layby about half a mile from here.'

'Somebody will remember seeing it.' She'd wondered why the bottoms of his clerical trousers were so wet, but had not carried the thought to its logical conclusion.

'I doubt it. It's a very ordinary car, and it's pouring with rain, as you may have observed.' He rubbed his hand across his forehead again, smearing blood over one eyebrow.

'Somebody will have noticed you walking here.'

'That's a risk I had to take. I was no more than five minutes on the main road, and after that it was the country lanes, and in this weather, there wasn't a soul about.' He frowned, reached somewhere inside his sleeve for a handkerchief, and wiped his brow. 'I'm bleeding,' he said, looking at the bright stain on the cotton. There was an initial H machine-embroidered in one corner. 'Anyway, I'd say God played into my hands, wouldn't you?'

'In what way?'

'By producing such heavy rain. It'll hide any traces.'

Traces of what? She wasn't going to waste time thinking up an answer to that question. 'You can't seriously think that you'll get away with it.' It was the classic line of the desperate victim, hoping to stop the perpetrator in his wicked tracks.

Nightingale smiled. 'I seriously think I can. Particularly when I've removed the evidence I know you've got here, which you picked up from poor old Mrs Farquharson yesterday. I've been trying to get her to hand it over ever since the Haden White woman first contacted me, but she wouldn't. Old people can be so stubborn.'

'When exactly did Lolly contact you?' All she could do was try to keep him talking. Was there going to be any escape from this? Even if she could get outside, he'd confirmed that because of the weather, there'd be nobody about to help her.

'After she heard me preach at St Bart's recently. None of this would have happened if I'd refused to come, but that pathetic idiot, Lightower, was so insistent that I couldn't think of a good excuse not to. Especially as I'm almost on the doorstep, in Oxford.'

'Tell me how it happened with Lolly.'

'I'd love to, but I don't want to be late. Marjorie Curtiss has gathered some ladies together for a luncheon party at which I'm the guest of honour. I really don't want to let them all down, and I promised to be there by one o'clock. I still have to walk back to my car.' He glanced at his watch once more.

Quicker than thought, Cassie moved so that the sofa was between the two of them. 'I expect the police have already worked it out, anyway,' she said carelessly. 'Sooner or later, they'll catch up with you.'

'Oh, come.' He smiled triumphantly. 'They haven't the faintest idea where to look for a suspect. I rang up and spoke to someone about it only yesterday.'

'Bad move.'

'In what sense?'

'That's suspicious in itself, isn't it? Telephoning to see how the investigation is going? You've given yourself away, all right.'

He looked smug. 'Naturally I didn't give my own name. I pretended to be from one of the national newspapers.'

'I'll bet they believed that,' said Cassie witheringly. 'They probably kept you talking while they traced the call.'

She watched him weigh this up, wonder if she was right. Then conceit at his own cleverness overcame him. 'Of course they didn't. I'm not that naïve.'

She raised a sardonic eyebrow. Made it clear she didn't buy it.

Obviously stung by her disbelief, he said. 'I'm *not*. And anyway, I never intended to do the Haden White woman any harm. She asked me to come and see her and it wasn't until she started talking about informing people, when she suggested that I turn down the chaplaincy at St Frideswide's, that I realised I hadn't any choice. All those years of ministry that I'd put in, to be tossed aside because of an old woman's ridiculous notions? She got away from me, escaped outside. It wasn't very difficult to kill her. She was rather frail, and I try to keep myself fit. I made sure she didn't suffer.'

'That's awfully thoughtful of you,' said Cassie.

'I'd been attending a dinner party that evening anyway,' Nightingale added. 'So it wasn't even out of my way.'

'A dinner party? So you were,' said Cassie. Was he so alienated from his fellow human beings that he didn't even remember which dinner party it was? Or who was there? Or that it was only just down the lane from here? Did he not recall that he'd been so impressed with the food served that he'd asked the cook to cater a similar dinner party for him?

The clock struck the half-hour. She wondered what was the best thing to do. If she could only get out of doors, she might have a chance. Brian Edgecombe should be here any moment to pick her up for lunch, and even the homicidally self-justifying Mr Nightingale might balk at killing her in front of a witness. Unless he killed the witness too.

But that was impossible. It had to be.

She edged backwards, towards the door into the passage leading to the front door. 'You can't possibly get away with this,' she said again. She thought of Lolly and the Farquharson letter thrust between desk and wall. Realising that Nightingale intended to sacrifice her on the altar of his ambition, had that been her last desperate act, taken in the hope that someone would find it and make a connection, however long it might take? Because it had always seemed odd that it should have been there. If it had missed the wastepaper basket, it might have been lying on the floor but there was no way it could have ended up where Cassie had found it unless it had been deliberately pushed into place.

'My problem has always been that I am too clever,' Nightingale said. 'You can't imagine how that bores and frustrates me. I've spent most of my life among inferior intellects. But I'm so close now to the kind of society I was born to frequent. An Oxford college, the scholastic ambience of our premier university, High Table, erudite conversation, philosophical discussion. It's all there now. I couldn't let her take that away from me.' He took a step in her direction.

Cassie wanted to point out that he was in for a sad disappointment. Last time Theo invited her to dine in college, she had rapidly learned that most dons were as dull and ordinary as the next citizen, that most of them are as concerned with the mundanities of life as everyone else. 'Don't touch me,' she said.

'And after four years or so, a life at the very top of the ecclesiastical tree. A diocese of my own. Perhaps, even – who knows? – an archbishopric? A chance to serve God as only I can do.' He moved closer to her.

'In your dreams,' said Cassie, reaching slowly behind her for the door handle which would lead into the passage and so to the front door. She was too scared to feel frightened.

'Precisely, my dear young lady. In my dreams. Except that my dreams are on the point of coming true. So I have no intention of letting you stand in my way. You do see, don't you?'

She wondered if those innocent black people, out in Nigeria, had seen the same implacability, and known that because their skin wasn't white, they had no chance, that this was the end of the line. There was a plant on the table beside her. She picked it up and flung it at him, catching him full in the face. At the same time, she turned the handle and whipped open the door, slammed it shut behind her, raced for the front door. Thank God she had not gone through the usual routine of shooting bolts and slotting in bars after letting him in earlier. As she got the door open and stumbled out into the freezing rain, he was already leaping after her down the flagged passageway, blinking, rubbing at his eyes, his face grimed with potting compound. She ran down the path which bisected the small front garden, vaulted over the gate and into the lane. Which way now? Was Quinn Macfarlane in residence yet, in Ivy Cottage? She thought not. In that case, the other way, towards the main road, in the direction from which Edgecombe was likely to be coming.

'Brian,' she shouted, knowing that even if he was coming round the bend, he wouldn't be able to hear her, but hoping to give Nightingale pause. 'Help! Help!'

As she ran from him, she imagined the repeated slash of a knife in her back, the rending pain of a bullet tearing through muscle and tendon, severing vertebrae. But he had neither gun nor knife, otherwise he would have threatened her with them before. He intended to strangle her, as he had Lolly.

Which, she told herself bravely, was a mistake, since she was neither as old, or as frail or as defeated as his last victim. She pounded along the lane, determined that, when this was over, she would join a gym. Despite an age gap of nearly

twenty years, he was catching up on her fast. Although rage
would give her strength, she wasn't sure how long she would
be able to fight him off if he actually attacked her.

*Neither gun nor knife ...* Oh shit: she remembered the
sound of him moving about in the kitchen, and the way he
had held something concealed in his hand. Her kitchen
knives, her expensive Sabatier knives in their own special
stand, kept at optimum sharpness, had been on the counter,
plain as could be. A knife. Oh Christ. Fear gave her a fresh
burst of speed. Panting, she reached the bend in the lane. And
at the far end, proceeding in stately fashion towards her, she
saw a lovingly polished, dark blue Rover, circa 1959.
Chrome and enamel badges from the RAC and the AA
gleamed on the pristine front bumper. Edgecombe sat at the
wheel. She waved wildly at it, and it added a mile or two per
hour of speed to its progress. Edgecombe drew up alongside,
rolled down the window and said with a smirk: 'Here, I know
I'm a bit late, but were you that eager to see me you couldn't
wait indoors?'

'Brian, for God's sake ...' She ran round to the passenger
side of the car and scrabbled at the door handle. As she did
so, Nightingale appeared. The fury on his face was terrifying.
She could see the glitter of a knife in his hand. 'Brian,' she
screamed. 'Open the damn door.'

Instead, he floored the accelerator and drove on down the
lane, dragging her with him until she thought to let go of the
door handle. He was heading straight for Nightingale. Was he
going to drive straight over him? Surely not. Surely he
wouldn't ...

He didn't. Not over Nightingale, but at him, until the priest
had no choice but to leap into the hedge. At which Edgecombe
stood on the brakes, tipped the steering wheel slightly and with

301

the car's bulk, held him trapped like a hunted stag among the dripping black thorns.

'How dare you?' Nightingale yelled, as Edgecombe got out and advanced round the side of the car towards him.

'Don't you give me none of that,' Edgecombe said.

'I shall report you for dangerous driving.' Nightingale pulled furiously at his cassock, which was caught and held by numerous sharp-spiked twigs. The potting compound still on his shoulders was slowly turning to something like mud, oozing down across his chest.

'You do that, chummie. I'll be more than happy to defend myself against any charges you care to bring.'

'Would you please move your vehicle immediately?' Nightingale tugged so hard that he partially freed himself.

Edgecombe raised a flattened hand and chopped the air in a menacing fashion. 'I can break a brick with this, you know,' he said. 'Want me to show you?'

Nightingale subsided. 'All I ask, my good man, is that you allow me to be on my way. Quite apart from the discomfort you are causing me, I have a luncheon engagement to attend.'

'Taking your own utensils in case they didn't supply eating irons, were you?' Edgecombe stooped and picked up the Sabatier knife which lay on the road. 'This'll look good in court, I'll tell you that much.'

'It's nothing to do with me.'

'Oh no? Then why did I come round the corner of the lane to find you chasing Miss Cassandra Swann down the lane, brandishing it like a maniac?'

'There's a perfectly logical explanation. Now if you'd just move your car and let me get out of this damned hedge, we can—'

'Did you call the police yet, Cass?' Edgecombe said.

'I'll do it now.' Cassie started towards her gate and then turned back. Her recent terror had given place to the kind of euphoria she'd thought only a recreational substance could give. 'Could I just say that I think you're wonderful, Brian? I don't know how we won the War without you.'

'Now you mention it, love, neither do I.'

## ♠ 16 ♠

*Underneath the arches* . . . The two figures shuffled in close formation across the dark stage, lit only by a single beam, *Underneath the arches*, blank faces turned to the audiences, hat brims flipped up in stylised foolishness.

The audience was rapt. For a moment, it truly seemed as though the familiar figures of Flanagan and Allan were there in front of them again, two old tramps traipsing across the unfriendly pavements, one's hand on the other's shoulder . . . *waiting till the daylight comes creeping* . . . Recognising Richard Craufurd's name from the programme, the audience had applauded when the couple first came on but there had been no preliminary or introduction, and the pair had launched straight into the song. Who, they wondered, was the one with him, smaller, softer looking, walking so close behind? Was it somebody famous, one of Craufurd's friends off the telly, was it someone they ought to know?

*Heralding the dawn* . . . the two figures reached one side of the makeshift stage and turned to troop slowly back again . . . *Sleeping when it's raining* . . . Even the children were silent, recognising something they could not have put a name to. Besides, there was the promise of Scott Lyall, heart-throb, star of the popular California high school series, to keep them quiet. For the older members of the audience, there was, quite simply, magic in the air.

To one side, a Christmas tree blinked on and off, red and blue and green and yellow, multicoloured stars in the darkness, annual promise of hopes which most of the audience knew would never be fulfilled but to which they nonetheless responded still with expectation. Paper garlands drooped from the ceiling, silver baubles turned and twinkled in the small warm currents set up by so many people being crowded together into one room.

*Pavement is my pillow* ... as the two voices sang the words, there was scarcely an adult present who didn't wonder, however briefly, what it might be like this Christmas season, to be one of the dispossessed, setting up their cardboard homes beneath the railway aqueducts, in cold doorways, on city streets, all the sad and lonely places where the homeless did their best to keep on living.

*Underneath the arches, I dream my dreams away* ... the song died into silence, the two old codgers turned and faced the audience, there was absolute silence and then a storm of clapping. If Crisis at Christmas had been here with their collecting boxes, they'd have made a mint.

The piano struck up again, and the old tramps stripped off their fur coats to reveal striped suits and bow ties. From the wings, someone tossed them each a cane and a straw boater and they went into another routine, songs that the old folk could join in, songs of their long-ago childhood, when they had never dreamed the years could pass so quickly. Nodding in time to the music, they sang happily along as the two launched into the perennial favourites: 'Lily of Laguna', 'My Old Man Said Follow the Van', 'There'll be Bluebirds Over the White Cliffs of Dover', 'It's a Long Way to Tipperary'.

When they had finished, and the ecstatic applause had died down, Robert Craufurd stepped forward. 'Ladies and Gentlemen,' he said quietly, 'I am more happy to be here than I can possibly say. Not only does my being here give me a chance to contribute to Mr Charles Quartermain's magical Christmas show which, as we all know, is in aid of the home's new facility, so all of you give generously, folks, because you'll be old one day, and maybe sooner than you think, I know I only look like a young sprig, but don't forget, I'm sixty-eight years old . . .' he paused so that the audience could join him in Harry Walkinshaw, OAP's, most famous catch phrase '. . . and I'm still going strong.'

After allowing a moment of applause, he held up his hand for silence. His rich actor's voice deepened into sincerity. 'But I have something of a far more personal nature to share with you. If I had not agreed to take part tonight, I would have missed finding my heart's desire, missed having my dearest wish come true. I won't go through the whole story – it's far too long and boring – but suffice it to say that after many years, I have at last been reunited with two people I loved very dearly and thought I would never see again.' There was a pause while his face crumpled slightly, then he recovered, took the hand of his partner and said into the vast hush which had settled over the hall: 'My friends . . .' his voice dropped with emotion, 'let me introduce you to my long-lost daughter, Elizabeth.' There were gasps from the enthralled audience. Liz Trowbridge stepped forward, swept off her boater, let her long red hair sweep the floor as she bowed theatrically. 'And, sitting among you, my other daughter, Serena Smith.' Craufurd held his hand out to the darkness. 'Serena, where are you? Come up here and meet the lovely people.'

The audience went wild. This was like Esther Rantzen and Cilla Black and *Lassie Come Home* all rolled into one. And what's more, it was better than the TV because it was real; it was three-dimensional; they were being allowed to share the true-life adventures of one of their screen heroes. As Serena Smith stumbled from a seat close to the front and took Craufurd's hand, staring dazedly over the heads of the people in front of her, Cassie could not decide. Had she known beforehand what Craufurd was going to say, or had he sprung it on her just a few moments ago?

She could hardly believe that Lolly could have deprived her daughters of their father, his parents of their grandchildren, because he was homosexual. Was her shame so great that she was prepared to deny them such a basic right as knowing their family? It seemed impossible, yet what other explanation was there? And if so, how unnecessarily cruel prejudice could be.

After warm and prolonged applause, Craufurd and his daughters left the stage and Tim Holloway, the local MP, recited 'The Green Eye of the Little Yellow God', with appropriate actions, much to the relish of those listening. 'I never realised he was human before,' Natasha whispered to Cassie, as they stood at the back of the hall. 'I'll vote for him next time.'

'Oh *please*. It'd take a lot more than that to make me vote for his lot,' said Cassie.

John Lightower appeared, cassocked and dog-collared, and thanked everybody profusely, particularly Mr Charles Quartermain, without whom none of this would have been possible and whose energy and enthusiasm had made the event such a success. He hoped that everyone would remember absent friends, would spare a thought for those less fortunate than themselves at this season of goodwill and for the victims of the recent tragic events which had shaken their little community so deeply. He ended by reminding them that it had all begun with an overbooked lodging house, some two thousand years ago.

Standing there, slightly shabby, wholly good, Cassie asked herself how she could have imagined that he would be capable of strangling Lolly or smothering Kenneth Langdon, in order to suppress a deed which he could not possibly have committed. Luckily, she had told nobody of her former suspicions about the Vicar. She'd probably have been lynched if she had.

Nightingale was awaiting trial on a charge of murdering Lolly Haden White. When the police arrived to extricate him from the hedge, he had adopted a pose of high indignation, demanding that Edgecombe be charged with careless driving and criminal assault. Taken to the police station himself and later formally charged with murder, he had insisted that a dreadful mistake had been made and that he would be vindicated when the case came to court, after which he had refused to speak without his solicitor being present.

'Mad as a bloody hatter,' Walsh had told Cassie. He spoke coldly, still unable to forgive her for having withheld important evidence from him. Words had passed between them on the subject. Harsh words. Cassie had tried to explain about Lolly's deep-rooted sense of privacy, about the need for the old to be allowed their dignity, but knew he hadn't understood anything of what she was trying to say. 'Doesn't look like it on the surface. He's very smooth, very plausible. But they always are. We've seen the type a hundred times before. They're all the same: they're right, the rest of the world's wrong. And that gives them the right to do what they want, regardless.'

'You're sure you can prove he did it?'

'Easy. He's so sure he's God that he didn't even bother to wipe his prints off the handle of the kitchen door or the back of one of the chairs – I told you there was one we hadn't identified yet. He accounted for it being there by saying that he'd often visited Mrs Haden White before, but we know from the daughter that the first time she'd ever seen him was in church, a couple of weeks before she was killed.'

Poor Lolly, seeing at last the chance to wipe clean her own personal slate and, at the same time, to make sure that Nightingale, as she had finally learned he was called, paid some kind of a price by resigning from his current post. Instead, she had added her own life to the roll-call of those who had been sacrificed in the furtherance of his ecclesiastical career.

'Raffle tickets are on sale,' Lightower said, the spotlight gleaming on his forehead. He smiled persuasively, turning his compelling gaze on the audience as they all began reaching for their purses. 'We have some magnificent prizes, as I'm sure you'll agree. The first prize is – and I can hardly express my gratitude to him – a brand-new car, donated by Mr Charles Quartermain.' Everyone clapped and cheered. 'Among the equally stunning other prizes I must mention a wonderful painting by a dear friend of mine, the Belfast artist and poet, Brendan O'Rourke, whose work has done so much to highlight the problems besetting his troubled country.'

Cassie's mouth opened in astonishment. 'Did he say Brendan O'Rourke?' she asked.

'Yes.'

'But that's impossible.'

'Why? It's a magnificent picture, much more worth having than a car,' said Natasha. 'I was looking at it earlier.'

'But . . .' Cassie shook her head. Weird, or what? She was under the impression that Brendan O'Rourke was a product of her own over-fertile imagination; perhaps she'd read about him somewhere.

John Lightower walked off and a troupe of sixth-form girls from Bellington Comp came running onstage in Edwardian cycling costume. As the piano banged out the opening bars of 'Daisy, Daisy', Robin Plunkett's Nanny's old bike was wheeled on by a young man that everybody under the age of fifteen instantly recognised as Scott Lyall, even though he was wearing the kind of kid-on-the-street cap favoured by Jackie Coogan. An enormous cheer went up from the younger members of the audience. This was more like it: this was *cool*. Even the old folks looked animated, though they had only a vague idea who Scott Lyall was.

'Dighsy, Dighsy,' he sang, in passable Cockney, 'give me yer answer, do,' and the girls all turned, fingers on chins, heads to one side, while they waited for Daisy to appear, which she duly did. Another sustained clap, and some enthusiastic whistles. Through his thespian connections, Richard Craufurd had secured for them the services of a TV weather girl whose marital and extramarital exploits had ensured her considerably more than fifteen minutes of fame in the tabloids. 'I'm 'alf crighzy,' said Scott Lyall, rolling his eyes lecherously as she simpered back at him, 'All for the love of you.'

The number was a riot, the girls moving swiftly into a can-can and back again, the bicycle being mounted and remounted, the tempo hotting up. When the song was ended, the girls were joined by the sixth-form boys, and together they did passable imitations of people sitting at small tables in a bar, while Scott Lyall swapped his cap for a bowler hat, took off his jacket and, with the weather girl, gave a spirited version of 'Frankie and Johnnie', complete with actions and gunshot at the end. To the huge delight of everyone present, a garishly waistcoated Charlie Quartermain took the part of the fat bar-tendin' man. 'Ah don't wanna cause you no trouble,' he droned unmelodiously, sticking his thumbs under his braces, 'don't wanna tell you no lies.'

'Encore,' a woman shouted – was it Petra Lewis? – and Scott Lyall said: 'Yo, man, take it from the top, Chuck.' So Charlie did it again. The show reached a climax with Christmas carols, leaving scarcely a dry eye in the Home.

There was a party afterwards. Scott Lyall worked the old folks like the pro he was, ensuring that on future Tuesdays, the audience for his show would be swelled by at least sixty old people bemusedly watching the antics of a dozen Californian teenagers.

Coming across Serena, Cassie impulsively embraced her. 'I'm so happy about you and your father,' she said.

'Strange, isn't it,' said Serena. 'I've watched all his programmes, and I never had the slightest idea who he was. And yet, just sometimes, he reminded me of someone. Liz, of course.'

'Wasn't she good?' Cassie said.

'I always knew she was.' Serena looked round the room a little tremulously. 'I just wish my mother was here.'

'Mmm.' Given Lolly's attitudes, that might not have been a good idea.

'You know,' Serena said, staring at Cassie over the rim of her wine glass, 'at one point, when you were asking all those questions, I wondered if you thought *I'd* killed Mother.'

'You?' Cassie gave a loudly disbelieving laugh. 'Good heavens. Why on earth would I think such a thing.'

'Silly, isn't it?' Serena's disconcerting blue eyes did not leave Cassie's. 'But I had the means, didn't I? And the opportunity. Not to mention a motive.'

'The thought never crossed my mind.'

'Mmm,' said Serena, in her turn. She moved away to speak to someone else and let Cassie let out a big breath. Phew: she had never realised before how much like Lolly Serena could be, and how little she herself wanted to get on the wrong side of her.

She made her way across the room to Liz Trowbridge. 'Thanks,' the woman said.

'What for?'

'Everything, really.'

'I don't think I had a great deal to do with it.'

'You did.' Liz put a hand on Cassie's arm as she was about to turn away. 'By the way, my mother's papers?'

'What about them?'

'I found them. In the lining of her fur coat. She'd stuffed them all in there. Amazing, isn't it?'

'Or sad. Maybe she knew she was risking her neck by inviting Nightingale to the house.'

'Yes. It makes it easier to . . . put her into perspective.'

'I'm glad.'

There was a sudden uproar close to Cassie's ear. ''Ello, darlin'. How's it going, then?'

'Wonderful, Charlie. Absolutely wonderful.'

'Good, innit?'

'Everybody's having a fabulous time. And you must have made hundreds for the fund.'

'It's looking good,' agreed Charlie. 'Looking really good.'

He took her hand in his giant paw. 'You too, Cass.'

'Don't start, Charlie, or I'll be forced to belt you.' She smiled up at him.

'If I had a bit of mistletoe, no telling what I wouldn't do under it.'

'Who with? Petra Lewis?'

'Look here,' Charlie said. 'I can explain.'

'There's nothing to explain.'

'Charlie, darling.' Petra arrived at Charlie's side. 'There're some people over here who're dying to meet you.' She put her hands round his arm, like a restraining device.

'You're a free agent,' Cassie said swiftly, lifting her chin. 'As I am.'

He looked back over his shoulder at he was led away. His eyes locked with Cassie's. 'I could change that,' he said.